SMOKE

Stephen Brooke

Arachis Press 2019

Smoke
©2019 Stephen Brooke

ISBN 978-1-937745-66-0

Arachis Press
4803 Peanut Road
Graceville, FL 32440
http://arachispress.com

An acknowledgment to any who were actually at the 2001 Florida Folk Festival, performers, volunteers, and audience. As the stock disclaimer goes, any resemblance of my characters to real persons is coincidental. But the smoke that year was very real!

I have included a map of the park and festival at the end of this book.

Chapter 1

It was leftover surf but that's better than no surf.

It was also my birthday. That counts for something — at least as an excuse to be out here on this Saturday morning, catching a few waves before going back to open the shop. I would usually avoid the pier on weekends. Too many kids in the water.

Today, though, nowhere else was breaking decently. I had staked out the second peak south of the pilings. It was mushy and pretty much impossible to paddle into except on a long board. I'd had enough sense to properly equip myself.

Someone paddled over to me, a youngish guy with long hair. I'd seen him around but wasn't sure of the name. Maybe not even a local. He wasn't on one of my boards, anyway. "Hey, man," he said, "I think those kids are trying to get your attention."

I followed his eyes to a clump of youngsters by the dunes, about a block south of the pier. Yeah, they were waving to me, weren't they? "Thanks," I replied. "Time I got out of the water anyway."

I caught the next wave, going left though the rights were walling up way better. It fizzled under me and I ended up paddling the rest of the way in. What did those kids want? A collection of local surf rats, boys mostly. Future customers, I told myself. It pays to be friendly to them.

Not that I wouldn't be anyway. "Look, Shaper," called out Jeff. I knew Jeff and most of these kids. Middle-schoolers who would hang out in the shop sometimes. Not much on buying anything but that was okay. He pointed to something in the face of the dune.

"We called a responsible adult," Robby put in. It was the sort of crack he would make. But it was good they had. Those were bones sticking out of the sand. Human bones. I could recognize that.

"Damn," was all I could say for a moment. "The storm must have washed away the sand."

The kids gave wise and solemn nods to this pronouncement. "Have you told anyone else, yet?" I asked. Solemn shakes of the head to that.

The police station was only a couple blocks away. I could run over there and get someone. Or find a phone. That would take almost as long. "Stand guard," I told them, "and watch my board." I dropped it in the sand and went up the nearest wooden stairs to the parking spaces. "And do not touch anything!" I called back to them.

Here I was in wet trunks and bare feet. Aw, folks were used to seeing me like that, including the local police force. I waited for a lull in the traffic to cross the road, Highway A-1-A. Oh, wait. There came the bike patrol. Who was riding today? Didn't matter. I waved to them. I may have looked a bit frantic.

Jay Johnson. I could recognize his tall lanky form from a distance. And Dave. That surprised me but it wasn't something I was inclined to ponder at that moment. I did fleetingly wonder if he would make it to my party tomorrow. *The* party I should say. I didn't really want to claim it as mine.

By the time they had pedaled up to me, I had settled myself a bit. "There's something you need to see down here," I told them, waving an arm toward the beach and the kids. "You're both gonna have to get sandy."

I'm not sure they believed that. "I'll check it out," Dave told his partner and followed me down to the sand. A few seconds later he was waving at Jay to join him, while simultaneously calling the station on his radio.

"I suspect this spot will be swarming in a couple minutes," he said, and gave the remains a look. "Nothing but bone. Must have been here a while."

"It was convenient of whoever he was to die so close to the station," I remarked.

"She," Dave corrected me. "I think. You'll have to stick around, Ted. Sorry. You kids too. You found her?"

"I did," volunteered Jeff.

"I'll get all their names," said Jay, and proceeded to do so.

I turned to Dave Blake. "I'm surprised to see you on a bike again."

"Filling in this weekend. Things are still in a bit of turmoil, you know." I did know. I had been a part of that turmoil when Chief Cotton had been accused of embezzlement. "And Jim has turned in his resignation. Moving on to bigger and better things."

I nodded. "He said he would, once Bill's name was cleared."

The yelp of a police siren in the lot above us. There was a fairly high bank here, higher than a man stood, above the broad beach of coarse brownish sand. Here and there, grasses and other vegetation had established itself, straggling down from the top, but much of it was barren, loose sand. A blue and white SUV, Bill Cotton's own vehicle, pulled in behind the row of parked cars. "There should be more of us cops along shortly," he called as he ambled over to the stairs. "I was headed across the bridge when I heard you on the radio, Blake."

He came down and crouched beside the remains. "Haven't had a body on the beach in years," he mused. "And never one skeletonized like this." Bill looked up at me and shook his head. "You do need to stop finding bodies, Ted."

"Can't blame me," I objected. "It was the kids." And I had only stumbled over a couple bodies in the past, after all.

"Okay," he said, rising. "Oh, by the way, happy birthday."

"Yeah, thanks." I might have expected the chief would hear about that now. I'd managed to keep the date secret for the ten years I'd lived in Cully Beach. Getting into a relationship had destroyed my privacy.

Not that I regretted it for a moment. Well, maybe an occasional moment. We all have those.

"You have all the kids' names, Officer Johnson?" he asked.

"Yes, sir, and statements."

"Okay then, you can go," the chief told the knot of youngsters. "If you want to stick around and watch, keep out of the way, alright? Maybe from up there," He waved an arm toward the parking lot. Cotton turned to me. "Let's get your statement too and send you home."

"Not much to tell you, Bill. The kids waved me over and I waylaid the bike patrol as soon as I got a look."

Another police car pulled in behind the chief's vehicle. "You might as well head home then," he said. "We know where to find you. And," Bill held out a hand, "I have to tell you again how grateful I am for all you did for me."

I shook and headed off with my board. A few minutes later I was pulling in by the *Cully Beach Surf Shop*. The front door was already hanging open, even though our official opening time was still a few minutes away. It didn't hurt to get business going early on a Saturday. I stowed the board, rinsed myself in the outdoor shower, headed in.

Charlie was at the counter. "I'll be out in a couple minutes, kid," I told her. "Where's your mom?" I'd noticed her van was gone.

"The bank asked her to come this morning. Filling in for someone, I guess. You're dripping on the floor."

"It's a surf shop. I'm allowed." But I went and got a towel and changed into dry shorts and tee before reappearing. No need to mention this morning's excitement to the girl. She'd hear eventually, from one source or another.

"Slow this morning," she informed me.

"That time of year." It was the weekend after Easter. The snowbirds had mostly flown north and summer vacationers were still weeks away from appearing. "Shouldn't you be studying?"

She gave me a look of disgust. Charlie had a talent for that. "I don't have to study all the time, Shaper. I know the stuff. I'm ready."

I knew she was. I wasn't really the one to push her, either. That I could leave to her mom. "We're going to celebrate after you take the test even if you don't have your grades yet. Finishing the course is accomplishment enough."

"Darn right it is." She smirked at me. "Almost as big an accomplishment as turning fifty-one."

"The only thing to celebrate there," I told her, "is that your mom took pity on poor old Ted and decided to stay with him."

Charlie snorted. "It was the best decision she ever made, Shaper. The best decision either of you ever made."

She might have been right.

Chapter 2

We'd had a private party, just Michelle and me, last night. No need to tell you more about that. This morning, I made her get up and go to church with me.

Not as early as I get up, mind you. I'm out of bed by five most mornings and walk across the street to look at the ocean while the coffee brews. Whether or not there is surf sets my agenda for the rest of the day. There wasn't any this morning.

I hadn't expected any but if the waves had been good my morning services would have been held in the water and Michelle would have been off the hook. "Father Paul should get a glimpse of you now and again," I had argued. "That way he'll recognize you at our wedding."

"I'll be the one in white," she informed me and then thought about that. "Well, ivory maybe, what with it being the third time around. I think I'd look better in it, anyway."

"Okay, I'll wear white then. It sets off my tan."

I was a bit peeved at Father Paul for canceling early mass after the Easter weekend. Yeah, he — and his predecessor at *Our Lady of the Sea* — did it every year and didn't start it back up again until winter residents began to return. It made it difficult for me to open the shop doors at ten. Not impossible. I just had to hurry back. I guess I could always make it to the Sunday evening Spanish mass.

Jaime Trejo and his family sometimes attended then but they were at the mid-morning service today. I figured I should talk to him after mass and he seemed to think the same. "So," immediately said Trejo, "you've come across yet another body."

"What's this?" demanded Michelle, turning to me at once. "You'd better not be getting yourself involved in more danger, Mr. Carrol."

"I sincerely hope not," I told her. "Maybe Jim can solve the case before he leaves us."

"That's only one week now," the policeman said. "Off to the big city."

"I think I will miss Cully Beach," chimed in Sara. Their infant was in her arms; little Stevie clung to her leg. He must be almost two now.

"Me too," admitted Jim. "But it's a step up and I can put more of my skills to use." He chuckled. "As much as I enjoyed it, I wasn't getting much of anywhere on bike patrol."

"Then I'll wish you luck in the big city," I said, shaking his hand. The 'big city,' I understood, was Orlando. "I'll miss you and your family. Hey, stop by my place this afternoon and you can have a piece of birthday cake."

"I'll see, Ted." I watched him and Sara head for their car. I knew it might be the last time I saw them.

"Okay, Ted, what's this about a body?" came Michelle's fierce whisper. I filled her in on the drive home. That's not very far but there wasn't much to tell.

Charlie's first words when we went inside were, "What's this about a body, Shaper? Jan says you found a body." So I had to give her my sparse tale as well. Jan got the news from her boyfriend, undoubtedly. That would be Dave Blake.

I'd be seeing both of them later. For now, it was just time to open the shop up to Sunday shoppers and maybe fix another pot of coffee. If things were as slow as I expected, I might go back to the shaping room later and work on a board or two.

Yeah, like I could get away with hiding in the workshop and avoiding the party my friends had planned. I'd settled myself down at the counter with a mug of Colombian — plenty of milk — and a scone when the phone rang. "Cully Beach Surf Shop," I announced. "Ted speaking."

"Um, yeah." It sounded like a young guy. Deep voice, southern accent. "Is there a Michelle, um — Michelle Jackson there?"

"Whom should I say is calling?" I figured maybe I should screen this call.

"Oh, she won't know me. Tell her it's about, um, her husband. The first one. Or say it's about Pam Huntley. She'll know who that is."

"Okay. I'll see if she can come to the phone." I went back to the kitchen, where Michelle and Charlie were goofing off. "Do you know a Pam Huntley?" I asked my girlfriend. I knew I had the name right because I'd jotted it down. Ted doesn't trust his memory that much.

"Pam's on the phone?" She seemed almost shocked.

"No, some guy. He said it was about her."

Michelle nodded and went up to the shop. I stayed. I figured it might be best to give her privacy.

"That's my aunt," volunteered Charlie. "My real dad's sister." She frowned at that. "My birth dad's sister. Bradley Jackson adopted me so I consider him my real father."

There had never been but a couple mentions of the man. "He died when you were little, right?"

"Yeah, I was like six. He and mom had already split when I was just a baby."

I only nodded at this. I did remember there was little love lost between this aunt of hers and Michelle.

Michelle came back. She looked thoughtful, but it was hard to read any more than that. Maybe bemused. "Your Aunt Pam passed away, Charlie," were her first words. "Cancer. I guess she had been ill for some time."

"I wish she had tried to stay in touch," Charlie put in.

"Yeah." A pause. "I also learned something about your father, something I never knew. Never suspected, even. He had a son from another marriage before he met me. Charlie," she said, "that was your brother on the phone."

Chapter 3

"Doug was an alcoholic. He died in a car crash four years after we split. Driving drunk." She sighed. "Again. I always worried about Charlie going the same way. I am so grateful she has straightened herself out. I thank God and I thank you, Ted Carrol."

"You can thank Jan Bell too, I think. And John Brody, for that matter." I thought on that. "And yourself. You are the one who chose to make a new life here. You're the one who took a chance."

"Yeah, it was pretty foolish of me, wasn't it? Will you go unlock the fridge and get a couple bottles of wine?"

"Sure 'nuff." I ambled back to the workshop. We kept all alcohol in the padlocked refrigerator there, out of the house because of Charlie, locked up so it wouldn't tempt any neighborhood kids hanging around. I wouldn't have put a lock on it for Charlie. It was best to trust her. It was also best not to tempt her. Hmm, I hadn't seen those bottles before. Jugs, actually. Michelle must have picked them up on the way home from work yesterday. I assumed they were the ones she wanted.

I slipped them into a cooler — barely fit — and locked the fridge back up. I'd best lock everything up. No more work back here this afternoon and it was time to hang the 'closed' sign in the shop. I'll admit, I would rather have worked on a board than attend this party. I had decided to pretend it wasn't for me. My birthday was yesterday, after all. This was just another barbecue in Rick Bell's backyard.

That was two houses north of us, on the corner. A fair way to carry three liters of wine. My shoulder was aching a tad! We crossed Alvaro Guzman's back yard to get there. It was good to have someone living in that next door house again. Not much more than half a year ago junkies were squatting there — and I discovered the body of one of them. But that's another story. I've told it enough times to too many people.

Al didn't mind us traipsing across his lawn. He even said he intended to put in a path for us all to use. I figured I might just continue that across my own place, now that I'd bought the house on the other side of the shop. Michelle and I had, that is. I would never have extended myself that way without her. I wouldn't have had any reason.

No Alvaro at his house. The big Buick station wagon was gone, carting his daughter Marty off to another surfing competition. Maybe they'd get back in time to come over for some cake or something. Maybe I'd even save some for them if they didn't.

Rick was at the grill, not cooking yet, just getting it ready. "Hey," he called, "no one else is here yet. Kay's in the house if you want to bother her."

"Will do," replied Michelle. I decided to stay and bother Rick. No need to take the cooler inside. But someone would have to bring a corkscrew out eventually.

"Do you like eggplant?" my friend asked, pretty much out of the blue.

I was cautious in my answer. "If it's prepared properly."

"Hmm. That's up to Kay, I guess. She found some recipe for eggplant patties and wanted to try them out on you."

Everyone else, of course, was a meat-eater. I hadn't been able to convert my new family yet. "The secret is to salt your eggplant slices first to draw out the bitter juices," I told him. "Then rinse 'em and pat 'em dry. I make eggplant lasagna now and again."

In fact, it was my go-to for holiday meals, when I bothered. I hadn't in some time.

SMOKE

"I'll remember that," Rick told me. I prevented myself from letting out a sarcastic 'sure.'

"You can just throw the slices on the grill," I said instead. "Brush 'em with a little olive oil. Serve 'em in a bun with some cheese, maybe."

Rick made a bit of a face at that. "With ketchup?" he joked.

I smiled but my answer was serious. "Spaghetti sauce would be better."

He stepped back from the grill to admire his work. "Bright and shiny," he proclaimed.

I shrugged. "It'll just get dirty again."

"A clean grill won't smoke as much. There's enough of that in the air."

"That's true," I admitted. It had been a dry spring, even drier than usual. This was always the season for that in Florida. Smoke would blow out to the coast from one wildfire or another, leaving a haze on the town, on the ocean. Making eyes smart some, too. "Do you hear bells?"

Rick nodded. "Something's ding-dinging. Up that way." He gestured toward the west, up Eighth Street. A moment later a bicycle came into view from behind the hedge, its rider alternately ringing her bell and waving.

"Patty."

"So it is," agreed Rick. "I thought maybe she'd ridden along with the Guzmans today."

I only nodded to that. I knew she liked Alvaro but not enough to sit watching his daughter surf all day. "She did threaten to get a bike."

"Did she? Not that far to her new place, is it?"

"Nope. It would be easy enough to walk it." I waved back. It was a nice looking bicycle, in white. An English-style three-speed, wasn't it? Patty wouldn't mind spending a little money for something decent.

"I'd best get the charcoal going," said Rick, turning back to his grill. It was a big brick affair he had built himself. Rick worked construction, at least from time to time. Carpentry, mostly. There were several neat stacks of lumber toward the back of his yard, under tarps. Much of it, I suspected, had been 'liberated' from one job or another.

I went to greet Patty. "Now you have to get a bike too," were her first words. "That was the agreement."

"I'll just steal Marty's," I told her. "She's going to have her license shortly and won't want to ride it anymore." Though I might look more ridiculous than usual on a girl's bike with a banana seat.

"Her and Charlie both, right? Hey, you got anything to drink?"

"We'll have to go into the kitchen for that." I picked up my cooler. "And yeah, Charlie should be able to get her license back this summer."

"It's about time you brought that wine in here," greeted me as I passed through the back door into the kitchen. The ground floor of the Bells' home was identical to mine, except flipped left and right, but at some point a wooden frame second story had been added on top of the concrete block structure. It might even have been built that way originally, back in the Fifties. And, as with my place, the front had been converted into a store — *Kay's Korner*, boutique, gift shop, and gallery.

"I think they're happier to see the cooler than us," I told Patty.

"We're always happy to see Patty," my fiancee informed me. "Here's the corkscrew. Get busy."

She handed it to me and I did get busy, first the red, then the white. "None of the kids around?" I asked Kay. Jan's Malibu was outside so I had kind of expected to see her.

"Jan's upstairs, as is Charlie," she replied.

Michelle felt it necessary to scold me. "You aren't very good at keeping tabs on your future daughter. Jan is helping her prep for the GED test."

I only nodded. I could have asked where Richie was but figured it didn't matter and might even get me in more trouble. I'd mentioned the kids just to be polite anyway. "Ready to pour," I announced.

Kay got goblets, I poured, we drank. I assumed Rick had beer out at the grill. If he didn't, he'd come in and get some. The burgers or whatever he intended to cook, too.

"I suppose the boyfriends will be along later," I said.

"That goes without saying," replied Michelle. "But we just said it, didn't we? This merlot is so-so. Let me try the chablis."

"This merlot is only so-so, but I won't throw it away," I half-sang. "Should I write the rest of that song?"

"I think not," felt Kay. Michelle and Patty seemed to concur. There was a clatter on the stairs as both girls heavy-footed it down. One of the dogs, a little brown long-haired one, scampered behind.

"Dave just pulled in," said Jan, and hurried out the back door. Charlie followed at a more leisurely pace.

"Stay," Kay told the pup when it looked like it wanted to follow. It came and settled by her feet. "Jan tells me Dave is going back to college to get his law degree. She thinks the example of your friend Sally prompted it."

I sipped and thought a moment. "Part time, I would assume." Dave wouldn't bail on his rising career at the Cully Beach Police Department. "I wonder if they'll be in the same classes."

"Might not even be in the same schools," Michelle pointed out.

Maybe not. If he took courses over in Gainesville, he'd have more opportunities to be with Jan. She was headed there in the fall, having finished up at the local junior college. "Or on the other hand, they might end up car pooling," I told her.

The subject of our conversation came in right then, Jan on his arm. I was too comfortable with my glass of wine to get up and shake, so I only gave him a wave.

"Mr. Guzman just pulled in," Charlie called from the open door. "I'm gonna run over there."

"I hope Alvaro comes over and joins us," said Patty. "Are we expecting anyone else?"

"Just John-boy, I think," Kay said. "And Richie and Cathy are around somewhere. We can get to cooking. Ted, make yourself useful and start carrying things out to Rick."

"Will do." I swallowed the last of my chablis and grabbed a platter of burgers and sausages. I didn't see any of the rumored eggplant patties.

Chapter 4

"We decided to go over and invite Karrie," Charlie told us. "Hope you don't mind." She didn't look like she actually cared whether we did. Marty, standing at her side, seemed a tad more apprehensive about it.

"She's still camping at your place?" asked Kay.

"And paying rent," Michelle told her, and then laughed. "Though it is next to nothing. Ted didn't want to charge her at all."

I shrugged. "She's just using a little electric in her van."

"And coming over to use our shower," Charlie reminded me. That was the outside shower, of course. Karrie Goodpaster was not coming into our home.

Michelle said, "If we decide to rent that place she will have to move on."

"Maybe Karrie could rent it," said Charlie.

Maybe, but I doubted it. "I'd rather move you into it. We're eager to get you out of the house, anyway."

"Mom, are you going to let him get away with that?" she asked Michelle, as seriously as she could manage — which wasn't very.

"You'll just have to accept that you have an evil stepfather, dear," her mother replied. "They happen when you have a fairy tale romance."

I had to kiss her for that. Then I said, "I do plan to convert the extra bedroom — your bedroom, Charlie — into more shop space. A board room, maybe, opening off the main shop area."

"And don't be surprised," added Michelle, "if the two of us eventually move into the other house also."

"Darn, just when I thought I was rid of you! Hey, here comes your dad, Marty."

The two girls went to meet Al Guzman. I wondered if Patty would too but she stayed put at one of the picnic tables. It was then that Dave Blake was able to get me to himself.

"I thought you might want an update on, um, what you found," he said, low, almost whispering.

"I didn't find it," I reminded him. Nor was I all that interested but I let him go on.

"The autopsy isn't done yet, of course, what with it being the weekend." His tone only slightly revealed his disapproval of the way things were done in small town Florida. "Definitely a woman, though. There was some jewelry but pretty much everything else had disintegrated. The coroner thinks perhaps nine or ten years in the sand. Total guess, I suspect."

"No idea who she was then. An accident maybe?" I pictured a drowning victim washing up and being buried by heavy surf. I wasn't sure how accurate the picture was.

"Unlikely. There appeared to be trauma to the skull." The slightest of shrugs. "That could, admittedly, be accidental. We'll have a better idea when we get the autopsy results."

"Murder? It seems like an awfully public place to plant a body."

"Easy enough at night, when you think about it, even there in the downtown. Just drive up and drop her over the edge of the dune, dig a shallow hole, and be done. No one could see you from the road."

I nodded, slowly. It was a likely enough scenario but in the wrong order. Dig the grave first and have it ready. One wouldn't even need a shovel in the soft sand. "And just far enough away from the lights at the pier."

"Yep. The chief would like you to drop by the station sometime and give a fuller statement. Not that you know anything, Ted. Just a formality."

"I'll be downtown tomorrow. Maybe I can stop in." I glanced up to see someone coming across the Guzman's yard. Three some-ones, in fact. Karrie, undoubtedly and — oh, Richie and his girl-friend. I wondered briefly what they'd been doing over there. Maybe they had followed Charlie and Marty.

The two youngsters were about Marty's age, but a grade behind her in school. I could see them hanging with her, or wanting to, especially in that all three were surfers. I should ask her how she did in competition this weekend.

No need. Alvaro was already boasting to anyone who would listen. "First place," he was telling us. Marty's first 'first' since moving up into the Junior Women's division on turning sixteen, and also moving into a new district with relocating here in Cully Beach. It hadn't taken her long to adjust.

"Another trophy? You'll have to build more shelves," Patty told Alvaro.

"There's a wall of them already," said Charlie. I hadn't been in the Guzman's house — not since they had moved in — so I took her word for it.

"Can I see them?" asked Karrie Goodpaster. "Oh, and thanks for inviting me."

I wondered if that was Charlie or Marty's idea. Didn't matter, I guess. "You'll need to cater to a second vegetarian," I informed our hosts.

Karrie shoved back her unruly straw-colored hair and gave me a bit of a skeptical look. "Don't you ever cheat, Shaper?"

"Not since I've known him," said Rick.

"Shaper sticks to things," Charlie added.

I tried to, these days. None of these folks knew of my past failures and I was willing to let it stay that way. Ted 'Shaper' Carrol had been reborn in Cully Beach, reborn ten years ago.

"Hey, there's John," noted Charlie, as her boyfriend's old pickup pulled in. "Now we can eat!"

Chapter 5

"There are classes you will need to attend," Father Paul informed us.

I knew about that. I might not have mentioned it to Michelle. "Locally?" she asked. A sensible question. I could depend on her for that sort of thing.

"The ones with me are," the priest replied. "Or meetings, if you will. Talks. The Pre-Cana conference is held in St. Augustine. The next is quite soon, in fact. There should be more dates available in the fall. That would be cutting it close for your desired wedding date."

"No way, Father," I said. "We're not taking any chances." So I had told him last week. I had come to talk with Father Paul as soon as Michelle had finally accepted my proposal.

This was her first time here. "September," she said.

"Or October," I added. "It would be convenient to get our honeymoon out of the way before we get busy with tourist season."

Father Paul's round face always seemed to wear a smile, but it was broader now. "Your husband-to-be is quite the romantic, Miss Jackson."

"Don't I know it? Call me Michelle, sir, um, Father." She gave me a quick sidelong look, wondering if she had said that correctly. "And I actually still call myself Mrs. Jackson, being a widow." Michelle's voice sort of trailed off on that.

"Yes, a widow." He glanced down at the papers we had brought along, laid out on a dark, rather battered desk. Father Paul had told me what we would need when I popped in last week. "Twice? My condolences to you, Michelle." Then with a definite twinkle in his eye, "And perhaps a touch of concern for you, Ted."

I'd heard this joke before. In fact, I had made it myself. "Third time is the charm," I told him.

"Maybe so. That's not exactly church teaching!" We both thought that was funny. Michelle didn't really get it, I think, but smiled anyway. "We should be able to manage a wedding date around what you want," the priest went on. "But you must make it to the class in St. Augustine. You might plan on attending a retreat, too, if you can. I'll get some dates for you."

He looked at the papers again, or squinted might be a better description. "Are these addresses right? I know yours, Ted. This other one — next door?"

Michelle jumped in. "A couple houses up." Since the motel had closed down, her mail had been delivered to the Bell house. We hadn't gotten around to changing that.

"Hmm. You know the church would not approve of you living in sin, if you'll excuse an old-fashioned expression. Do keep that in mind. Especially you, Ted."

"Certainly, Father." My conscience was quite clear on that. Loving Michelle would never be a sin.

A couple minutes later we were stepping out of the little office in the rear of the rectory. "Time to stop for coffee?" I asked. It was around opening time for the shop but Charlie had promised to take care of things till I got back.

"No, I'd better get to work." We headed toward our rides. We had come over separately, Michelle after already stopping by the bank. "I feel odd calling someone younger than me 'father,'" she said, and then snickered. "And way younger than you."

"He's just a baby-face," I responded. "Looks younger than he is." Still, Father Paul was younger than either of us, somewhere in his thirties, I would guess.

SMOKE

Michelle headed back to the bank, a few blocks south of the church. There was no point in going somewhere to sit and drink coffee by myself, so I followed right behind in my truck but continued across Main Street — the Scott City Road — after she turned aside. I might as well stop by the police station as Dave Blake had suggested.

A small blond woman was manning the front desk this morning. Or womanning it. They seemed to be using Anna Church all over the place, maybe because she was the newest member of the force. They would need someone to replace Jim Trejo, wouldn't they? I wondered what sort of duty he was pulling this last week in Cully Beach.

"Oh, Ted," she said, spying me. So she was finally willing to call me Ted, eh? That was okay with me. "Chief Cotton wants to talk with you himself. Let me see if he's busy." She buzzed his phone, exchanged a few words. "Go right ahead," said Officer Church. She rightly assumed I knew the way.

That Bill Cotton would handle this himself was not at all surprising. It was a small force, after all, and a murder case was pretty important stuff. The door to his office was standing open.

"Hi Ted, have a seat." He waved me toward one of a pair with splitting vinyl upholstery. Sort of maroon. Might have been brighter once. "All I need is to get something down on paper with your signature. I probably could have come by the shop."

"There was enough of that the last couple months," I replied. The chief chuckled appropriately. We'd had a few early morning clandestine meetings when he was under suspicion.

He got up and brought over a clipboard with a couple sheets on it, handing it to me and sitting down in the other chair. "Just look it over and if it's correct, sign. Or if you need to add something, write it in and I'll initial it."

There was little to read and it all seemed correct. I put my signature at the bottom and handed it back to him. He signed too, witnessing it. "Any word yet on who it was?" I asked. "Or whether it was or wasn't murder."

He slid the clipboard onto his desk and leaned back. "Nothing yet. Probably before the end of the day. I don't know how much they can tell from those bones. This isn't one of those television shows, after all. The doc will be doing well to determine a cause of death."

I was glad Bill was old-school enough to use the words, rather than say COD. I hardly ever heard him use cop jargon. "Dave said there was some jewelry. Learn anything from that?" I was only mildly curious, you understand. I might as well ask while I was there.

"That went with the body. Or the bones, I should say. We took some pictures —" He stood and rummaged through the folders on his desk. "Here."

He handed it to me and leaned back, sitting on the edge of his desk, as I opened to a pair of glossy enlarged photos and some handwritten notes. That necklace —

It must have showed on my face. "What is it, Ted?"

"I know this necklace." I looked again. Was I sure? Yes. It was one of a kind. "I think — I think I might have known the victim."

"Just from the jewelry?"

"Yes. I made it."

Chapter 6

What had Alyce been doing in Cully Beach? I had known her, yes, but that was long ago, down in the Miami area. I told Cotton this.

Of course, someone else might have been wearing the necklace I had made for her. It might not have been Alyce Noble in the sand. That seemed unlikely, didn't it? It was a pendant I had crafted from bits of leftover fiberglass and resin, for a 'stained glass' look, back when I was doing contract glassing on other shapers' surf-boards. I made only a few and each was unique. I could recognize the one I put together to give to Alyce.

It was kind of clunky, really. I think she was the only one who actually liked it. Anyway, I had been able to give Bill Cotton a name before driving home. The phone rang almost as soon as I got in the door.

It was Bill. "Hi, Ted. The coroner's report came right after you left. Definitely murder, she says. A blow to the head."

"Damn," was all I could say. I hated to think of it.

"The doc says the victim was almost certainly African-American. Does that fit what you know?"

"It does. Alyce was black. A tall woman too." Taller than me.

"Hmm. Yes, the report says probably around five-ten or eleven. I guess that's our victim then. I'm sorry it was someone you knew but, um, you know we'll have to talk to you more about it now."

"Understood. I'd like to get to the bottom of it myself." I'd liked Alyce. We'd never seriously dated or anything like that but we did have our moments.

"We're following up on the name you gave us. So far, no one seems to have any record of her."

"Someone should remember her. She made a bit of a splash in Miami fifteen years or so ago." I wasn't going to say she was pretty much a high-class prostitute. The police would figure that sort of thing out on their own.

A few pleasantries and we hung up. Nothing more I could do there, not right now.

My old college friend and surf buddy Mike Gainey had introduced me to Alyce, hadn't he? Or to one or another of her friends. He hadn't really moved in the circles they did, but there were mutual acquaintances. I could give his name to Bill if they still had trouble with her identity, but I didn't much want to pull him into any of this. Other names, too. Some of them even still alive and safely behind bars.

Charlie was already at her studying, books spread on the kitchen table. "Can I help any?" I asked her. "I'm not as smart as Jan but I know a little something about this and that."

She sat up straight and gave me a look. Other folks give me that same look sometimes. I'm not certain why. "I study with Jan not because she is smart but because she makes me work. You're the smartest guy I know, Shaper, but you would let me get away with, um, malingering. That's one of the words I learned in class. I hope it's on the test!"

"It definitely should be. It's not used nearly enough. I'll go malinger up front now and let you work."

Darned if she didn't give me that look all over again. "Yeah, sure. I know you can't stand to be doing nothing."

I knew it too but didn't feel like admitting to it. I went into the showroom and looked things over. Not a single customer on a Monday morning in the off season. Maybe I should start an inventory. I'd sort of relied on Jan to help me with those these last few years. I'd miss her when she went off to the University of Florida in the fall.

Did I really belong here myself? I wasn't young anymore, and I'd taken on a family. It felt a bit odd, being older now than the parents of the kids I surfed with. When I thought about it. I tried to avoid that. But what else could I do? Michelle obviously expected me to stick with what I was doing. She wouldn't have invested in the property next door otherwise, wouldn't have taken a job in Cully Beach. Wouldn't be with me.

I guess I couldn't disappoint her, now could I? I pondered how I might rearrange the place if I knocked an opening through the wall into what was now Charlie's bedroom. Formerly the guest bedroom, in theory, and the place where all my clutter ended up in fact. Put the boards in there? Maybe, but people liked to see surfboards when they walked in. That's how they knew it was a surf shop.

Ha, I should put together a surf team and we could use the space for all our trophies! I'd have to poach young Marty from Kim Timble. I should certainly talk to the girl about working in the shop. She was as responsible as Jan Bell.

Hazy outside. Smoke from inland wildfires. The afternoon sea breeze would send it back, I hoped. The weather was nice, otherwise, though already getting hot at the end of April. That was Florida. I would still refuse to run any air conditioning in this place. In the back, in our living quarters, yes, but not up here in the shop.

And that only at night to make sleep possible. Michelle and Charlie hadn't spent a summer in my home yet. I anticipated complaints.

Was that somebody knocking at the back door? Or thumping. I went back into the kitchen to see Charlie let Karrie Goodpaster in. Karrie looked over the array of books and papers. "Your GED test is this week, right? Hi, Ted." She leaned her thin frame back against the counter.

"We're reviewing tonight and Wednesday," said Charlie. "Test on Friday. I'm thirsty. Would you like anything?" She peered into the refrigerator.

"No thanks. You should take a college class or two after you get your diploma. I've signed on to teach through the summer. English One-Oh-One! You could be one of my students."

"That assumes I pass," replied Charlie, pouring herself a glass of iced tea. It wasn't surprising she would start to have jitters about that now, with the test so near.

"Jan would never let you fail," Karrie assured her. "Nor would Mr. Shaper."

"Darn right," I put in. "I'll be driving her over first thing Friday morning."

Charlie nodded, sitting down again. "Testing is available all through Friday and Saturday to fit everybody's schedule. I'm going in as early as I can on Friday and getting it done!"

Karrie turned to me. "Which brings me to why I came over, Ted. I think I'd like to stay next door longer. I really like the privacy. But not if I'm in your way, okay?"

"Not so far. Maybe I should put put a 'no trespassing' sign to keep it private."

Charlie snickered. "You could use it in one of your poems."

Jan had once shown us a poem by Ms. Goodpaster, consisting of words copied from road signs. The author termed it *bricolage*. I won't tell you what I might have called it. "I'll have to put it up in Spanish, too," I said. "*Prohibida la entrada!*"

"Ooh, I like that one," said Karrie. "But it's cheating to use it unless you actually put up the sign."

"Far be it from me," I informed her, "to inhibit the artistic process."

"I know you're kidding me, Shaper, but I know it's also true. Hey, do you have any new aloha shirts in the shop? They inspire my artistic process too."

"Then come on up and I'll show you."

"That I will," Goodpaster replied. "And you," she said, addressing Charlie, "keep studying. I do expect to see you in my class." Karrie's air of seriousness was surprisingly convincing — to someone who didn't know her.

"Yes, ma'am!" Charlie grinned and returned to her lessons.

Chapter 7

"May Day! May Day!" I called out.

Charlie poked her head out of her room, at the end of the hall. "What's the emergency?"

"No emergency. Just letting you know it was May Day. Time to frolic around the May Pole and crown the May Queen!"

"Sheesh." She slammed her door shut again. Michelle hadn't even bothered to check what the commotion was about. I'd bet Karrie Goodpaster would appreciate a celebration of the day, but her unicorn-bedecked van had pulled out a little while ago, off to her job as an instructor at the junior college in Scott City.

She'd be busy. This was exam week, the end of the semester, so everyone there would be busy. Jan would need to concentrate on her own studying. Her two years at the college were coming to an end. The same for John Brody. He'd have little time for Charlie.

I glanced up at the kitchen clock. Well past Seven. The girls would be up and ready to go soon. Michelle anyway. I started a new pot of coffee brewing for them and considered going back to the workshop until opening time. The phone rang up front.

More often than not, at this hour I would let the machine handle it. No real need to answer outside of business hours. Ah, might as well. "Cully Beach Surf Shop," I said. "Ted speaking."

It was Pat Edwards. He would know I was up and about but he should have known as well I might not answer the call. We gabbed about nothing much for a bit, catching up on the whole week and a day since I'd last seen him. Then he said, "You know it's just a little over three weeks to the Florida Folk Festival. Are you planning to make it this year?"

I would have said four weeks, but whatever. "Dunno," I admitted. "Maybe for Friday. Especially if Michelle can get the day." I thought a second or two and added, "And Charlie is willing to watch the shop."

It's not too far to White Springs, but I'd mostly missed the festival these past ten years. Memorial Day weekend was not a good time to shut down the shop, not even on Friday, though I had done that a couple times.

"Oh, Charlie should come too," he told me. "Anyone and everyone is welcome at my place in Ruby. It's only a hour drive from there."

The way Pat drove, yeah. Make that an hour and a half for me. "I'll mention it to her," I promised. "Um, you never met Alyce Noble, did you?"

A short pause. "I don't think so. The name sounds familiar."

"I probably mentioned her to you sometime. Someone I knew in Miami, way back."

"Oh." Another pause. "A friend of Mike?"

"Yep. It's not important. I just found out she was dead."

"Does Mike know?"

"Not yet. The, um, police might want to contact him. Alyce was murdered."

"Then I'll leave it up to them to contact him. Don't have a number for Mike anyway."

"Me neither. I think Patty might." Yeah, I would ask her the next time I saw her. I could even walk over to her house.

"Okay. Let me know if you have any festival plans. I'll be playing again this year. Oh, and Bran says he's going to come."

"I thought he always avoided it."

"His latest girlfriend is a folkie. Guys will change for that sort of thing."

Temporarily, maybe. "Alright, Pat, I'll let you know. And I'll mention it to Patty, too. Unless you already called her."

"I would have but now I don't need to. Hey, good to talk to you Ted. See you in three weeks, I hope!"

"Bye," I said, and hung up.

The Florida Folk Festival — hadn't I promised to take Alyce there, way back? It never happened. Lots of reasons why. I'm not sure she took me seriously about it, anyway.

Michelle was up and pouring herself cold cereal. "That was Pat, wasn't it?" she asked. "I can usually guess when he's on the line with you."

"Sure 'nuff. Do you think you could get the Twenty-fifth off to drive up to White Springs?"

"Maybe. I'll see. The festival, right? Betty and I gabbed about it when they were here."

I glanced again at the clock and wondered if Patty was up this early. I could call her — no. "I'm going for a walk," I let Michelle know. "If I'm not back by opening time, Charlie can take care of it. Or not. Doesn't matter much."

"Okay. Headed anyplace special?"

"Patty's place. We should get bikes like her, shouldn't we?" I figured if I posed a question immediately she might not ask me why I was going.

"Bit of an expense." Her forehead furrowed just slightly, as some thought or another made its way into her head. "Unless we rented them out, like you do with the old surfboards."

Don't think I hadn't considered that. "Liability could be a problem. We'd need more insurance."

"Oh. Yeah. Going to invite Patty to your folk festival?" She hadn't forgotten.

"Among other things." I hesitated over adding more to that. "Some of them having to do with that body they found. I need to fill you in better on that." I hadn't told her anything of what I had learned the day before.

"Yes, you do," Michelle told me. "Now get along."

I popped a cap on my head — it was already getting pretty sunny — and headed out, crossing the Guzman and Bell yards to Eighth Street. There I took a left, west toward the river. They call it a river but it's really a bay, separating Cully Beach from the mainland. I needn't go that far.

Patty's newly-purchased house was several blocks back, none the less, and it took maybe ten minutes to walk the distance. More if I ambled along like some. It was a pretty big place, wood frame, on stilts. Not particularly new.

The house was set on a large parcel of land too, double lots. A lot more yard than I'd want to take care of. I could see her gray Miata parked underneath. There were outside stairs front and back. I went up the front ones and rang her bell. Knocked too, just to be sure.

Patty answered at once. "Hey," she said, "if you'd been a couple minutes later I'd have been off on my bike. I'm riding it all over town now! Come on in."

The place was something of a jumble, partially unpacked boxes sitting around, the furniture sparse and placed out from the walls. I didn't think she'd brought any to speak of with her from Atlanta. "You need any help with this, let me know," I told her. "I'll send Charlie over."

"I'm in no hurry. Come look at my studio. You'll be the first visitor."

"Not Alvaro?"

"Hasn't been here yet. I think I'll have to invite him. He doesn't drop by unexpectedly like some people."

The room she had made into her studio was well suited, large, plenty of natural light, on the north side of the house. It was probably labeled the 'family room' by whoever drew the plans. A drawing board sat angled in the middle of the space. Patty might not have decided on a final position for it yet.

"Nice." I was a tad envious, even if I hadn't painted in ages. "No easel?" I asked.

"On the shopping list. So what brings you here, Ted?"

"Aside from your fascinating personality? I need to get in touch with Mike Gainey. Neither Pat nor I have his number. We probably could have found it but we're not that ambitious."

Then, of course, I had to sit down and tell her the story of Alyce Noble. Not the whole story, mind you. "I'll call him myself," she said when I finished. "I'll give him your number too, if he wants to talk, okay?" I noted she didn't offer to give me Mike's number. Maybe she thought she should ask him first.

"That's fine. Now, how do you feel about folk festivals?"

Chapter 8

"So there was never any sex?" asked Michelle. "Not that it matters to me, you understand." Sure, Michelle. I believe that.

"Nope. She needed a friend, not a boyfriend. Though who knows what might have happened if we'd stayed in touch?" It was a valid question, though not a very serious one. I couldn't resist adding it.

"Why didn't you?"

"I went home to be a caregiver for my parents. Back to Genoa. They both passed within six months of each other. Then I came here."

She nodded. "Time to break with the past? Just like me."

"Pretty much."

Michelle put her book aside. "I'd best let you get your beauty sleep, Ted. You look bushed. I won't even suggest fooling around."

"I'd give it my best," I promised.

"Your best would have been a couple hours ago. I missed my window of opportunity."

She was right, of course. I tended to run all day and crash in the evening. We flipped off our beside lights and snuggled. It was a bit warm for snuggling, to be honest — I told you about me and air conditioning. We had only a sheet for covering and that was almost too much.

It would cool down. We might need to pull a spread up by the wee hours. The windows were open and the cool Atlantic waters were near. By midsummer, the ocean would be like bathwater, the nights too sultry.

I managed to sleep through most of the night. I've never been good at doing that. At five, I slipped out, leaving Michelle to slumber on, started the coffee maker, walked across the highway to look at the ocean. My usual routine.

It was flat. That was expected. There would be a lot of flat days through summer. I stood and looked out over the dark Atlantic for a while anyway, breathed in its fresh salty scent. Not much smoke lingering this time of morning. To my left stood the low seawall of the demolished *Easy Breezes* motel. Burkhardt Development seemed to have canceled their plans to erect a condo on the site. Their billboard was gone. Michelle would probably know if it was up for sale again. That sort of thing would be talked about at the bank.

The new security lights were out too. As was the old one. It was pretty darn dark. I should complain again about there being no street lights this far south. I headed back, crossing A-1-A at the corner. Sometimes the Bells' dogs would bark at me, sometimes they wouldn't. No noise this morning. Rick could sleep in.

No one much parked along the roadside this morning. John hadn't been spending the night, what with both Charlie and him facing exams. When he went off to the University of North Florida in the fall, none of us would be seeing much of him. He was a good kid. I hoped he and Charlie could make it work.

But they were young. Shoot, I had to wait till I was fifty before I could make anything work.

A car was parked across the road, at the abandoned filling station. That was unusual. Maybe an early surf-caster. Or a late one. No matter. I turned up my own driveway.

The sound of a car door closing — I spun around at once, wary. Oh, a police cruiser had pulled in beside the car and was checking it out. I couldn't make out who it was, only that a flashlight was in his hand and that it was probably a guy. I decided to stand there and see what was going on. It was starting to get a little light out.

Jack Saunders. That's who it was. His short reign as second in command at the station had ended with Bill's reinstatement and now he was back on patrol. I suspected Jack wasn't entirely happy about that. A tall man had gotten out of the car. I couldn't make out anything about him but he was gesturing in my direction. I ambled down to the edge of the road but didn't cross. I wasn't going to insert myself in police business.

But Saunders waved me over. "This man and his friend were sleeping here," he informed me. "Says they had come to see you and were waiting until you opened up."

I peered at the fellow. A stranger to me, tall, young, hair sort of a dirty blond. It almost looked gray but that could have been the light. I could make out the form of a second man inside the car. Old and greenish. The car that is, not the man. "I don't think I know you," I said.

He gave me a crooked grin. "We talked on the phone. I'm Charlotte's brother. Her half-brother." He held out a large hand. "Sebastian Furr." With a jerk of his head he indicated his companion. "That's my friend Al in there. Al Brown."

"Alistair," came a muffled voice from within the vehicle.

I shook Sebastian's hand. "I'd invite you in but I don't think anyone else is up yet. Maybe you *should* wait until shop hours." There was no way I was letting these strangers in my house right now.

Saunders gave an approving nod and turned back to Furr. "I don't want to come across you sleeping by the road again, young man. You'd better find a place to stay if you don't want to be arrested for vagrancy." There probably wasn't much to that threat.

The police would be more likely to just tell them to move along again.

Sebastian nodded. "Yes, sir. It was a long drive and we got here kind of early. Overnight from Virginia."

"Very well. But I would suggest you go down to the corner and park there an hour or two. Get some coffee." He meant the convenience store across Eighth Street. When Sebastian just stood there, he added, "Now."

"Oh, right." Furr got in and cranked the engine for a few seconds before it turned over, then eased into the street.

The policeman watched them go and then turned his attention to me again. "Will you be okay with them coming back, Mr. Carrol?"

"Sure, if it's light out and folks are around. I thank you for checking them out, Officer Saunders."

"Someone called about the car sitting here. It might have been your neighbor." He nodded in the direction of Alvaro Guzman's house.

"I wouldn't be surprised," I replied. I *was* surprised he didn't come out to see what was going on. Al was a pretty early riser too. "Thanks again." I crossed the highway back to my place. Charlie was already drinking coffee in the kitchen.

I decided to say nothing to her about her brother. Better to wait until Michelle joined us.

A rap on the back door. I hoped Furr hadn't returned. "Who is it?"

"Alvaro!"

"And Marty!"

I opened up to the Guzmans, father and daughter. "Is everything okay, Ted?" asked Al, before I could even say good morning.

Charlie was curious but said nothing. "Sure, Al. Come on in." I gave Marty a look. "This is still a school day, right? You're not out yet."

"Two more weeks, Shaper."

"A little more than that," said Alvaro. "But summer vacation is coming. We may travel and allow Marty to surf in new places."

"And be seen in new places," I said. The girl had a reputation to build.

"A little publicity doesn't hurt anything," he admitted.

"Yeah. Make sure Kim Timble is paying for part of it," I told him. "I'm waiting for Michelle to come out before I talk about our visitors."

Charlie looked even more curious. "Understood," said Guzman. "As long as all is well with you, we needn't stay." He ushered his daughter out before I could even ask them to sit down and have a cup of coffee.

"Something going on, Shaper?" asked Charlie.

"A lot of somethings," I said, filling myself a mug. I splashed a fair amount of milk into it and sat. "But a new something this morning."

"Gee, and we hadn't even finished with the old somethings."

"There's only one something I want you to concentrate on."

"Oh, you know I'm going to do okay on the test. And I took Karrie's advice and applied for admission at the college. I'll need to have the GED in hand before I can go any further there."

"Then you'll have to concentrate on that. You won't have any time for poor John-boy."

"We'll work something out," she assured me. "Good morning, Mother."

"Is it?" muttered Michelle. "What's all the commotion been out here? Was that Alvaro?"

"It was." I decided to volunteer no more than that.

Michelle drained the last of the coffee into her cup. "One of you get busy and make some more of this. I'll need it."

"I suspect you will," I said, getting up.

"We have a new something to deal with," confided Charlie.

"And that something is down at the corner right now, also drinking coffee," I told them, as I chucked the used coffee filter into the compost bin. "Charlie's brother is here."

Chapter 9

He looked a bit like Charlie. Except for the nose. Charlie had her mom's aquiline beak. Michelle blamed that on her French grandmother. Sebastian Furr must have had about four years on his half-sister. His hair still looked almost gray under the showroom lights.

I hadn't been able to get a good look at Sebastian's traveling companion until now. Alistair Brown was a good head shorter and somewhat thicker. Not fat so much as deep chested and big boned. His skin matched his name. I wasn't too surprised when Sebastian called him 'Brown-Bear.'

"They're a couple, aren't they?" Charlie whispered to me. I nodded agreement. It wasn't hard to figure that out.

"We won't bother you right now," Sebastian had said. "Just wanted to introduce ourselves before you had to be somewhere else."

"Only I have a job to run off to," Michelle assured him. "In fact, I need to go right now. You all work out some time for us to get together later." With that, she abandoned us and went out to her van. It started once again. That was always a bit of a surprise.

"Charlie needs to be busy this morning too," I told our visitors. "She's cramming for her GED test on Friday. How long are you staying?" We were standing around in the shop. I hadn't invited the pair into the back yet.

Sebastian seemed to hesitate. Just a little. "A day or two. Then we head down to Miami. My mom still lives down there." He looked like he had swallowed something he wanted to spit back out. "And her husband."

Not 'my step-father.' "You lived with your aunt?" I asked.

"She pretty much raised me. Hey, Brown-Bear, how about hitting the beach?"

"Okay with me," Alistair replied in a surprisingly high and mellifluous voice. He looked around the shop. "We'd buy something, sir, if we had any money."

"Wouldn't we all?" I said. "Call me Shaper."

"Come by this afternoon, maybe," said Charlie. "I have my last class tonight so I can't go anywhere this evening."

"It seems we arrived at a most inopportune time, Bear," remarked Sebastian, in a faux-British accent.

"Indeed so, my dear Sebastian," responded Alistair Brown. He might have pulled it off a little better.

"At least it's a great day for the beach," I told them. "Except for the smoke."

"We drove through some pretty bad patches last night," said Furr. "Some stretches of the Interstate were closed."

"No rain in sight, either. We need a tropical storm to put out all those fires."

"Oh, you just want one for the surf it makes," said Charlie. "I'm gonna go crack the books now. Later, guys." She disappeared into the kitchen.

"I like your sister," said Al Brown.

"She seems okay," agreed Sebastian. "I didn't know what to expect. Hey, thanks for putting up with us, um, Shaper." He held out a hand to shake. "We'll try to pop by later." I shook with him, and Alistair too. A minute later, their dark green Granada was headed uptown.

Still more than an hour to opening time but the door had been hanging open. I left it that way. A few minutes later, a pair of policemen in bike shorts wandered in. Jim Trejo and Jay Johnson.

"Hey, guys," I greeted them. "Haven't seen you on a bike in a while, Jim."

"I finishing up my last week on beach patrol," responded Jim. "I like the duty and there wasn't much point in assigning any case-work to me."

"I'm gonna miss him, even if he is a hard ass," Jay said. "With Jim leaving and Blake moving up the ladder, I'll be senior officer on bike patrol for a while."

"He'll have to put up with the out of shape partners Millie assigns him."

"Some are okay. Anna Church works hard but her legs are too short!" Both men chuckled at that. "The Martian says he might like to try it out."

"Martian?" I was fairly familiar with the members of the force but that was a new name to me.

"Marvin Dobbs. Haven't you met him?"

"I don't think so."

"Sure you have, Shaper," came a voice from the kitchen. Charlie came in to join us. "He took your statement the morning those thugs attacked you."

"Oh." I pictured a fairly young, fairly nondescript man in my mind. "Didn't know his name." Nor was I likely to call him 'Martian.'

"He tried his best to get him to go to the hospital," she said, and shook her head. "Shaper's just too stubborn."

"And cheap," I added. "Don't forget cheap."

"Impatient, too," said Jim. "I can't see you sitting around to be checked over, Ted. Even though you should have."

Jay was impatient too and wanted to get to the next subject. "Is everything okay here, Ted? Saunders asked us to check on you. Suspicious characters lurking or something like that."

That was good of Officer Saunders. "A relative of Charlie," I told them. "Seems like an alright kid. His friend too. Um —" I wasn't sure how to say this. Or whether to say it at all. "You guys getting along okay with Saunders?"

Some of the force — these two especially — had seen Jack Saunders as disloyal when he was acting deputy chief, reporting infractions directly to the mayor. Yes, she had ordered him to. He could have gotten around those orders, had he wished. Others did.

Trejo answered. "Saunders let his ambitions drive him, to be sure, but he's also a by-the-book sort. He'd never let anything get in the way of duty."

Johnson sort of snickered. "That's one hard ass complimenting another one," he said.

Jim could only smile at that. "You know I was willing to bend the rules a little. I think my time here in Cully Beach has helped me be a little more, well, flexible. That's necessary if one aims to move up."

"Then I'll wish you good luck in moving up, Jim," I said.

"Thanks. You were a part of it, you know. You and all those surf rats that hang around the beach. I think I'll even miss them!"

I suspected a few of them might even miss Officer Jaime Trejo. We shook hands and he and Jay peddled off, north into the haze.

Chapter 10

I was on the phone with Patty when Michelle pulled in after work. Charlie had already headed out for her class. Her last class. John Brody chauffeured her, as oft he did.

We said goodbye as she came in through the front door of the shop, hanging open as I preferred. There were a couple girls wandering around looking at stuff. My afternoon part-time employee didn't mind keeping an eye on them.

"That was Patty," I told her, though she might not have cared. "She'd just been talking with our college friend Mike."

"The one who knew the murdered girl, right?" She said this low, so the shoppers wouldn't hear.

"Right. He didn't know much more than we did but he did say she had disappeared and the police asked around about her for a few days."

"Oh. Did the Furr boy and his friend come back?"

"They did. We talked for a while. His Aunt Pam didn't exactly like you, did she?"

"Pam disapproved of my remarriage." She sighed. "And she was probably right to do so. I knew Bradley had problems from the get-go but he did well for a while. Life was good with him for a few years." Michelle frowned. "A couple years. So Pam raised Sebastian?"

"Pretty much. His step-father disliked him. Even more so after he came out."

"Came out where?" It took a moment for it to soak in. "Oh."

Apparently it hadn't been apparent to Michelle. "He and Brown are already on their way south. They say maybe they'll stop by again if they head back to Virginia. I'd guess there isn't much to hold them anywhere."

"And there is nothing to hold me back from a hot shower," she said. "I'll never be able to thank you enough for putting one in, Mr. Carrol."

"It was the only way to get you to agree to marry me," I reminded her. "Speaking of which, Father Paul called with some dates for us."

"Okay. Make sure you have some wine waiting when I get out of the shower."

With that she disappeared into the kitchen. "Keep an eye on things," I told Josh. "That pair over there looks kind of shifty." The girls giggled and Josh reddened a little. "I'll come back before it's time to close."

I'd been lucky to get Josh Tuddle to take a shift this afternoon. The end of the school year was throwing off any attempts at a schedule. In a couple weeks, everyone would have to be shuffled around for the summer. And I would lose Josh, most likely; if not then, by summer's end. He was graduating high school and might be thinking about a real job. College, too.

I had a glass of zinfandel waiting when Michelle exited the shower, drying her hair with a moss green towel. It didn't match her pink bath robe well at all. "That's what I needed Ted." She sat down at the round table and took a couple sips. "Our last night with Charlie not underfoot and I'm too bushed to take advantage of it."

"Not that she's likely to hang around here in the evenings when she's finished with the class." I sat down across from her and poured myself three or four ounces of the red.

"True enough. I guess she'll be studying all day tomorrow."

I looked at her over the rim of my glass. "Nope. Tomorrow is for recharging. Charlie knows what she knows and she should take it easy the day before the test." A sip of the zinfandel before adding, "She knows that."

"Okay, so you two can have a beach day while I slave at my job. That reminds me, I heard today the *Easy Breezes* site has been sold again."

"Any idea what's going to be built there?"

"Another motel." We both had to laugh over that. It should actually be good for business, though, shouldn't it? My shop would be about the first place guests would see. Mine and Kay's.

"How did — Mike, you said? How did Mike know this woman, anyway?" Michelle asked.

"From his job as a social worker. He worked in some of the bad areas of Miami and knew some of the bad people there." I sipped a bit and thought of those days. "In the long term, I got to know Alyce much better than Mike ever did." I didn't explain that and Michelle didn't ask about it.

I suspected I might have to talk about all this to someone at the police department, sooner or later. I'd worry about that when they contacted me.

"You're daydreaming," she said.

"So I was," I admitted. "I hadn't thought of those days much for a long time."

"They weren't really good times, were they?"

"No, they weren't."

The back door was propped open so the air could flow through. It also allowed neighbors to wander in. In this case, Marty Guzman.

"Hi, Mrs. Carrol," she said. "Hi, Shaper."

"Not Mrs. Carrol. Not yet," Michelle reminded her.

"I'm practicing for later!"

"Just call her Mrs. Shaper." Some of the kids were known to do that.

"Just call me Michelle." Michelle looked our young visitor over. "Hmm, we need to get you into the wedding, Marty. A bridesmaid, maybe?"

The girl smiled. It looked more like a polite smile than a pleased one. "As long as I don't have a meet that day. I have my priorities."

Her father had his priorities, anyway. But I went along with it. "If the surf is good, I may play hooky too."

"That goes without question," said Marty. Before Michelle could come up with a suitable rejoinder, Marty went on. "I thought maybe you would be in your shaping bay."

"Stuff got in the way." I lifted my glass. "And wine."

"You need to think about the wedding too," Michelle told me. "Will you ask Pat to be your best man?"

Best man? She was right, I did need to think about it. "Pat — hmm, yeah. I think so." Or maybe Branford Perry. Yeah, we'd been out of touch recently but we'd been buddies since we were kids. I might see him at the folk festival. And there was always Rick. "We'll need a guest list, huh?"

Michelle laughed. "We haven't thought about it at all, Mr. Carrol," she said. "I guess we have lots of time."

"And I have time to do a little work out back," I said. "Apparently Miss Guzman wants to admire my shaping skills."

"You know I just want to learn stuff, Shaper." Marty tried not to sound too serious about it but I knew she was. "I've never had much chance to watch Kim shape."

"Maybe she doesn't shape her own boards at all. She leaves blanks out overnight for the elves."

"I'll be sure to tell her that's what you think. I do know she doesn't glass them herself, like you do."

"I've had a lot of experience in glass work," I said. "Want any more?" I asked Michelle, picking up the wine bottle. She shook her head and I pushed the cork back in. I carried it out the workshop. I had left the big front doors hanging wide.

But the refrigerator was locked up, of course. I opened it and slipped the zinfandel back in before turning to my shaping racks.

"A production board?" asked Marty, looking over the blank I had laid out. The outline had been cut with a reciprocating saw but nothing more.

"Yep. A straight-forward thruster." That is, a three-finned board. "I keep it pretty neutral. Square tail, wide point at center."

"No concaves, right?"

"Not unless they are requested. Flat bottom forward, a mild vee out the back. A bit thicker, a tad straighter in its rocker line than you might prefer, but suited to the average surfer."

I got out my power planer, put on my headphones, and forgot everything else.

Chapter 11

We wouldn't know for a while how well Charlie did. It was a long test and took time to score. We intended to celebrate anyway.

So did lots of other people. It was Cinco de Mayo, and everyone likes an excuse to drink margaritas and eat tacos. "They don't even celebrate this day in Mexico," Charlie informed us. She was full of facts since taking her course.

She was also full of breakfast at last. A late breakfast — Charlie had slept in this Saturday morning. I'd already opened the shop by then. She wandered up after a while.

"Can we expect John to join us this evening?" I asked her.

"Huh-uh. We're going to Sunday dinner at his folks' instead."

With their big family at their big McMansion out the Scott City road. I didn't ask whether the Brody's were still in favor of the two marrying, and soon. John's parents were big on marriage. John and Charlie, not so much. The world had changed since teen-aged Adele and Stan had gotten hitched.

Anyway, Charlie and her boyfriend seemed to have an understanding that they wouldn't think about that sort of thing till John had finished college. He would be headed off to North Florida, in Jacksonville. Now Charlie was planning further education too.

"Want to invite anyone else along? Your tutor?" Meaning Jan.

"I suspect she'll have better things to do on a Saturday night, Shaper. But you can ask anyone you want."

"We'd best check with your mom about that. I do believe that is Cully Beach's one and only unmarked police car pulling up out front." Aside from being painted black, it was identical to the blue and white Tauruses the force drove. "And Dave Blake at the wheel. Are you and Dave speaking this week?" There had been some ups and downs between Charlie and her best friend's boyfriend.

"Yeah. But don't invite him to dinner." She went into the back before Dave came in the front.

He got right into it. "The chief asked me to come down and fill you in on our murder victim. See if you'd come up with anything new also, stuff you might have thought of since he talked to you."

So I told him about Mike, which wasn't much. Dave jotted down the name anyway. "Okay, I've got something here." I had noted the padded envelope he carried in. He slid the contents out on the counter. "This is evidence now but if we don't find a next of kin we might turn it over to you. Or if the next of kin doesn't want it."

It was the necklace I had made for Alyce. There were three pieces to it, medallions one could call them, the central one larger than the other two, with a little surfer figure set in a translucent resin circle of wave and sky. Almost a circle. I didn't try to be exact. The two smaller ones were more abstract, but all three suggested a yin-yang design. They were edged with twisted fiberglass cloth and attached to a chain. That I had purchased.

I could only shake my head. The memories were almost too much. Damn, what had happened to Alyce Noble? I had kind of let her slip out of my mind these last few days, with all the rest of life going on.

"Okay if I handle it?" I asked.

"Sure, Ted. It's been thoroughly processed, not that it mattered. After a decade in the sand no usable evidence survived."

I picked it up. Not really good work. I'd just been experimenting, amusing myself. The girl had liked it and I had given it to her readily. I turned it over. "What's this on the back?"

"Something was scratched onto it. Letters and numbers. We can't make any sense of them. Probably have no bearing on the murder, anyway."

What with the pendant being translucent, the marks did show some from the front. The whole thing was pretty badly weathered now so it didn't matter, but I couldn't see Alyce intentionally marring it without reason.

"SF" I read off. "And a dash. I think. OMS?"

"We think that's a five, not an S," said Dave.

"Hmm, maybe so." I should put on my glasses. "Whatever was used wasn't very sharp. A nail file maybe?"

"As good a guess as any. We can't make out the next bit at all."

It wasn't a letter but a crudely scratched square with a line sticking out of one side. The left side, facing it, and closer to the top than the bottom. I could only shake my head. I wrote the numbers and letters down, though they were meaningless to me and likely to remain so. I also copied the little picture.

"Being investigated again?" came a cheerful voice from the front entry. "You just can't keep out of trouble, can you Shaper?"

"You should write a book about him," Dave told Karrie Goodpaster. "It could be a best seller."

"And get me away from being stuck teaching at a branch campus of a junior college? Sounds like a great idea, Officer Dave."

"I demand a cut of the royalties," I told her. I picked up the junk jewelry I had made and looked at it once more before slipping it back into its envelope. Karrie, to her credit, didn't ask about it. She had heard enough gossip to probably figure out what it was.

An older couple had come in while we spoke and were now browsing among the tee-shirts. Older couples always like the tees. They make inexpensive gifts for grandchildren or whomever, and prove they actually went somewhere and did something. "I'll let you get back to business," said Dave. "Thanks for the info." A nodded goodbye to Goodpaster and he was out the door.

And Charlie was in the other one. She was avoiding Dave, it seemed. Maybe just didn't want to bother with the necessary small talk. "Hi, Karrie. Mom's down at Kay's," she informed me. "Hey, we both have to remember Mother's Day is next weekend."

"Only one of us has to, to be accurate."

"Okay, I'll depend on you to remember and you can depend on me! I think I'm going to go back to the workshop and get my paints out. I've neglected art while I was studying."

"I don't suppose you know your grades yet," said Karrie. "Not to be nosy or anything."

"Nope. Monday or Tuesday."

The older woman nodded. "I have to get all my grades in this coming week. Then a well-deserved vacation! Summer classes won't start till after Memorial Day." She paused. It was an intentionally dramatic pause, I am sure. "I do expect to see you in one of them."

My business should start to pick up again then. It was slow this morning. I glanced outside. Not much traffic. Smoke again.

"If I passed," Charlie was saying. "And whether I did or not, we're going to go out and celebrate tonight anyway. Wanta come along?"

Goodpaster glanced at me. I shrugged. It was okay with me. "Excellent idea," she said. "I can pick Shaper's brain before I start on the book!"

Chapter 12

Three things happened on Tuesday. Charlie got her grades and, yes, she passed all five sections of the test. Bill Cotton himself called up and asked me to drop by the station sometime soon.

And the surf came up. That had priority and I was already in the water when the other two events occurred. It was a pretty good swell, especially for that time of year. I played hooky and didn't get into the shop till Eleven.

There was Charlie, both happy on account of her news and a bit steamed that I hadn't gotten back earlier. I think she wanted to run around the neighborhood shouting about it or something. She had jotted down the chief's message. Tomorrow morning, I decided. If there wasn't any surf.

Things had fallen back into their normal rut. That was fine with me. I guess Alyce Noble was still in the back of my mind. I still wondered a little about what she had scratched on the medallion. Maybe it didn't matter. Maybe it meant nothing. I didn't think I wanted it back. I'd tell Bill that. Better to bury it with her. I thought I would like that.

Would someone claim her body? I'd take care of it if no one stepped forward. I'd tell him that too. But she must have folks somewhere.

Fortunately or unfortunately, depending on whether you were me or Bill, the swell had dwindled overnight so I drove up to the station at Eight. I knew the chief liked to get in early.

"Your friend in Miami was able to point us the right direction," he told me, motioning me to one of the chairs and again seating himself next to me instead of behind his desk. "It turns out our victim used the name Alyce Noble, um, professionally, but was born Alice Norbert."

"I never knew that." Not that it surprised me.

"Now we know who she is, the police down there are interested too. Not just the police, it seems, but the FBI as well. But she was found well above the mean high tide line. There's no arguing that it's our case." He paused before adding, "The murder, at any rate."

"There is more than a murder involved?"

"Jewel theft. A big deal a decade ago and none of it ever recovered."

"And Alyce was involved? Or someone thinks she was?"

"She was, as we cops say, a person of interest. But she disappeared and now we know why."

"How. We know how. Why still needs an answer."

"Very true." Bill cogitated a moment or two, staring at the framed pictures and certificates on the wall behind his desk, before he went on. "You realize you were our prime suspect up until now, don't you? An old flame of yours found buried a few blocks from your home, murdered right around the time you moved here. It was pretty darned suspicious, Ted. Not that I ever thought you were involved."

Neither did I, until now. "Thanks. I do hope the Miami police or the FBI or whoever doesn't start thinking I was involved in a heist."

"I would doubt it. You had already moved here. Hadn't been in the Miami area for some before that either, had you?" He knew the answer to that so he plowed on. "Still, someone is going to come up here and will certainly want to talk with you."

"I'll do what I can. I'm, well, kind of bothered about this whole thing, Bill. It's personal." I almost stopped right there. "Alyce was a friend. And — and why would she have been in Cully Beach unless she came to see me? It's like she was asking for my help but I didn't hear her until ten years too late." I shook my head. "I hadn't meant to blurt out so much rubbish."

Bill Cotton chose not to comment on that, not directly. He probably understood. "We'll keep at it, Ted, you can be sure of that. But it's been a long time. There might not be much any of us can do now."

"Yeah. Life goes on and all of that." If I sounded a tad bitter, so be it.

"It does, and that's mostly a good thing. Like you and Michelle. Have you two set a date yet?"

"Looking at the last weekend in September." I rose. "Right now, I'm more concerned about this weekend."

Bill got up too. "Mother's Day. Yes, the women expect things from us, don't they?"

"Even though they aren't our mothers. In a perfect world, it would all be on Charlie."

"Unfortunately, our kids have scattered. Joan can't expect much more than a phone call from them."

I'd met a couple of them. I wasn't sure how many there were in total but they wouldn't have much in the way of ties to Cully Beach. They'd mostly grown up elsewhere. But then so had Charlie and she showed no signs of wanting to leave.

That, I knew, could change. "Let me know when you need me again," I told Chief Cotton, shook his hand, and left.

Alyce. I could certainly believe she might have gotten mixed up in something of this sort. She had the wrong kind of friends. Maybe I counted as one of those, maybe I had let her down, but I hoped to be the right kind now. The sun was bright when I stepped outside, and it was already hot.

Chapter 13

"The chief has put Jack Saunders and me on the case. Hopes we'll work together and patch things up. Or so he told me."

Dave and Jack were the two main contenders for Jean Stuart's position as Deputy Chief when she retired next year. Bill might have been thinking a little competition between the two might not hurt, as well. It could help him make a choice.

"So no more bike patrol for you?"

"Nope. Jan says your friend Miss Singer has taken to bike riding."

"I might myself. I was a big bike rider as a kid," I told him. "I rode all over Columbus when I was like twelve, thirteen years old."

He gave me an uncertain look, sort of a frown. "Georgia?"

"Ohio. Yeah, I know my accent doesn't have much of the north in it these days."

"It reminds me sometimes of Kentucky, maybe," said Dave.

"That might be my southern Ohio roots showing. It's a different culture down there from the rest of the state."

"I'll take your word for it, Ted. Anyway, why I stopped by — we expect someone to come up from Miami tomorrow. Not sure how early."

"And you'll be escorting them around?"

"Him, probably. I think they're only sending one man." Dave's tone seemed to become just a little less conversational and a little more professional. It was subtle. Or it was my imagination. "Sooner or later, he'll want to talk with you. We could steer him over here if you'd rather not go to the station."

It didn't matter much. I'd be more comfortable here but it might be better if the investigator were the comfortable one.

"Whatever works best for you," I said. "You'd best not keep Jan waiting any longer."

"Right. You know, this is the first time I've actually sat down and had dinner with her parents. There have been those cookouts but this feels different."

It probably was. "You're lucky you don't have to take the whole Bell family out to a restaurant," I assured him. "By the way, I have an appointment tomorrow morning, fairly early, if you and the visiting cop want to get hold of me. I may be back here by the normal opening time."

He nodded. "Good enough. I'll head over to the Bells' place now. Wish Michelle a happy Mothers' Day for me." With that he was out the door — the front door of the shop — and headed up the sidewalk toward Kay and Rick's house. I assumed his car was parked there. Time I closed and locked that door. I did that, doused the lights, went into the back. Neither Michelle nor Charlie seemed ready to go yet.

I sat at the kitchen table, gazed out the window toward the Guzman house. There was no Mothers' Day there. Marty's mom had passed years ago. Maybe we should have invited her along. Alvaro too, for that matter. Hey, why not?

I got up, then hesitated. Should I clear it with Michelle? I could see Alvaro now, sliding a pair of long black surf-casting rods into the back of his Buick station wagon. He had plans for the evening. Out I went. He greeted me almost as soon as I came into view, around the corner of my place.

"Fishing on your own this night?" I asked him. I spoke loudly; Alvaro's hearing was not so good after a career spent working on jet engines.

"I am afraid so, Ted," he replied. "Marty is not too interested and, too, she needs her sleep. Tomorrow is a school day."

So he hadn't invited Patty. Or he had and she turned him down. "Last week, right?"

"It is. There will be final exams, Marty tells me, but she is ready for them."

I was inclined to agree with that. Marty seemed ready for anything. "Then would she like to come with us to dinner tonight? It will just be me and the girls."

He turned from the car, planted his feet securely, almost like a boxer's stance. "You would include her in your Mothers' Day? That is kind of you, Ted, and of Michelle."

I was not about to inform him Michelle knew nothing of it. "Sure. If she wants to."

"I shall ask her." He at once turned toward the house.

"Just tell her to come on over if she wants. We'll be taking off in a while." So that was that. I slipped back into the kitchen, leaving the back door open. The bugs weren't bad yet, though yellow fly season was upon us. I do not like yellow flies at all. They will follow you way out into the water to bite you.

Charlie showed up first. I suppose she had dressed for the night out but looked the same as ever to me. Her hair was still dyed black. I wondered how much longer that would last. The natural dark brown roots showed, if one looked for them. "I invited Marty along," I told her.

"As long as you're the one paying," she replied.

Marty peeped in the door at that moment. "Do I need to dress up? Oh." She took a look at Charlie's shorts and tee. "I guess not."

"We'll need the van with all four of us," Charlie pointed out. That would be Michelle's aged Dodge. Admittedly, it wasn't as old as my truck but I trusted it a lot less.

The Guzman girl came on in. "My dad says there are suspicious characters lurking again," she informed me. "I think he was glad I wouldn't be alone this evening."

Alvaro probably worried too much about things like that, but I didn't mind having a personal 'neighborhood watch' living next door. Michelle joined us at last, dressed much nicer than we were. To her credit, she did not comment on that fact.

"Marty's coming with us," Charlie informed her. Marty only smiled. I think she might have been a little embarrassed to be included in our family celebration. But happy too.

"Okay with me. Where are we going?"

"No place that takes reservations," I told her. "How about *Dee's*? You get to choose today."

"Mom always gets to choose," commented Charlie. "There's no point in pretending otherwise."

Michelle gave us another looking over. She might have thought we weren't presentable enough for a place like *Dee's*, not that it was exactly high class. "Let's make it *The Fiddler Crab*," she said.

Charlie hadn't been there since our encounter with Ray Manuel. "Is that okay with you, Charlie?" I asked. "I know you might have some unpleasant memories of the place."

"No problemo, Shaper. That water's gone under a whole bunch of bridges."

Marty turned to her friend. "That's where you ran into the gangster, right?"

SMOKE

I could have chuckled at the word 'gangster' but held it in. It was as good a description of Manuel as any. "You've been telling Marty tales of our exploits?" I asked her.

"Some," she admitted. There were things in her past she would not want to revisit, at least not with this kid. I knew a lot of them. So did Jan.

"Then the *Crab* it is. Let's go."

It was still plenty light outside, between being almost summer and that darned Daylight Savings Time. I don't like DST. I would not be surprised if I have said that before. Michelle's minivan was parked at the curb so my truck wouldn't be blocked in the drive.

"One of us could take to parking next door," I said, as we climbed in, the kids in the back, Michelle beside me. They expected me to drive though I don't care much one way or another. "Now that we own the place."

"It might be better than the street," admitted Michelle. "But you have to cut down that hedge first so we can see it." I had intended to. Eventually. It might take me as long as it had to give her an indoor shower.

I pulled away from the curb. There was almost no traffic. We were pointed the right way, as *The Fiddler Crab* lies beyond the southern edge of Cully Beach, about two miles south of my own shop. It was a low building on the west side of the highway. The gravel parking lot looked about half-full. We wouldn't have to wait for a table.

The young hostess ushered us into the dark, paneled dining room, showed us to a booth, handed us menus. Slow-turning fans hung from the low ceiling. As we settled in, a dark, diminutive woman get up from a table somewhere behind me and hurried to the counter. Was she someone I knew? Maybe. She did seem familiar, didn't she? Whoever she was, the necessity of choosing food put her out of my mind.

"Should we order the Captain's Platter for your mom?" I asked Charlie. "If we can get it away from the captain, nyuk, nyuk." It was an old joke and I would probably trot it out every time we came here.

"Along with the Chef's salad," she replied without a moment's hesitation. Our companions ignored us.

I glanced up. The woman was gone. I still thought maybe I knew her, though I had caught only a glimpse of her face.

Our waitress appeared, bringing iced water and her order pad. "Happy Mother's Day," she said to Michelle. "Are you and your daughters ready to order?" Charlie snickered. Marty didn't look much like the rest of us. She's pretty dark, between her Puerto Rican father and Philippine mother. A heck of a lot better looking too. I think we could all admit that.

"We're going to adopt you," Charlie whispered to her young friend after we had ordered. "At least for tonight."

"But you would have to work for the family business," I added.

Marty considered that. "I'll have to see if Kim can make a better offer."

"Undoubtedly. But seriously, if you would like to work in the shop I'd be glad to put you behind the counter. After school, come fall, maybe. Or sooner if you are interested."

"Hmm. Okay, Shaper." The girl was not prepared to commit to anything at that moment and I did not blame her one bit. She would talk with her dad about it, of course.

Our dinners appeared shortly. Not one of us had chosen to deprive the captain of his platter but there were plenty enough scallops and shrimp and fish fillets to go around. Those last are not part of my vegetarian diet but I'm willing to partake of most shell-fish. Except cephalopods — squid and octopi are just a little too brainy for me to feel comfortable eating them.

Dessert? Well, of course, I had told the waitress. We couldn't let Michelle escape an occasion such as this without thoroughly stuffing her. I tried the coconut pie. So-so.

Marty leaned forward, a bit hesitant about speaking. Self-conscious. "My father slipped me money so I could pay my part," she told us.

"That's like Alvaro," commented Michelle. I nodded agreement. We'd only been neighbors a few weeks but we knew the man.

"Shaper invited you so he pays," stated Charlie. "That's the way it works."

"Unless previously agreed," I added. "But it's never a good idea to trust the guy who invited you to have enough money."

Michelle shook her head. "You are sooo good at seeing what might go wrong. I think you lie awake at night and dream up worst case scenarios."

"I'm just being prepared. I have to make up now for not being a boy scout as a kid. All ready to go?"

We were. Marty did insist on adding a couple dollars to the tip. Ha, maybe Alvaro thought I was the sort who might run out of money. Back into the van and north into the dusk. One could not see the Atlantic along this stretch of A-1-A. Further south, yes, as one approached Jumento Inlet and the state park there. North, not until one was past our shop, well into town. Oh, glimpses along the way of the distant horizon, water meeting sky, above the tops of the dunes and the thick patches of silvery palmetto, but the highway did not run right beside the beach here. It was dark out over the ocean now anyway, though a faint glow lingered along the western horizon, behind the tall trees that overhung the highway in places. Some of those grew in front of our new house.

Our new old house. Built in the the Thirties of good cypress, well before the concrete block structure that housed my home and shop. I would have plenty of time to work on it through the summer. It was coming up on our left now. "What do you say to going on up to the pier first?" I asked my passengers. I didn't really feel like bringing the evening to an end this soon.

No objections. Wait — was there someone standing there in the shadows of that unruly hedge? Two someones I realized as I slammed on the brake. It couldn't be Karrie. I was pretty sure of that.

What I wasn't sure of was pulling in with these three. I didn't know what was going on but I would not put them in any danger. I hit the accelerator again and drove on to the corner, turned on Eighth and pulled in beside the Bells' house. Dave's car was still parked there. I was pretty happy to see that.

"All of you inside," I said. "Tell Dave. He can call the station if he thinks its a good idea."

Michelle gave me a suspicious look. Well deserved, I suppose. "And what are you going to do?"

Not get out, that was for sure. Shaper isn't that stupid. "Cruise by again," I told her. "Get another look."

I guess she thought that sounded reasonable. "There were two of them, right?"

"Yep. That I saw." By then, the back light was on and Kay was sticking her head out the door. "Get on in." I dislike ordering anyone to do anything but I was in a hurry.

Was Alvaro still out fishing? I thought it likely. I backed out and pulled up to the corner. A small dark car sped by just as I turned onto the highway. It took me a moment to realize its lights weren't on. Dangerous. It was completely dark out now and, as I have previously complained, there were no streetlights. I inched south, past the Guzman's house. No sign of Alvaro's wagon. I slowed to a near stop at my own drive. Nothing going on, no one to be seen.

It was pretty likely my lurkers had been in that car. Maybe pulled into the drive next door. Could they have bothered Karrie? I was apprehensive about pulling in to check. Damn, I felt responsible for her. I shut off my own lights and crept up the remains of an old oyster shell driveway. It was even darker under the trees. Ah, Karrie's van wasn't behind the house. That relieved me considerably.

But I would have to warn her when I saw her. I should warn her as soon as she returned, no matter how late. There was no way of telling what the prowlers were after, which house they were interested in. My guess was thieves, hoping to break and enter at the *Cully Beach Surf Shop*.

A flashlight. I tensed up as it swung back and forth. Someone pushing through the hedge from my back yard. Its beam focused on the van. "Ho, Ted!"

Dave. I stepped out. "No sign of them," I reported. "I think they were parked over here."

He looked toward my vehicle. It was too dark to make out his expression. I should leave a light on over here, I decided, if only the one by the back door. "If there was any evidence from their car you're likely to have wiped it out."

"I think I saw it, heading north. All I could tell was it was small."

"Okay." He swept his flash back and forth a couple times. "Nothing more to do until morning."

"Hop in. I'll take you back."

A couple minutes later we entered the Bells' kitchen. There were still remnants of their dinner on the table but the family seemed to be in the midst of clean-up. "Charlie and Marty are going to stay over here tonight," Jan informed me at once.

It seemed like a good idea. "I'd better leave a note for Alvaro. We wouldn't want him to think we'd kidnapped his daughter." A siren whooped outside. "You didn't call for backup, did you Dave?"

"Afraid so. Best to be safe. We'll get a statement quickly and send everyone home. But be sure to lock up securely tonight, okay?"

I did. As always.

Chapter 14

"There is a bit of an age gap between you, isn't there?" asked Father Paul.

"Ten years," replied Michelle. "Not that big a difference at our ages."

"We're all growed up," I added.

"I am, anyway."

The priest only smiled at the exchange. "You are right, Michelle. It is not a big difference. But keep in mind that women live longer than men, on average, and add those ten years in." His expression suggested only friendly concern. "Just something you should recognize and know you may have to deal with someday."

I had no intention of letting Michelle outlive me. "Anyone can go anytime, Father. We all know that."

"A bag of money could fall on me at the bank," said Michelle, getting into the spirit of it. "Leaving poor Mr. Carrol as a widower."

"Not poor for long. I'd sue 'em!" I gave her a reasonably wicked grin. "And then not a widower for long, with all that money."

"Very well. Let's move on from the age difference," decided Father Paul. It was a wise decision, I felt. He spoke directly and seriously to my fiancée. "Have you given any thought to joining the Catholic Church?"

She was surprised and only shook her head. "I asked," he went on, "because of your daughter. She has spoken to me of it."

"Charlie wants to — to convert?" asked Michelle.

"She has only expressed interest. Curiosity, perhaps."

"But when — I mean, she came to see you, Father?"

"She comes here for AA meetings sometimes," I reminded her. "In the parish hall." Charlie would have run into Father Paul.

"Just so. I am sure Ted has something to do with it, too," the priest added. "Now, do you think you will make it to the encounter this weekend?"

Encounter was a fancy word for some kind of class, to be held in St. Augustine. We said we'd try to make it. Saturday was not at all good for me, of course, but just this once I could leave Charlie in charge.

There wasn't much else to go over. Father Paul had given a test of sorts, a self-assessment, when we stopped in before, and we went over that. We were supposed to take it before our class in St. Augustine. I think we passed.

As we stepped out into the morning sun, Michelle asked, "So who *would* you marry if I kicked the bucket? Or ran off with Alvaro?"

"Hmm, with Alvaro out of the picture there would always be Patty."

"Hmmph. She knows you too well."

"True. I guess I'd have to woo Karrie Goodpaster. She thinks I'm cute, you know."

"She thinks a lot of people are cute. Of both genders." A slight smirk transitioned to a more thoughtful look. "Still —"

"Still?"

"I could actually see you as a couple. She's smart. Smarter than me, Ted. I know you like smart girls."

"So you're jealous of Karrie's brains."

"Well, I certainly wouldn't be jealous of her looks." She stopped walking and gave me an exaggerated raised eyebrow. "Or should I be?"

"I think a lot of people are cute too," I told her. "But only women."

"Thank goodness for that." We resumed the walk toward our vehicles. They were a fair distance from the rectory, in the church parking lot. "Maybe we should set Karrie up with someone."

"I'll leave that to you and Kay. But look for someone a lot younger than me."

"Yeah, I don't think she's more than thirty."

"Younger, I'd say. She's only a couple years out of grad school."

We were at our separate vehicle, ready to go our separate ways. At times I wished Michelle hadn't taken a job, that she stayed at the shop all day and helped me run it. After all, wasn't the offer of a job how I talked her into staying in Cully Beach — staying with me — when she was ready to throw everything away and head somewhere else? That offer had let her save face. Maybe it did the same for me.

But now she wanted to prove herself. Shoot, I understood that. I didn't completely like it, though. I kissed her goodbye. She drove off, I drove off.

There was knot of people on the front steps of the shop. One was in a uniform but the patrol car parked at the curb already told me the police were there. I pulled up my drive. Alvaro, and Charlie. Jan. She was out of college for the summer now and maybe at loose ends.

The officer was 'the Martian.' That was stuck in my head now and I couldn't think of his actual name. Oh, Marvin. A last name did not come with that but it didn't matter. He had a name tag. M. Dobbs.

He was as polite as at our last encounter. "Officer Blake already wrote up a report, sir," he informed me. "I'm just following up."

"Not much to follow up on, is there?"

"I'm afraid not. No tire tracks. Even if you hadn't driven in yourself, there is too little open ground for any impressions."

In other words, the place was overgrown with weeds. I might need a bigger mower now. And definitely should get onto taking down that hedge. Especially up front here. What was Dobbs saying?

"And you can't identify the automobile you saw?"

"Nah. It was small and I don't think particularly new. Dark but I couldn't say what color. Maybe if we had streetlights down here." I would keep mentioning that to anyone and everyone. "And I definitely can't identify the men except to say there were two of them. I can't even guarantee they weren't women."

"One was a good bit taller than the other," Charlie put in. "I could see that."

"Oh?" I thought about it. She might be right or maybe she'd just put the idea into my head now. "Maybe so."

"Very well," said Officer Marvin. "Someone lives over here?" He pointed toward the old house with his pen.

"Not yet. A friend had her van parked behind the place but she never came back last night." I had checked a couple times and finally given up on Doctor Goodpaster.

"She's holed up at the college," said Jan. "Getting her grades in."

Dobbs closed his pad. "I can't think of anything else," he admitted. "If you do, call the station. Um —" He searched his pockets for a few seconds. "Here." A card with his name. The number was the desk at the police station. I knew it by this time.

"Good enough. Any sign of the police from Miami yet this morning?" I asked him.

"Not when I left the station." There was an awkward moment while we all stood there. "I'll be on my way, sir," said the Martian, and headed for his cruiser.

Alvaro collared me at once. "I thank you for taking care of Marty last night. It was smart to have her stay with the Bells."

"We were just being careful." Or Jan was, and the rest of us thought it was a good idea.

"It is sometimes exciting to live next to you, Ted. Maybe too exciting."

Worried about his daughter. That I could completely understand. "Just a couple burglars probably. Would be burglars. Even if we knew who they were they couldn't be charged with much but trespassing." I thought the police were making a little too much fuss about it. But I admittedly had been a bit shaken myself last night. "Still," I went on, "it doesn't hurt to keep an eye out. You have stuff someone might like to steal too."

Alvaro smoothed his mustache absentmindedly, thumb and forefinger. "Hmm, yes, this is so. Maybe I should get a gun. I do not like guns but maybe I should."

"Shaper has a gun," volunteered Charlie. "Mom told me."

Of course I had informed Michelle early on that there was a revolver in our bedroom. It was the sort of thing she should know. I had not intended her to blab it to Charlie. "I do not like guns, either," I stated. "I am a nonviolent person but others are not."

Guzman nodded. "Unfortunately, this too is so. Oh, Marty told me you offered her a job."

"If she wants to take an occasional shift in the showroom. Nothing more." As my other high school part-timers.

"So I understood but I wished to make certain. I have no objections is she wishes this. But," he continued, "you understand you can not use her name for promotion."

Her arrangement as a member of Kim Timble's surf team. I suspected there was no written contract involved. The kid was an amateur, after all, simply being sponsored by Kim. "I am far too lazy to do any sort of promotion," I assured him.

"And too cheap," Charlie added.

"Yeah, that too. By the way, Jan," I said, turning my attention to my number one assistant of the past few years, "are you interested in taking shifts this summer?" She'd be just the person to show Marty the ropes. Wherever those ropes are kept. I could never find them myself.

"I might as well, Ted. No sense in looking for a new job for three months!"

And then off to college, never again to be the little surfer girl who watched my shop. But who knows? Maybe Marty could fill that post for a while.

Chapter 15

It had been Saunders who called on Monday afternoon, asked me if they could drop by in the morning. "We've been going over the case with the detective from Miami," he informed me. "Figured it was too late to come bothering you today."

No problem, I had told him. I didn't really mind if we met here or at the station, honestly, but it was more convenient to stay at the shop. Even if I had to fix them all coffee.

The black Taurus pulled up a bit before Nine. It was an hour yet to opening time but I had the door hanging open while I puttered in the tiny front lawn. I was eyeing that hedge. Not quite up to tackling it yet. Maybe clip it some first.

Blake and Saunders, as expected, and a heavy-set black man in a tan suit, up front on the passenger side. The Cully Beach boys weren't in uniform but had opted for short sleeved shirts in this weather. I would have worn shorts, too. In fact, I did.

I didn't know the Miami cop. There are lots of people in Miami I don't know. I could see the bulge of a shoulder holster under his jacket. I guess that was why he was wearing the suit.

Did Jack and Dave have guns somewhere on their persons? I would think so but not their service revolvers. Those were too hard to hide. No matter. I didn't expect them to shoot anyone in my front yard.

"This is Lieutenant Jones," said Saunders. "Ted Carrol."

We shook. "Boris Jones," said the detective. "Pleased to meet you Ted."

"Come on in," I said. "Dade must have a high opinion of you Boris, if they only sent one man." I had hoped for a contingent of cops to solve Alyce's murder.

"Don't know about that, sir. I'm afraid it's not considered a high priority case anymore."

"It is to me," I replied.

"To the FBI as well," said Dave. "They've been in contact but aren't sending anyone."

"Anyone they've told you about," Boris said. He gave the surf shop interior a quick scan.

"Come on back to the kitchen," I told them. "Anyone want coffee?"

"Sure," said our visitor from Miami. The others were noncommittal but I knew they'd drink it if I made it. They were cops. I did not, however, have any donuts on hand.

I busied myself with the coffee maker while they arranged themselves around the table.

"We ran your name," Jones informed me, "and it didn't pop at all."

"I could have told you that." I added water and turned the machine on.

"So how did you happen to know Ms. Norbert?"

I should have brought the fourth kitchen chair back. It tended to end up in the showroom much of the time. I perched on a stool instead. That let me look down on these three policemen. Whether that was good or bad, I had no idea. "I knew some of the people in her, um, world. I worked on their boats."

"Crew?" asked Saunders.

"No, no. I actually worked on the boats. Custom fiberglass jobs. Just a bit of it here and there, once it became known I did that sort of thing. My college friend Mike, Joseph Gainey that is, introduced me to Alyce and to some of the others."

Boris looked at his notes. "Hmm, yes, Gainey is clean, as far as we can tell. He liked to party a bit back then."

"He did have a weakness for women," I admitted. And they seemed to have a weakness for him. "But not a high-roller by any means. Mike was always at the edge of things."

"But not you?"

I could only shrug. "I wasn't even part of any of it. I'm not a fun guy and they all saw that pretty quickly."

"Yet —"

I had to laugh. "There's always a yet, isn't there? I think some of those guys — hmm, the women too — saw me as someone they could talk to, confide in, outside their regular circles."

"Including Alice Norbert." I only nodded to that so he went on. "I never knew you in those days, Ted, but I knew — and do know — people who did. Do you remember Dorothea Dominguez?"

The name rang one of those bells, but the tower it hung in was pretty distant. "Dotty? The cop? Um, policewoman?"

"She was. Dominguez is in the private sector now. Insurance investigation."

"Damn," I said pretty quietly and mostly to myself. "That's who I saw the other night. I *knew* she looked familiar." The coffee maker had stopped wheezing. I went to find cups.

"She's interested in recovering the jewels, of course," said Boris. "So are we but there is also this murder. And yeah, I know that is you guys' jurisdiction," he said to his companions.

"And we've gotten nowhere with it," admitted Dave.

"At least we've got some names now," Saunders said.

"Yep. Hey, Ted, did you know a Donny Morales?"

I placed sugar and a jug of milk in the middle of the table. "I did. Not well. Isn't he in prison?" Or was the last time I had heard the name.

"He's out," Boris informed me. "He confessed to the robbery but got a shorter sentence for naming his partners." He held out his cup and I poured it three-quarters full. He drank it black. "Claimed he had no idea where the loot was. I was part of the original investigation, which is why I'm here now. Sergeant Jones then. That's City of Miami, by the way, not Miami-Dade."

"Miami-Dade?"

"I guess they still called it Metro-Dade when you were down there."

So they did. Not at all important. Dominguez was Metro-Dade; that I remembered and that was also unimportant. I filled the other two cups while he went on. "We had suspects at the time. Ms. Norbert was one of them. When Morales talked we knew who the other was. A Rex Stoddard."

The name meant nothing to me. "He disappeared as thoroughly as Norbert. It has been theorized that Morales killed both of them and stashed the jewelry somewhere."

That didn't sound like Donny. "I would not be inclined to believe that." My own cup. A splash of milk.

"The finding of Norbert's remains way up here makes it seem less likely. Morales tended to stick to the Miami area. Not that we can be sure of that. It does make you seem, um, a little more of a possible suspect, though we know you weren't a part of the scene down there anymore."

"So that leaves this Rex guy, doesn't it?" I asked. "I'm pretty sure I don't know that name."

"Stoddard. He and Norbert were an item at the time. Or had been."

It felt like there was an implied question there. "I had been out of the picture for a long time," I said. "Well out of the picture. Maybe I shouldn't have been."

"You think you could have done something?" asked Dave.

"Who can say? I could at least have been a friend to Alyce. I can't help feeling I abandoned her."

Boris remained impassive. I couldn't tell whether he knew what I meant. "This Rex Stoddard was not a good guy at all. History of violence." He shuffled through a thick folder he had carried in. laid it out, open, when he found what he wanted. "Biker type. And you never had any contact with Ms. Norbert during this period?"

I'd been waiting for that question. Why else would they even want to talk to me? "Not for, um, a couple years at least. Maybe three. After moving back to Genoa I never even visited that area again."

"Yes, Genoa. Family concerns, right?"

"Right. And then I came here."

"And you've no idea why Norbert would have been in Cully Beach?"

I shrugged. "To see me, I'm sure. But I couldn't say why."

"She never wrote you, phoned you, anything of that sort?"

"Nope. I wouldn't have thought Alyce even knew where I was."

"Uh-huh." He stared at his papers for a moment. I suspected they had nothing to do with his questions. "Were the two of you lovers?"

"We never had a physical relationship of any sort."

Lieutenant Jones raised an eyebrow at that but made no comment. He sipped his coffee. "You served us the good stuff," he said. "Too good for cops."

"Don't I know it. Consider it bribery."

A laugh at last. Boris put away the professional demeanor of the last couple minutes. "I wouldn't be surprised if Donny Morales came up here, now that he knows what happened to Alice Norbert. He won't forget about those jewels. You'll let these guys know if he shows, won't you?"

"Absolutely. And they'd better let me know if they learn any more about what happened to Alyce."

"Will do, Ted," said Dave.

Chapter 16

Most of the work was to be left to Blake and Saunders. Boris Jones headed back to Miami shortly after talking to me. I think he was disappointed by how little I knew.

Maybe he half-believed I knew something about those stolen jewels. Maybe Jack Saunders had suspicions about me too. No matter.

Dave Blake did give me a few other details later that day. He might as well as long as he had come to pick up Jan Bell for an evening out. And as long as I had gone over to their house and waylaid him. "She disappeared right around this time of the year back in Ninety-one."

So ten years, almost exactly. Is there such a thing as 'almost exactly?' It seems a bit of a contradiction of itself. Whatever. Ten years, anyway. More or less. There's a better phrase.

"Do you think I could get a picture of this Rex guy?" I asked him. "In case he shows up."

"Sure. I'll leave one at the desk for you to pick up." He considered this a moment. "You know, I ought to print up a bunch and distribute them to the force. Maybe the other guy too."

"Morales."

"Morales, right. The one you know."

"It's been a dozen years since I've seen Donny. I might need a picture of him too."

"Of course," said Dave, "Rex Stoddard may be dead."

True. For all we knew, he could be buried a few feet from where we had found Alyce's remains. I wasn't going to start digging.

"Doctor Goodpaster has returned," Michelle informed me on my own return home. "Charlie went over to fill her in on all the excitement we had while she was gone."

"Maybe to announce that she is going to be one of her students, too," I pointed out. "Already into the sauce, are we?" A bottle of pinot grigio rested on the table. I got a glass and poured myself a little.

"How was your day?" I asked, settling down in one the chairs. "I was grilled by surly policemen, you should know."

"I did know. They didn't leave many bruises, did they? My day was just another day. Had to drive to Scott City to pull records again. I do hope they digitize those soon!" I wasn't sure what 'digitize' meant. Something to do with computers.

She refilled her own glass and took a seat across from me. "I don't think I can take May Twenty-fifth off. The Friday you wanted to go to the music festival."

"So be it, kid. With all this smoke we might not even want to go. It's worse around White Springs than here." I could see the festival being canceled or postponed if wildfires threatened it.

A noise at the open back door, right behind me. "Karrie says she might drive over to your festival, Shaper," said Charlie, stepping into the kitchen. "Hmm, I guess I need to call her Doctor Goodpaster if I'm going to be in her class."

"Tell her there won't be any camping available near the place if she's thinking of staying in her van. That would all have been reserved long ago."

"Wouldn't that depend on how far she was willing to drive?" asked Michelle. "Like the hour or so it takes from Pat and Betty's place."

I couldn't imagine Pat wanting Karrie Goodpaster's unicorn-adorned van parked at his place. Even if he was as good-natured a guy as you could hope to call a friend.

"We've been discussing finding Karrie a girlfriend," I informed Charlie. "Or boyfriend, depending on which she prefers at the moment."

Michelle gave me a sour look. I believe she felt I shouldn't have shared that.

But Charlie apparently thought it a grand idea. "I'll get right on it," she proclaimed. My fiancee shrugged and sipped her wine.

Charlie found herself a soda in the fridge and joined us at the table. Someone should probably think of cooking dinner eventually.

"Doctor Goodpaster needs someone solid and dependable," she decided.

"Like her ex?" asked Michelle. It is not to be denied there was a certain amount of sarcasm in her voice.

It didn't phase Charlie. "Maybe we should find someone for Sally Stuart while we're at it," she said.

I had news for her there. Maybe for Michelle too. "She and her boss are an item. Teresa Carver. Her Aunt Millie told me." That was Jean Miller Stuart, Deputy Police Chief. "I just may need Teresa Carver to defend me if this murder investigation takes a wrong turn."

A joke, of course — I didn't really see that happening. Still, I reckoned I could depend on her and Sally to dig into things if I needed help. I'd done the same for them, hadn't I?

"What a bunch of gossips we are! Pour me a little more, will you Ted?" Michelle held out her glass. "And then lock it away."

As I obliged, Charlie began to list Karrie's selling points. "She's young," she said. "That's a good thing to be." She snickered a little at we old folks' expense before continuing. "A little goofy looking but not ugly. Not even homely. Smart, of course."

"She does have a PhD," admitted Michelle. "That's pretty good."

"Having a doctorate in English lit is no guarantee of a good job. Or a job at all," I said. Not to mention a good life — so I didn't mention it.

"Better than art history," she replied.

"True, but I never pursued a career in that."

"Why not?" asked Charlie. "You could have been Doctor Carrol."

"And then I would never have met your mom, would I?"

"Sure you would. It was fate!" She grinned, knowing full well I did not believe in fate. I had made that clear in the past.

No matter. "By the time I had the degree I realized I would rather make art than teach about it. Even if it were only surfboards. But I did date a professor of English lit for a while, back in the Eighties," I let them know. "Or adjunct professor or instructor or some title like that. My friend Branford was in her classes, in fact, at USF."

"We learn more of Shaper's mysterious past," commented Charlie.

"Nothing mysterious about her," I objected.

"So what was her name?" asked Michelle.

"Let's just call her Anne." I didn't mind telling them. I didn't see any reason to either.

Charlie made a bit of a rude sound. "Anne the Professor. That's great, Shaper."

"Isn't it? It was kind of long distance, what with me spending time both in Genoa and on the east coast, and her teaching in Tampa."

SMOKE

Anne Paley. Not Doctor Anne Paley when we first met. She was still a grad student. Teaching Assistant would have been the title then. I hadn't thought of Anne in a long time.

Not that I had any reason to. "I'll get this put away," I said, rising and picking up the half-emptied wine bottle. "Then I'll fix you both a decent meal. Vegetarian, of course."

"Of course," sighed Charlie.

Chapter 17

"They are going to discuss the plans for a park across the road," Alvaro told me. "You should attend."

He meant the City Council meeting tomorrow. Probably I should attend and probably I would were I retired like Alvaro Guzman. "I'll see what I can do," I told him. "Kay and I may need to depend on you to represent the neighborhood." Guzman understood we both had businesses that needed our attention. "And remind them we need streetlights down here if you get the chance," I added. A park would almost guarantee those, wouldn't it?

"Maybe we should do like Rick and have security lights."

"If they don't shine in our windows and keep us from sleeping." I got back to the hedge. I had a tool for lopping off the branches — new from the Brodys's hardware store — and meant to take out everything I could with it before tackling what remained with a saw. I had just started on the roadside end when Alvaro came over to supervise. Who the heck would haul all this away? Maybe Joy and Susan could bring a chipper over. Their *River Road Nursery* wasn't too far beyond Patty's new place.

"I think that one is too thick," observed Alvaro. I had been straining to squeeze the cutters through a heavy branch.

"Possibly," I agreed, turning the lopper to cut afresh from a different angle. It went through this time. "Now I know about what the limit is, huh?"

A car was crawling by, halfway into the parking strip. Maybe checking whether I was open yet. Yeah, I had the door open to let the morning air in but it was a good hour and an half to opening time. They pulled in and stopped anyway. The car was small and old and dark and I suspected I had seen it before.

SMOKE

"Alvaro," I said in a low voice, "there might be trouble." Just to warn him, you know? I did not expect him to be much help. I could see a black man on the side facing me, the passenger side. Light gleamed on his hairless head when he got out and stood. He didn't stand very high.

And crawling out of the driver's side? Donny Morales. He was heavier but not that hard to recognize. He'd lost his mustache. "Ah," was all I said and not very loudly.

"You know them?" whispered Guzman.

"I do. The police would like to know they are here, I think — hmm, but not right away. They might have things to say." It wouldn't do to scare Donny away by having cops show up.

"I understand. I will watch from my house, okay?"

"Good idea." I stepped forward as Alvaro casually ambled toward his place. As casually as is possible for him. "Donny," I said. "It's been a very long time." I could see his companion better now. He looked like someone I might have known.

"Hey, Ted. You remember Small Change?" He gestured toward the other man.

Small Change Robinson. He was still small but Change had changed. Old, he looked. Way balder. He had been a petty hustler and sometime dealer, and never more than a casual acquaintance of mine. But Alyce had liked him for some reason.

I nodded to the man and turned back to Donny. "I take it you were the ones hanging around here the other night."

"Yeah, that was just me and Change. We wanted to talk with you alone, you know? We didn't know who all was in that van so we bolted."

I wondered if — no, I suspected there was more to it than that. I wouldn't have wanted to talk with them alone in the night, that was for sure. I didn't trust either. Not that Donny and I had ever had any trouble. Nor Small Change for that matter.

"Well, we can talk now. Right here." I was certain it was best if we stayed out here in the open. Best for me. My limb-lopper was still in my hand. "While I work." I turned back to the hedge.

"Cuttin' that 'cause we was hidin' in it?" asked Robinson.

"Been planning to take it down for some time, Change," I replied. "I bought the house next door and want to be able to see it."

"It's a good lookin' old place," he allowed. "I, um, snooped around a little bit."

I was glad Goodpaster wasn't there. "I assume you are here because of Alyce," I said, snipping off another limb. "The police told me to expect you, Donny."

"That's none of their business. I'm done with prison, done with parole. I'm free to go where I want."

"If you are looking for the missing jewelry it definitely is their business. You know that."

Small Change piped up. "I don't know nothin' 'bout the jewels and don't wanna know nothin'," he proclaimed. "This is 'bout Alice."

"I had no idea what happened to Alyce until you found her body," said Donny. "I'm admittedly pissed. I figure Rex did it." Small Change nodded a vigorous agreement.

"That would seem likely," I agreed. "And I didn't find her body." Damn, this pruning was slow work! Maybe I should just rent a chain saw and take them all down in one pass.

"Me and Alice go way back, back to the fields down 'round Homestead," said Small Change Robinson. "I always tried to look out for the girl."

When not pimping her out. Ah, I shouldn't judge him so harshly. He seemed sincere about it. Donny, maybe not so much.

"No one knew where Stoddard was all these years," said Morales. "There wasn't a trace of him."

"I heard he was ridin' with a biker gang out West," offered Robinson.

"So did I." Donny shrugged. "We can be sure he's headed back here now. And he'll be looking for you, Shaper. Anyone can figure she came here to see you."

Small Change did something like a classic double-take. "You're Shaper? Alice told me to get a message to Shaper just 'fore she disappeared but I didn't know who that was."

We both stared at the little man. "So what was it?" I asked

"'Tell Shaper to meet me at the festival,' she said. 'He'll know what I mean.'" Short Change shook his head. "You might know what it mean, but I sure don't."

"Festival?" wondered Donny.

I knew very well what festival but didn't see any reason he should. "Maybe the Snowbird Festival they hold here?" I could see that didn't convince him at all. Too bad. "Whatever it was, we never connected."

Donny wasn't happy. "Why didn't you say anything before?" he snapped at Small Change. "I didn't even know you saw her."

"Didn't. It was a phone call. The girl hung up soon as she give me the message."

"That's the breaks," I told him. "Don't worry about it." I turned to Donny. "Rex might be looking for you too. You did spill about him to the police."

"Rex will hold a grudge," agreed Robinson.

"I suppose so. I reckon he doesn't know where the — items are either." Donny gave me a squint. "So Alyce must have stashed them somewhere."

"And you think she told me." Rex Stoddard might think that too. The murderer of Alyce Noble might very well come looking for me.

"It looks like she didn't get the chance." Donny said this with some reluctance. I think he wanted to believe I knew something. Maybe he could even convince himself of it.

Something else came to me. "Stoddard might think you know something too."

"It's likely. We both need to watch out for him, Ted. He's a bad dude." A twitch of a smile, just at one corner of his mouth. Maybe Donny realized 'bad dude' sounded kind of silly. "Not likely to show himself though, huh?"

"I wouldn't think so."

"You should tell your cop friends if he does. You're gonna tell them about us, right?"

"Yes, I am. But not necessarily everything about you." And not what I had learned about Alyce. Not yet.

"Tell 'em whatever you think you should. We'll be keeping an eye on things."

Donny turned to his car without further words. Small Change Robinson, however, extended a hand. "Good to see you, Shaper. Shaper — why didn't I ever know that was you?" He shook his head and I shook his hand. "We'll do Alice right." A few seconds later the pair drove away.

I gave a wave and a smile toward Alvaro's house so he would know everything was alright. Then I went into the shop and called the Cully Beach police station.

Chapter 18

SF-OM5. That and the little pictograph. I stared at the note paper onto which I had copied Alyce's scratched message.

Saunders and Blake had come over Wednesday afternoon, after I had phoned. I told them everything that had happened. Yes, all of it, even that Alyce had attempted to make contact at the Florida Folk Festival. That was what she meant, of course. I had promised once to take her there. Someday.

That day had never happened, nor did I make it up to White Springs that year to meet her. Somewhere in the midst of all of what had happened, I had to take a little blame. I had deserted her. I could have kept track even if I did have other obligations tugging me elsewhere at that point in my life. I could have made an effort when those obligations had been fulfilled.

No, I had run away, up here to Cully Beach. I had wanted to start over. Maybe I left too much behind in doing so.

What I didn't tell my two cop visitors was that I had an idea now what the message Alyce had scratched on her medallion meant. SF — Stephen Foster? The park on the Suwanee River where the festival was held. If I was right, that message had been written for me and I should be the one to follow its directions.

A car door slamming closed. A customer? No one parked out front. Early afternoon was the deadest time of these dead days. Ah, Alvaro was back, and Patty with him. She had ridden over on her bike this morning and then on to the city council meeting. Most likely had lunch somewhere too. How serious were those two?

I guess I would find out when they found out. They parted at Alvaro's door with no signs of affection and Patty rolled her bicycle out of the carport. She then rolled it on over to my front door.

"It looks good for your park," she announced as soon as she entered the shop. "The council voted in favor a study, anyway."

"They're afraid to try to sell the property again, after the whole Burkhardt thing was exposed," I said. I thought I was probably right about it, too. "Public opinion wouldn't stand for it."

"I suppose we need to thank you for all of that." Her dry tone belied the words to some degree. She meant it anyway, I was sure.

"Thank Sally Stuart first. I just helped some."

"Yeah." Even drier. "Maybe they shouldn't name the park for you."

"Well, if they insisted I would have to go along with it."

"Vicky says she is going to suggest they call it Wayne Davis Park." Vicky Ward was her friend on the city council. Represented this part of town, too. Davis was was a fixture in Cully Beach politics. An elder statesman, as they say. Or someone says. He'd been an ally in the Bukhardt affair, and in clearing Bill Cotton's name.

"I'd be okay with that. If they do intend to pass me over. How's things with you? Getting moved in?"

"The house *is* starting to look lived-in."

"I grew up in houses that looked unlived-in," I told her. "We moved just about every year. As soon as my parents built a new house, it would be on the market, so it was kept neat and bland. Beige walls."

"No wonder you turned out the way you are," she commented. "Neat and bland. But I knew your dad was a builder. I guess you are also, in your way." In my way. Yeah, I made things — the family business. When I didn't comment, Patty went on. "You're a craftsman. Your own boss too."

I had to smile at that. "Yeah, me and my dad were both too independent to work for someone else." I looked down at my shorts and flip-flops. "We got to dress the way we wanted, too. My father's preferred work uniform was khaki trousers and Wellingtons. Later on, a guayabera."

"Oh, you should wear a guayabera. It would look good on you."

"Not as long as aloha shirts are hanging in the shop. I should wear what I sell." At the moment I had on a somewhat stained *Secret Surfboards* tee-shirt but that was beside the point. I sold those too.

"Speaking of which, I may have a customer." A sedan had pulled up out front. "That's gonna interfere with my siesta."

I couldn't tell you what kind of car it was. It was about as nondescript, as generic, as an automobile can be, and neither particularly new nor old. It *was* white.

The driver sat there for a while. I couldn't see what he was doing or even what he looked like. Maybe he was checking me over. Maybe he was reading a book. Okay, she, not he. I recognized her when she slid out and stood up. Dorothea Dominguez.

Aside from her graying hair — longer than she used to wear it — Dotty hadn't changed much. She was a diminutive woman. Dark. More makeup than I remembered. That might be because she was no longer a cop or just a change in fashion.

"Hi, Ted," she called when about half way up the drive.

"Hello, Dot," I returned. "For a second time."

"Oh, you recognized me at that restaurant. I did not anticipate you and your family coming in." By now she had reached the steps up into the shop. They aren't very high but neither is Dominguez, so Patty and I were looking down on her. Dot's eyes went to my companion.

"Patty Singer, this is Dorothea Dominguez. An old friend from Miami."

"Pleased," said Patty. She didn't sound it. "I'd better get on my bike and ride home, Shaper. See ya later."

"Come on in," I told Dot. The two women passed, nodded at each other. "She's protective," remarked the former policewoman as soon as she came in. "Not the girlfriend, right?"

"Nope. She's at her job."

"Yes, the bank. I've studied up on you, Mr. Carrol."

"You took long enough to drop by. Would you like to come back to the kitchen? I can fix coffee."

She shook her head. "Not now. I have to run along on other errands. But what do you say to going out and talking over dinner? You and Ms. Jackson, my treat." Dot gave a half-smile. "I can count it as an expense."

"Tonight?" I wasn't big on springing something like that on Michelle.

"Or tomorrow. I'll give you a call around six and you can tell me, okay?"

I nodded. It seemed reasonable.

As reasonable as anything I'd heard recently.

Chapter 19

"I had just arrived and pulled into the first place I saw, driving north. And then, of all the seafood joints in all the towns in all the world, you walked in."

We were are at Mama Toni's, out by Scott City. I had made certain we met there, going in separate vehicles. I didn't want Dot Dominguez driving us around.

"You're not yet another old flame I have to worry about, are you?" asked Michelle. "It's bad enough having Patty around."

"My husband would have greatly objected to me dating Ted." Dot hesitated, maybe thinking how best to phrase what came next. "But we need to talk about another old flame, don't we Ted? A flame that went out."

I tried not to make a face over that bit of heavy-handed poetics. Dominguez had a penchant for it I remembered. Maybe it's a Latin thing. Maybe it's just her.

She continued. "The police told me Donny Morales visited you. Boris asked them to keep me informed."

Maybe I should ask them not to. "Small Change Robinson too," I said.

"He was not involved in any of this. We are quite sure of that. Ah, thank you." Our orders were being set before us by Toni herself, Joan Antonia Charles. Her bright primitive paintings hung around the dining room, signed Toni Tomaso. I poured a little red into Dot's glass.

"They like you at the Cully Beach Police Department, by the way. You probably know that."

"He saved the chief's professional skin," stated Michelle.

"I keep him supplied with aloha shirts too," I added.

"But one of the officers who filled me in has his doubts about your part in all this, Ted. I think he half-believes you murdered Alyce." Dot called her Alyce, not Alice. She had known the girl back then. I wondered if she had know her real name.

"Saunders, I would assume."

"It certainly wouldn't be Dave," Michelle put in. "Oh, this linguine is marvelous. You're missing out, Mr. Vegetarian."

"No, not Blake," agreed Dot. "Saunders seems to be a minority of one around the station."

"That's just Jack being ambitious again. And this clam sauce is just as good as yours, Ms. Carnivore."

"Not too ambitious, I hope. There's a reward for recovering the jewels and I hope to get it. Intend to get it. Though," Dot said, "it can certainly be shared if you come up with anything, Ted."

I sipped some of the chianti before speaking. "I don't know a darned thing about the jewels, Dotty. Or jewelry, right?" She nodded. "Alyce's death is all that's really been looked into here."

"But Morales is interested."

"So it seems. Small Change just wants to get the murderer. Rex Stoddard, presumably."

"Presumably. Right. He does seem good for it." Dorothea did not sound all that convinced, however. "You know, I have been tailing you a little. Not that you go much of anywhere. You've gotten pretty boring, Ted!"

"I always was," I maintained.

"He just has a talent for being in the middle of interesting situations," said Michelle. She held out her glass. "More."

I obliged.

Dot watched the two of us for a few seconds before starting up again. "I wasn't involved in the original investigation of the theft, of course. The robbery, strictly speaking. I was still pretty much a glorified beat cop then. You know that, Ted."

"But not in uniform."

"No, I'd already been plainclothes a while when we first met, I think." She shook her head. "Beside the point. Anyway, I asked for this case when your name popped up. When I informed my bosses I knew you, they gave me the go-ahead. I've thoroughly familiarized myself with it now. It was a rather small amount of jewelry but very valuable stones."

"What did they do, break into someone's house?" There was plenty enough tempting jewelry in safes scattered across Miami.

"That they did. More or less. The items had just been taken out of a safety deposit box. We have Alyce to thank for that fact. She talked their mark into letting her see them. Mmm, wear them, actually, the owner eventually admitted, while they had sex."

"And then her accomplices showed up," I guessed.

"Yep. Tied our disappointed victim up and left with the jewels. Nothing but the jewels, though there was plenty else of value. They were focused."

"I never knew Donny to be focused." Nor Alyce for that matter.

"Stoddard's lead, no doubt. The most important stone taken was big enough and valuable enough that it even had a name — the Santo Antonio Emerald." I don't know if she expected any reaction to the name. I'd never heard of it.

"There were other stones, diamonds, rubies. Some of the diamonds were top quality blue-whites. Not huge but plenty valuable and easier to sell. None of the gemstones ever turned up." She leaned back and took a sip of her wine. "All of them together, even with the settings, could fit in a shoe box. Valued at somewhere close to half a million back then, and that's being conservative. Probably more now."

"But not to the thieves."

"No, not to the thieves. But they would make a decent-enough haul."

Michelle pondered all this. "So we need to look for a shoe box full of jewelry, eh?"

Dominguez ignored the joke. "Unless the pieces were scattered. Stashed in separate places."

"You think they are up here?" I asked. "Around Cully Beach?"

"It's the best guess. I mean, we do know now that Alyce came here and we assume she had the jewelry. Donny Morales claimed at the time that she and Rex Stoddard cut him out and he had no idea where they went."

"So, at least in theory, Stoddard could have gone off somewhere with the loot and still be sitting on it."

Dot nodded. "In theory. I kind of doubt it."

"You're going to stay around, then?" asked Michelle.

"For a while. I'll be keeping an eye on your husband-to-be."

"Not for the first time. You were a pretty good cop. Why the change?"

"I decided to take a pension at twenty years, while I still had time to try out something else." Dot's laugh was a bit self-conscious. Self-deprecating too, perhaps. "So I ended up a private cop!"

Toni came over, pulled a chair up to the table, and sat with us. We were used to that. We were old friends now. "You're the visitor from Miami, aren't you? Patty told me about you."

"That was pretty quick," observed Dorothea. "I'm Dot."

"Toni. Patty and I talk."

SMOKE

"Fellow artists," I put in as a not-very-good explanation.

"Maybe more than that," she responded. "Patty's thinking of investing in a gallery with Kay Bell. Maybe even with me if they can get me to part with some of my hard-earned cash."

Kay's Korner was not anything like a real art gallery, even if Kay did hang paintings by both women, as well as my old buddy Pat Edwards. More space at a better location would be needed — if Cully Beach could support an upscale business like that at all.

Toni knew that. No point in bringing it up.

"So how do you know our Shaper?" asked Toni.

"I'm still not convinced she's not an old girlfriend," Michelle said.

"She used to arrest my friends down in Miami," I told both.

"Not really your friends, were they?" murmured Dot. I think this talk made her a little uncomfortable. She wasn't one to go along with the lighter tone the rest of us had slipped into. Not while she was working — and have no doubt, Dorothea Dominguez was working this evening.

"A few of them," I replied. To the others, I said, "Officer Dominguez was another acquaintance of my old friend Mike. Work acquaintances."

Dot sighed. It was a theatrical sigh. "How many times did I tell you to call me 'detective,' not 'officer?'

"A whole bunch. Calling you Dot was simpler."

"But not respectful. Or so my colleagues on the force thought." She turned to Michelle. "I believe your Ted has a problem with authority."

"Always have," I admitted. "In truth, I am halfway inclined to consider it immoral to hand over ones god-given freedom to another."

"This does not bode well for our marriage," said Michelle.

"I never would have expected Ted to commit marriage at all," Dot told her, "but having done the crime, he's the sort to willingly do the time."

Yes, another of Dorothea's ponderous metaphors. That didn't mean she was wrong.

Chapter 20

It is true I find giving up ones free will to be morally questionable. This is one reason I do not gamble. I will *not* leave things to chance.

Surfing those big waves, you ask? Isn't that a roll of the dice? No, that is totally me in charge. Surfing on a big day is about exerting control in chaos, even when the rest of the world is more than one can handle — to paddle out into something over which no one has power, a force of nature, yet be in control of your own fate. Is it an illusion, a momentary escape from 'real life?' Or do we glimpse who we truly are?

Beats me. Maybe getting married was akin to it.

We were a step closer to marriage now, Michelle and I. Yesterday had been spent at the *Center for Family Life*, attending our Pre-Cana conference. We'd arrived home late from St. Augustine. It looked none the worse for being entrusted to Charlie and Jan for the day. It was good to have Jan around for just a little longer.

The paper from Gainesville was spread on our kitchen table, getting in the way of Charlie's breakfast. I'd picked it up on the way home from church this morning, at Pat Edwards's recommendation. He'd told Charlie on the phone, she told me. Michelle had disappeared into our bedroom, yet to reappear. For all I knew, she had gone back to sleep.

Ah, here was what Pat wanted me to see. I read aloud.

"Spring in Florida – fireflies vie with a sky full of stars to light up the night. A chuck-wills-widow calls from somewhere out there among moss-draped trees. Spread across a grassy hill, an attentive crowd listens to an even sweeter voice rising from the stage. This is the Florida Folk Festival." I put down the paper. "You know the guy who wrote that, Charlie."

She looked doubtful. "Not Mr. Edwards."

I had to laugh at that idea. "Someone much younger. His parents own a motel in Ruby."

"Martin Groves? No wait. His brother, right?"

"Absolutely right. Jeff Groves." I handed her the section.

"Hmm." She picked it up, looked it over, read the rest of the article. "It says he's a journalism major at University of Florida. Just like Jan is planning." She frowned at the page. "I only knew he was into photography when I stayed there." That was when Patty Singer had taken her over to the Gulf side.

I didn't know the Groves kids myself, nor their parents. They had moved to Ruby well after my most recent visit. Maybe I'd meet them at the festival. Jeff had obviously attended last year.

"Time to open the doors," I announced. The correct time, for once, Ten AM sharp.

Not that folks would be lined up, waiting to get in. Charlie followed me. I was pretty sure she didn't rinse her cereal bowl first. Despite the many times I had mentioned it.

"Still going over on Friday, Shaper?" she asked.

"Definitely." Now that I had figured out the message on the medallion — sort of — it seemed imperative. Not that I couldn't visit the Stephen Foster park before or after the festival, but that might arouse suspicions. And going when the grounds were crowded seemed safer.

I was glad Michelle couldn't make it. I wouldn't want her along now. Was I an idiot to go looking on my own? Maybe I should have laid out my theory to someone on the force.

"Patty is pretty sure she will drive over on Saturday," the girl was saying. "She has invited me along."

"No room for anyone else in her little sports car," I observed. I propped the front door open. The outside air was pretty warm. No improvement on the inside air, there. Still smoky too.

"Lisa Deland stopped by," Charlie continued. "She's back with her dad for the summer. I think she wanted to ask about working but she's too shy."

I nodded. She certainly was. As shy as I was at her age. "I could probably use her. If I don't see her first, you ask her if she wants a job, okay?"

"Sure. Oh." She was staring out the front window. "My brother is back." The green Granada was doing a U-turn in front of the shop. It was a good thing Officer Saunders wasn't watching. "I'd better warn Mom."

Leaving me to deal with Sebastian and his friend. Not that it was any trouble. They had much better tans than when last I saw them. Yes, Alistair too.

"Good morning!" called Sebastian Furr from the driveway. "We aren't intruding, are we?"

"It's never intruding during business hours," I called back from the doorway.

"Or any other time," called Michelle from behind me. I hadn't heard her sneak up. "We're family."

"We will be sort of related when I marry Michelle, won't we?" I asked as they stepped into the shop. "You're half-brother to the girl who would be my step-daughter."

"Dad!" said Sebastian. I think the rest of them thought that was funnier than me.

"But not legally my daughter, as she was to Bradley Jackson when he adopted her."

"Yes, Bradley Jackson. Aunt Pam never had a good word for him, I can assure you. Don't you have Jackson relatives around somewhere?"

"In Georgia. We got along with them okay, we just didn't keep in touch." Michelle glanced toward the kitchen door. "Charlie? Are you coming out?"

"I'm fixing fresh coffee, Mom," the girl called back.

"Then we might as well go back and drink it," I decided. I left the kitchen door open so I could keep a watch on the empty showroom, and we settled around the table. I'd made sure to bring along the stray kitchen chair this time, but with five of us I still ended up perched on the stool.

Michelle poured. "Too early to offer you wine," she joked, "and I'm not sure there are any of Ted's scones left."

"I ate the last," volunteered Charlie. "I could run to the corner and buy some donuts."

"No need for me," said Alistair, his first words since arriving.

"Nor me," seconded Sebastian. "No wine either! Aunt Pam was strictly no alcohol. I think my dad's problems were part of that. My Uncle Carl had to go elsewhere for a beer, when he was home."

"Home?" I asked.

"Career navy, so he was out at sea for extended periods. Carl was an okay guy. Anyway, I don't drink."

"But he doesn't prevent me from having an occasional beer," Al added. "This is a nice town. We may loiter in it for a few days, what with Ted here being buddies with the local constabulary."

"The founder of this town was named Sebastian," Charlie informed them. "Sebastian Cully. That was in the Twenties. There's a statue of him."

"Oh, on the road that crosses the bay? We saw it but didn't know who it was."

"I figured it was another Confederate general," said Sebastian. "Seems like there's one in every little southern town. Now I'll have to take a closer look at the old boy." He sipped his coffee — sugar and milk — and went on. "You know, we do like it around this area but we wouldn't, um, stay if it made you uncomfortable."

Alistair Brown admitted, a tad sheepishly, "I already have a possible job lined up. Security guard at the town up the road."

"Banner Beach. With his credentials it wasn't difficult — military police and a marine, to boot! I'm another matter."

"Not that we intend to make this our permanent home," said Al. "A base, maybe, for now, while we look around the state."

Michelle nodded. "So what kind of work would you be looking for, Sebastian?"

He shrugged. "Pretty much anything. I just got my degree but I've never had a, well, *real* job, you know?"

"In general business," added Brown. "The degree."

"We could say something to John-boy, couldn't we?" I asked Charlie. "The family business might be able to use him."

Charlie giggled. "Do you think he knows which end of a shovel to hold?"

"You're sister is altogether too much like you, dear Sebastian," remarked Alistair.

I saw someone come into the shop. Just a local kid. I gave him a wave and settled back on my stool. "Are you thinking of getting into law enforcement?" I asked Brown. "As you pointed out, I am friendly with the police. I could say something to the chief." I wondered how Alistair would do on a bicycle.

Sebastian gave me a bit of a sour look. Maybe even a scowl. I do not believe he approved of the suggestion.

"I think he'd still have to take some courses," said Charlie.

"It doesn't matter," Al told her. "I'm not looking for that sort of career." Sebastian settled back, apparently pleased to hear his boyfriend state this. "To be honest, the only thing the two of us are sure about right now is that we have no reason to ever go back to Norfolk."

I assumed that was where they met, Furr growing up there, Brown being stationed. "You have a place to stay?" I asked.

"We're in a motel across the bridge," Sebastian said. "A cheap one. We'll look for a rental if we stay on."

"Or they could camp in our backyard like Karrie Goodpaster," quipped Charlie.

"If they get a van with unicorns dancing along its side, I might consider it," I told her. "Is she still thinking of camping at the festival?"

"Not sure. That would make three with her and me and Patty. We could all ride in her van!"

"Festival?" asked Sebastian.

"The Florida Folk Festival. One of the oldest in the country and not so far from here."

"Way down upon the Suwanee River," Charlie put in.

"Except that's *up* from here. I'm going Friday only." I waved an arm toward Michelle and Charlie. "The women folk haven't made up their minds."

"I'm not going," declared Michelle. "Too much on a holiday weekend."

"And I think I am," Charlie said. "At least one day."

SMOKE

Sebastian and Alistair exchanged a look, and then a nod. "Maybe we'll check it out, as long as we're around," said Furr.

"After all," added Brown, "it is, as you said, Michelle, a holiday weekend. And officially we are still on holiday."

Chapter 21

Any swell at all was nice at this time of year. It was small but could be ridden, breaking with decent form on the sandbars around the Cully Beach pier.

Of course, every kid in town was out riding on their first Monday free from school. That included my neighbor Marty, whom I had chauffeured here at the crack of dawn.

Also of course, Marty didn't exactly surf with me. She hung with the other hot surf kids over closer to the pier, sharing the peaks that came wedging off the pilings. I sat down a way, as usual, preferring the longer — if mushier — walls there.

But here she was, paddling my direction. She wasn't ready to go home, was she? "It's Kim," she called, pointing toward the beach.

I'd seen the van before, down at Jumento Inlet. It was hard not to recognize it with the big 'Kim-Tim' logo on the side. I could also make out Kim Timble's blond hair as she stepped out to look things over. Alone, it seemed.

A couple minutes later she was paddling out to join the fun. "Hi Marty. Shaper Ted! I'm invading your home break."

"Maybe we should vandalize her van," I suggested to Marty. "Spray paint 'locals only' on it."

Both ignored the suggestion. Nobody takes poor Shaper seriously.

"I've been searching for surf. I drove up to Jumento but it wasn't breaking well, so I just kept going." Kim surveyed the water south of the pier, the surfers strung out over a couple blocks, the kids congregated near the piles. "I surfed here a lot as a kid."

"I visited a few times back then, well before I decided to move here."

SMOKE

Twenty years or more ago that would be. Since those days Kim had grown up, become a professional champion, and then retired. She was still likely to be the best surfer in the water, whatever break she rode.

"I don't remember it ever being this smoky. Going left!" She paddled into a small peak and did, indeed, go left.

I watched for a few seconds. Can't really tell much about a ride from the back of a wave. "Are you competing anywhere this weekend?" I asked Marty.

"Nope. No one wants to go to a meet on a holiday weekend. Too much else going on!"

That made sense. An amateur meet, anyway. Kim stroked back out to us. "I see you're logging it, Ted. One of your own?"

"It is. Brand new." I had decided to give myself a freshly shaped long board for my birthday.

She looked it over. "Would you let me give it a spin?"

I was a tad surprised by the request but why not? "Sure." I undid my ankle leash and slipped off. Kim did the same, not that I was likely to even catch a wave on her little potato chip of a board.

I turned it over and checked the bottom contours before flipping it back and climbing on. One must keep an eye on what the competition is up to. There were no big surprises nor even little ones, concave into double concave, thruster fin set-up.

Kim had ridden both left and right before I managed to drop in on a steep little peak that had popped up. To my credit, I didn't fall off but I am sure I didn't impress anyone on the shore. It had just the sort of handling I disliked, great for fast flat turns but hard to push into any sort of power move.

We switched back then. "No side fins, I noticed," Kim commented.

"I don't need training wheels," I responded. That's a pretty old surfing joke, mostly mouthed by pretty old surfers on single-fin boards.

But Marty laughed. She'd apparently never heard it before. "A lot of long board contests don't allow but one fin anyway," Kim mused. "I think it would be a pretty good competition board. A modern performance long board. Not quite what I expected from you, Ted."

She was quite right about that. I had not built myself a traditional cruiser, nor a 'nose-rider.' It had turned-down rails with a definite edge to them and a vee out the tail. In many respects, similar to the mid-sized boards I often rode.

"I'd like to see your shaping bay, Ted. Do you mind if I stop by on the way home?"

"Not at all. You can even use my outdoor shower if you want."

"That sounds great — and I'll remember it anytime I'm up here! Hey, Marty, let's paddle over by the pier and show those little kids how it's done."

It was still early. I could hang a couple hours more if I wanted. I might not want. Traffic had momentarily thinned, up on Ocean Avenue, Highway A-1-A. That probably meant it was Eight and no one was rushing to work at the moment. I don't wear a watch. They aggravate me.

A motorcycle pulled into the parking area, slipping in between two cars where the rider could get a view of the water. Make that riders. There was a girl seated behind him. I assumed they were he and she — I couldn't swear to it at that distance.

We saw lots of those guys when they had their Bike Week down at Daytona. Not so many the rest of the year. I grabbed another wave, faded left then cranked a bottom turn right, on my backhand. Step forward to bring the board into trim. I'd rather have set up for another turn but the wave was too mushy. There's nothing wrong with just gliding. A big roundhouse cutback as it got even mushier, bring it back into the petering-out wave and then pull out.

The biker was still watching us, still sitting on his chopper. I could see his long hair and beard now, from a little closer. Couldn't make out the woman. He seemed to be staring right at me. Then he revved up and backed out, and headed north.

I knee-paddled back to the break. That's one of the great things about long boards, one can get up on ones knees and paddle much faster. And stay dry on cold days! That wasn't a consideration this morning. A half-hour later Marty caught a wave my direction and then paddled by me on her way back out. "If you want to go, Kim can give me a ride home later," she said.

Normally I wouldn't go for that. Marty had been entrusted to my care and Alvaro would take that seriously. Never mind that I had been leaving Jan Bell at the beach to find her way home when she was younger than Marty. Rick and Kay were a different sort of parent and relied on their daughter's resourcefulness. But Kim Timble was another matter. Alvaro Guzman trusted her.

"Good enough. I am just about ready to go." And I did, ten or fifteen minutes later.

Alvaro wasn't even home so I needn't explain anything. Michelle was gone too, off to work. I'd probably just missed her. I slipped into my outdoor shower. It didn't have the charm it used to before I redid all the plumbing. Give it a few years and it would look as well-used as ever it did. Lived in. As hot as the day was already, I used only cold water.

"You forgot someone," said Charlie from the other side of the shower curtain. That was new also. I hadn't bothered before the girls moved in.

"She's with her friend Kim," I replied.

"Oh, your nemesis."

"Is that another word you learned in class?"

"Maybe."

"Kim Timble is not my nemesis. We are friendly competitors." I chuckled, though the comment didn't really deserve it. "Who operate far enough apart to remain friendly." It was a half-hour drive or more down to her shop in Vasco. "There are still waves if you want to get into the water."

"Maybe when I start driving again. I don't like to get going as early as you, Shaper."

I finished drying off, wrapped the towel around me, and came out, leaving my wet trunks to hang atop the shower stall wall. I'd get them later if I noticed them.

"We need to get Patty in the water too," I said. "I'll be right back." Into the bedroom, grab the tee and shorts on top of their respective piles in the dresser drawer. It would be too much trouble to figure out if they matched. A minute or so later I was back in the kitchen and ready for a second breakfast. Or brunch might be a better way of putting it, or even tiffin. I'm willing to eat all of them.

"I should start putting iced coffee in the fridge," I told the girl. "I like it on hot mornings like this."

"Me too. I sometimes go down to the corner and buy it bottled."

I said nothing about that. I didn't even shake my head, though I considered it a great waste of money. I'd have to be satisfied with iced tea for now. I poured a glass and went up front to open the doors, more than half an hour early.

Traffic was light along the highway. The throaty sound of a motorcycle engine came from the north, growing louder. The same guy as at the beach. He and his passenger did not look my way as they roared past. A different sort of bike appeared in their wake, traveling along the sidewalk at a leisurely rate.

At least Patty wasn't dinging her bell at us this morning. "No Alvaro?" she asked as she came to rest in my drive.

"Good morning to you too, Patty," I said. "I don't know where your boyfriend is."

She frowned at that and came over, walking the white bike. "Not boyfriend, Shaper. I like Alvaro but I don't think we're going that way."

That was how it had looked to me. Maybe they were just too different. Maybe Patty's divorce, as long ago as it was, bothered the very Catholic Alvaro Guzman.

"Come on in," I said. "No one will steal your ride." In fact, it was not unusual for several kids' bikes to be left lying on my front lawn.

"I think I'll take it around back anyway." I walked back with her and, as long as I was there, opened the big wooden doors on my shaping room. I'd built those myself, two hinged four-footers. Well, with a little help from Rick Bell who had just moved into the neighborhood. It would have been harder to hang them on my own.

The first couple years I was here, before I had a shaping space, I just worked on sawhorses in the back yard. Nothing wrong with that and nothing new to me.

"Remember your board is here anytime you want it," I reminded Patty. "And free rides to the beach." Her little Miata was in no way suited to transporting a surfboard.

"I should get a trailer for the bike," she said. "You remember kids getting their boards to the water that way?"

"I do indeed. It really wasn't needed when they got shorter and lighter, was it? You could peddle to the beach with a little board under your arm."

"True, but I don't think I'll try it. Who's this coming up your drive?"

The van rolled to a stop. Marty popped out of the passenger side, gave us a little wave, and hopped over the hedge to her own property. I saw her stop for a moment in the carport, crouching down a little by her father's yellow Mustang. There was a hidden key, I realized. A few seconds later she was inside.

Kim was more leisurely in coming over to say hello. She took a look at my companion. "I keep running into your woman on the side, Ted." So had Patty described herself when the two met. "Will this supposed fiancee ever turn up?"

"She's at her job. Someone has to work so I can surf all day."

"Makes sense. I have a husband for the same reason." Buzz was probably minding their shop in Vasco. "Now where's this shower of yours?"

"Right over there." I waved an arm in its direction.

"Hi Kim," from the back door. "Need a towel?" How did Charlie know her? I puzzled for a moment before remembering she had once ridden down that way with Marty and Alvaro. She'd even met Buzz, whom I knew only by repute.

"I have my own." Kim held it up. A change of clothes too, though I didn't mind seeing her deeply tanned athletic body in its current bikini. Hey, what do you expect? Shaper is neither blind nor dead.

But never fear, Shaper has a heart too and that belonged to Michelle. We might have joked about Patty or Karrie taking her place, but I knew if I ever lost her I would go back to the same single existence I led the first half-century of my life.

Best to give Kim privacy. As I said, I am not blind. I went on inside and up to the shop. Let the women attend to whatever needed attending back there. It was maybe a quarter of an hour before all four of them came to check on me.

"Charlie and Marty gave me the tour," reported Kim. "Nice efficient setup, even if the rooms are small."

"Works for me."

She turned to her protege. "You should get Ted to build you a long board," Kim told her. "You could compete in an extra division that way."

"Not you?"

"I don't know long boards well enough to shape you a competition model. I'll admit that." Kim gave me a thoughtful look before saying, "Would you be interested in shaping a few long boards under my label?"

I wasn't terribly surprised by the idea. I did provide boards to other shops, mostly basic stock models, to sell under their own names. "As long as I can initial them." That was something I insisted on no matter whose brand was on the boards. I believe in signing my work, both for my sake and the buyer's.

"Or you could just rip off Shaper's design," suggested Patty. "No one would be the wiser."

"There is an honored tradition of it," I admitted. "I was copying every new idea that came along when I started."

Patty laughed. Or maybe it was closer to a snicker. "He was building strange boards even in his college days. He'd go home for the weekend and come back with something new."

"And all of them equally bad," I told them.

She nodded. I didn't think Patty needed to be so eager to agree.

Kim Timble glanced at her diver's watch. "Time I headed home," she announced. "I'll get in touch with you, Ted. And I'll definitely remember to use your shower the next time I'm up this way."

"*Mi ducha es su ducha*," I told her.

Chapter 22

"I'm driving over tomorrow morning," Karrie announced, "and staying through the whole weekend."

I wasn't going to ask her where she'd be camping. That was Karrie's business. "It was going to be just me and Ms. Singer on Saturday," said Charlie. "Now other people are talking about joining us. Maybe John's sister." That would be Shannon, the youngest of the Brody brood. I will *not* call them the Brody bunch.

"Then you'll need a roomier vehicle," I pointed out.

"Yeah. Jan thinks maybe she'll go too and write about it."

"Our budding journalist," commented Goodpaster.

"Right. She could drive all four of us. Then new experiences after the weekend. College!"

"So, are you going to be in my class?" asked Karrie Goodpaster.

"It looks that way. I've only signed up for the one. Sort of to try the whole college thing out. And," Charlie went on, "not only will I be attending college but I also start my new job at *Coastal Coffee*. I was promised one once I had my GED."

"We expect free lattes on cold mornings," I told her, presuming to speak for Goodpaster.

"Her boyfriend never gave me one," sniffed Karrie. "And he was even in my classes. You'd think he would try to bribe me!" John-boy was a manager there. Not much longer.

I didn't mention what an inconvenience it would be not to have Charlie available to watch the surf shop. I'd kind of come to depend on her. She needed some independence. I knew that.

"This festival is part of who Shaper is," Karrie was saying. "If I write a book about him I need to understand these things." I had no inkling whether she was serious. Maybe she didn't either. "I need to absorb more of his surfer *zeitgeist* as well."

Michelle came out of the bathroom. She said nothing about Doctor Goodpaster being there so early. Karrie had actually waylaid me on my morning walk and followed me home.

I was beginning to feel a little apprehensive about those walks. I was vulnerable then, alone while it was still dark out. And, yes, there were no street lights. I couldn't help thinking about Donny and Small Change hanging around somewhere, or the possibility of Rex Stoddard showing up. But I'm a creature of habit, even if it might prove a bad habit.

"There are lots of places you can read about surf culture," I told her. "Even Tom Wolfe though he got much of it wrong."

Michelle poured herself some coffee and sat down with us. Karrie was perched on the stool where I normally might be. "Were you a surf rat like those kids that hang around here?" asked my fiancee. "I can't see you being as obnoxious as some of them."

"Umm." I wondered if I should make up something. "No. Not at all, really."

"The quiet but crazy outsider, right?" asked Karrie. "There's always one."

"They didn't call him Berz for nothing," stated Charlie. She let Karrie wonder about that a moment or two before explaining. "That's short for Berserk."

"Ah. So you weren't the laid-back stereotype, cruising in a convertible and listening to the Beach Boys?"

I snorted in contempt and derision. Yes, both. "True surfers back then listened to hard core surf music. Dick Dale and his disciples. Not pop bands catering to teenage girls." The true surfer subculture of the early sixties was more akin to the punk of a decade or more later. I could have gone on at length about that but didn't feel like it.

SMOKE

Karrie Goodpaster apparently didn't feel like commenting on it either. "So it's just you and me on Friday, Shaper?"

"And my friends from Ruby. Pat and Betty Edwards."

"Your friend from when you were a kid too, right?" asked Michelle. "The one with the odd name."

"Branford." His parents had named him after a town they liked. They'd passed through it on their honeymoon. "Pat claims Bran will be there." I'd believe it when I saw it.

"Sebastian and Alistair said they might go," Charlie reminded me.

"Yes, they did." I probably looked thoughtful after saying that.

"What's on your mind, Ted?" asked Michelle. She had drained the last of her coffee and was rummaging in one of the kitchen cabinets. "Shredded wheat all we have left? I'd better stop at the Pig on my way home." The Piggly-Wiggly was convenient to the bank, only a couple blocks away.

"I was just thinking I ought to talk to those two and see what they have planned."

I should indeed.

Chapter 23

I had a picture of Rex Stoddard, an old mugshot. Nearly a decade and a half old. He was unlikely to look the same. Long dark-blond hair, fairly good-looking aside from a receding chin. The drooping mustache only served to accentuate that feature.

As usual, I was up early. Unlike usual, I had not walked across the street. The truck was packed with most of what I would need today — snacks mostly. I was pouring the freshly-made pot of coffee into a thermos when Alistair and Sebastian showed up.

"We parked on the street," Al informed me. He hesitated to step in. The back door was hanging open, as I had been expecting the pair. "That okay?"

"Best place," I assured him. "Throw whatever you're bringing into the truck and we'll be on our way." I figured the three of us could fit comfortably enough in the cab, even if Brown was a bit wide. Five minutes later I was backing out into the deserted A-1-A.

Regardless of Alistair's size, I was glad to have him along. Or maybe because of his size. A bulky ex-marine as a bodyguard was not at all a bad idea. He and Sebastian didn't know that was why I had asked them to ride with me, to be sure, and maybe they never would. I'd as soon they never would.

But I did feel safer. There was going to be more than just music today, for me. Alyce had left me a clue, and it was entirely likely someone would follow me as I followed it.

West on the Scott City road, across the bridge. Within minutes, it was mostly agricultural land on each side, though that was giving way to development, to gated communities, to golf courses. All the stuff I had come to sleepy Cully Beach to escape. A faint hint of dawn was in my rear view mirror.

SMOKE

So was the haze of smoke, settled close to the ground overnight, a thick blanket on the fields around us. The air was still. "We'll angle toward Palatka," I told my passengers, "and then up through Starke." I could have picked up one of the Interstates, I-95 or I-75, but I preferred the scenic route. Maybe on the way home.

"Good enough," grunted a sleepy Sebastian. I doubted either had any idea what I was talking about. The coffee remained in its thermos. If I drank any now I would need a restroom before hitting White Springs and those were few on my chosen route.

Northwesterly we went from Palatka. It was getting light but smoke still obscured the way. Farmers were out on the road, moving their tractors from field to field. We had to slow down for them more than once. Even got stuck behind one for a minute or so. "You can tell it is spring," I informed my companions, "because the tractors are migrating." That did not receive the appreciation it deserved. Maybe it was still too early for these two.

But I wanted to arrive early, get into the park as soon as the gates opened. I could perhaps get in even earlier than that if I mingled with the performers. Pat could get me in. I would have to find him first. That might take more time than I wanted. I needed to do something in the park and I needed to do it before there was much of anyone around.

Or wait until really late when it was dark. I didn't much like that idea.

SF-OM5. If that SF really did mean Stephen Foster I could make a guess about the OM. Old Marble. The Old Marble Stage was one of several spots that would host performances this weekend. I also had suspicions about the 5, thanks to the accompanying picture. The Old Marble Stage was where I needed to be, before any of those performances started.

"Starke?" mumbled Sebastian, staring out the window. "Don't I know that name?"

"The big state prison is located near here," I informed him. "Raiford. Famous or infamous, depending on how you look at it."

"Oh." He subsided into silence. Starke was actually a rather nice little town. I'd driven up here one Sunday when Pat did an outdoor art show on its streets. Soft snores filled the truck cab. Hadn't Michelle's ex — Bradley Jackson, not Sebastian's father — done time here? I was fairly sure she had told me so. Furr might have heard the name in that regard. His Aunt Pam, from what I had gathered, might be the sort to repeat the news.

I turned left in Starke, toward Lake Butler and Lake City beyond it. It was bright out when I pulled onto Forty-one north. There was a bit of morning traffic too. Lake City is a pretty good sized town.

"Highway Forty-one," said Al, glimpsing the sign. "Hey, like in the Allman's song."

I'm old enough to know what song he meant. I was surprised Alistair Brown was even aware of the Allman Brothers. "It will take us right by the park," I told them. Both, since they were wide awake now. "Would one of you pour me a little coffee from the thermos? Have some yourselves if you want. Paper cups behind the seat."

It would be with plenty of milk and no sugar, the way I liked it. In half an hour we should be at White Springs and they could buy coffee any way they preferred.

Sebastian was the one who rummaged to find the cups. "Hey, snacks too. Can I open something?"

"May I open something," Al corrected him. "You must learn the proper Queen's English, dear chap."

SMOKE

"Your junk food isn't very junky." There might have been just a hint of complaint in Sebastian's voice. "I think we're riding with a health nut, Alistair."

"You can stuff yourself with greasy fried foods and root beer floats at the festival. Thanks." Al had passed a cup of coffee to me. It was still hot enough.

"I look forward to it. We're going to miss the big headliners today though, aren't we? Some of them."

"Not that big," said Brown.

I could agree with that. "The well-known names are just to draw in the general public. I care more about the folk community here in Florida."

Fifteen minutes later we cruised into White Springs and past the south entry to the park. Moss-draped oaks lined our way. "In years past, I parked along one of the residential streets here," I told them. "I think I'll go on around to the other entry this time. There's an official parking area there."

"Little town," remarked Al. "That was the Suwanee we drove across, wasn't it?"

"It was and we have been paralleling it since. This was one of the biggest resorts in Florida, a century or so back. People came for the springs."

The other entry was beyond the town limits and one had to double back a bit to reach the park. Hardly anyone was parked yet. I was able to pull in close to the gate. It would be good to be able to get to the truck quickly, if necessary. Quickly enough. There would even be some lighting here, if we stayed till after dark.

We were there. My plans for what came next were sketchy at best. So be it.

"Gather what you need," I said. "We walk from here."

Chapter 24

"I didn't know it was so *big*," commented Sebastian.

We were only as far as the Heritage Stage, where they were setting up for a day of string bands and clog dancers and such. I hadn't been thinking of how far it was to the Old Marble Stage from the north entry we used. I would have been much closer had I come in through the other gate.

"I have some private business down that way," I told the two, waving an arm in a somewhat easterly direction. "You can hang here and wait for me. Or whatever. We don't have to stick together all day."

"And lose our guide? We expect you to direct us to the best acts today, Mr. Carrol. And —" Al got quite serious. "We promised to keep an eye on you. Charlie insisted and so did your Michelle."

"We've heard some about this murder and all that," added Sebastian.

I resisted the temptation to shrug. "Very well. I need to get to the Old Marble Stage." I started walking that way, and not slowly, across the grass and beneath the tall pines. The park's rightfully famous carillon tower stood off to our right. It made a useful land-mark if one misplaced oneself here.

"Smoke is even worse here than in Cully," remarked Al. "You have a map there?" He peered at the program Sebastian was holding.

"I don't think we need it with Shaper leading us. Hmm, oh here it is, across from the Seminole Camp. I'd like to see that. And the river. It's over there." He flung an arm wide toward the right.

A long paved entry road stretched ahead of us, mildly twisting, mildly rising and falling. I carried a little folding camp shovel under my arm. It might get some odd looks if I continued to tote it around all day. Not enough of them to be a problem, I was fairly sure. I had considered also carrying my revolver, my rarely-fired nickel-plated Harrington and Richardson, but decided against it. I had no business messing with firearms.

"That's the gate house up ahead," I said. Today, the rangers weren't posted there but further along the way, right down by the highway. "The stage will be to its right and back a way."

Also to the right was a village of vendors, most busy getting their merchandise out for the day. Tie-dye, jewelery, that sort of thing. Crafts. No one I recognized so I needn't stop and say anything. Down a long shallow slope, beneath the oaks. The Old Marble Stage was also being set up for the day. A tent canopy was erected above a low wooden stage, which rested on the old marble slabs that gave it its name.

I thought I knew the older goateed musician gabbing with the volunteers. Maybe he would MC this morning. I didn't have time to stop and think about any of that. The best thing to do was keep walking like I belonged here.

Like I knew what I was doing. "Around on the far side," I told Alistair and Sebastian, speaking as casually as I could. I couldn't resist pulling out my paper even if I knew exactly what I had written on it. The Old Marble Stage — that was what Alyce's drawing was supposed to be. And the 5? The fifth slab from the corner, I was guessing. From the back corner, going by the picture. Something was buried under it. I hoped. We marched right on around there, which put us almost backstage.

I realized as soon as I looked at it that Alyce couldn't have turned over that chunk of stone. It was granite, by the way, not marble. Maybe from the same quarry that had supplied the venerable *Bank of Cully Beach* its building materials. So nothing could be under it.

Not directly under it. I unfolded my shovel and began digging by its edge. One of the volunteers meandered over and watched us, but said nothing. I guess we looked like we were supposed to be there. "This may take a lot of digging," I said to no one in particular. I doubted it would be very far down. Whatever 'it' was. Yes, yes, I was hoping the jewelry was there. And that the reward was substantial.

I'd have to share it with these guys. Should share it — that would only be fair. I could see more of the crew around the stage giving us looks now. A clank as the little shovel's olive-green blade hit something. I got down and dug more carefully around the object. A small cylinder of some sort?

"A thermos," said Al. So it was. Not quite shoe box sized — maybe not big enough for all the loot. Unless it was just the stones. I stood and brushed the dirt off it.

And started kicking the dirt back into the hole I'd made. Al and Sebastian joined in and in half a minute you'd never have known anyone had been digging. I gave the thermos a little shake but nothing rattled. That was disappointing.

A small audience was gathering now for the opening act, here and there on the folding chairs or picnic tables beyond them. "Let's sit down and see what we have," I said. The top did not want to come off. After ten years that wasn't too surprising.

"I may have to give it a few whacks with my shovel." Or wait until I got it back to Cully Beach. Whatever was in there was going to the police anyway. But I felt a considerable bit of satisfaction in figuring it out and finding what Alyce had hidden. What she had intended me to find.

SMOKE

Some guys started singing 'You Are My Sunshine.' "Let me," said Alistair. He strained with as little success as me. "Here Bastian." Al turned to me. "He's got big hands." A moment later, the lid was off and Furr passed it back to me.

"We loosened it for him," I informed Al. No jewels inside. A piece of paper? Folded notebook paper with a fairly long message penciled on it, crossings-out here and there. I peered into the thermos. Nothing else. "I'll keep this on me," I told my companions, tucking the paper into a zippered pocket on my cargo shorts. "The thermos doesn't matter, I think, but I should probably give it to the police." I screwed the cap back on.

As far as Alyce's message went, that could be read later. I had done what I came to do and now I could enjoy the festival. So I hoped.

"I don't think I want to stick around for this," said Sebastian. "Can we go visit the Seminoles?"

"Sure." As we rose, I noticed a couple standing a good distance back, the man leaning against one of the big oaks, the woman leaning against the man. Both were in denim, kind of heavy clothing for a day that was already almost too hot. Did they seem familiar?

Oops, they realized I was staring at them. And I realized I had seen that bearded man. Twice. He was the motorcycle rider from Cully Beach. The long dark-blond hair — though the face was partly hidden by beard and sun glasses I had a pretty good idea that was Rex Stoddard over there. They moved away, avoiding looking my direction, as I was avoiding looking theirs.

"We may have trouble," I whispered to the guys. "The biker couple over to our right." Al sensibly didn't look toward them. Sebastian did.

126

"They're leaving," he whispered back.

I glanced their direction. They were walking away, quickly, toward the food pavilions further east. "If they saw me dig out this thermos we may see them again."

"That's one of the jewel thieves?" asked Al.

"It is." And maybe the man who murdered Alyce. "I could call the cops. He's a wanted man." I doubted it would do much good but someone should know, shouldn't they?

Al gazed in their direction a while. "Probably not worth hurrying to do it right now. When we get a chance." I was forgetting Alistair Brown had law enforcement training.

We crossed the road to the Seminole Camp. There was a small stage there too, with split logs for the audience to sit on. The Seminoles themselves were not doing much but Sebastian sauntered around anyway, looking things over. I perused the program.

"I like these ones," I said, pointing them out to Al. "They're going to be right here in, um, an hour and a half. Yodeling."

Brown didn't seem very eager to hear yodelers. "Maybe. I don't know any of these names. Oh, him. He's famous. But it's a workshop."

"I think he performs in the evening. Yeah, at the amphitheater. Tomorrow night. Sorry."

"That's life. I don't know how to play the fiddle anyhow. You ready to move along, Sebastian?" The tall young fellow had finished his rounds and ambled up to us.

"Sure. Any sign of that pair?"

They had completely disappeared. "Nope," I said. "But that doesn't mean we won't see them again."

"I think you should count on it," spoke someone behind me.

SMOKE

"Hi, Dot," I said. I knew who it was before I turned. "Are you tailing me or Stoddard?"

"You. He's a bonus. Not following you, exactly, I just knew you would be at this gathering. It was common knowledge at the police station." I wondered who blabbed. No, I didn't. Not really. "Your friend Blake was talking about it. His girlfriend is coming over tomorrow, I understand."

So I could blame Jan. Charlie too, as long as I was at it.

"She is, with a bunch of friends. Maybe I should warn them away."

"No one is going to care about them, Ted. It's you that has everyone's interest." She looked my comrades over. "It was smart to bring backup."

"I thought so." I gave the pair a grin. "And they didn't even know. What do you say we go back up the road and see what's going on?"

It seemed agreeable to all, including Dorothea Dominguez. She had apparently attached herself to our group. "What's with the dirty thermos?" she asked.

"I'll explain on the way."

I did. All of it.

Chapter 25

A group of school children were on stage as we passed the amphitheater. "The big evening shows will be down there," I told my companions, having taken on the role of tour guide. It was the largest stage of the festival, set at the bottom of a long shallow slope, natural theater seating. "My friend Pat's gonna be playing over at the Azalea Stage. Okay with going there?"

Sebastian turned an eye toward the food vendors' tents strung along our way but raised no objection. Making plans for later, maybe.

"Fine with me," said Dot and turned her attention to Sebastian. "You're Charlie's half-brother, right?" He nodded. I think his mind was more on all that was going on around us than any conversation. Music arose from several directions, vying for our attention. Dominguez persisted in her attempt to talk with him and Al. "And planning to stay in Florida?"

"Yep. There was nothing for me in Virginia. The house I mostly grew up in went to my cousin after her mom died. That would be my Aunt Pam."

"And he'd just finished college and I was fresh out of the service. We pretty much intended to take off anyway," added Brown.

"Alistair was military police back in Norfolk," said Sebastian. I think there was a note of pride in his voice.

"Master at Arms?"

"No, ma'am. That's navy. I was a marine."

The Azalea Stage was a canopy erected on the lawn near the carillon tower. Plenty enough open folding chairs for us to claim places. Yep, there was Pat tuning up — as if banjos are ever really in tune — with a small group of musicians. I was a tad surprised that a couple of those were kids. I only waved in his direction. He was busy.

Someone took seats right behind us, making a good bit of clatter. "Hi Shaper!" I turned to see Karrie Goodpaster. There was a dark skinny girl with a rather large nose taking the seat beside her. "This is Tiffany," she said. "From Ruby. Her boyfriend's in the band."

Tiffany didn't look like she was going to say anything, but then blurted out, "Martin Groves. He's on the bass."

"The cute kid in shorts," Karrie added to this. "He sings too."

"I know the name," I informed them. "Charlie's met him. Is his brother around?"

"Over there." A young man with a camera slung around his neck was checking different angles for the best view of the stage. A man standing near him, a dark-haired guy in slacks and a loose short sleeved cotton shirt, seemed to catch Dot's attention. She waved for him to come over.

He hesitated only a few seconds. Despite a relatively nonde-script appearance, I immediately thought 'policeman.' The haircut helped me there. He slid onto a metal chair in the row in front of us.

"Meet Gordon Rivers," said Dot, "of the FBI. He undoubtedly knows who all of you are."

"That I do." Agent Rivers gave Tiffany a tilt of the head. "Except this lovely young lady." At risk of sounding like a dirty old man, I will say that Tiffany was rather attractive, in a Cher-like way.

"This is Tiffany," I told him.

"Theophilopolous," added our Doctor Goodpaster. "Tiffany Theophilopolous."

"I won't ask you how to spell that."

I asked outright, "So, someone else following me?"

"No, sir. I followed Donny Morales and his friend. Whether they followed you, I am not quite certain."

"They're here?" asked Dominguez.

"Somewhere. I could see rather quickly they had no actual plans so I needn't keep a close watch on them." He nodded toward me. "Chances are they'll be looking for Mr. Carrol so I'd do better to stick close to him."

"Rex Stoddard is here too," Dorothea said. "They spied him earlier."

"Ah! I should arrest him, shouldn't I?" He looked like he might want to smile but resisted the urge. "I'd rather find out what he is up to also. Or, for that matter, what you're up to, Carrol."

"Call him Shaper," Karrie put in. "Now shut up. They're going to play."

All eyes turned forward. A master of ceremonies was at the mike, looking at his clipboard. Dot leaned in close to me. "No need to tell Gordy about what you dug up," she whispered. "He'll find out from the police soon enough."

I whispered back. "I thought the FBI was keeping its involvement sort of, um, unobtrusive."

"I've seen Rivers meet with Officer Saunders." She glanced toward the agent, maybe to see if he was eavesdropping. "At that coffee shop Charlie likes to frequent. No doubt that is how he is keeping tabs on the investigation."

Coastal Coffee, where boyfriend John worked and she hoped to shortly. It was popular enough with the police force, being within three blocks of the station, pretty much across from the pier. I felt fairly sure Jack Saunders wouldn't be meeting with this agent without the knowledge of Chief Cotton. Bill was the one preferring to keep it private.

"This smoke is something, isn't it?" the MC was asking.

"It's all the hot musicians!" someone called out. It might have been a member of the band. The banjo player.

"Maybe so! Let's get them up here and playing music. Here's *Friend of a Friend!*"

"Which explains how this group was put together," announced their fiddle player, apparently the band's spokesperson. They launched into a fast instrumental piece.

Alistair leaned across Sebastian to ask me, "Is that bluegrass?"

"I think they call it 'old-time,' None of that syncopated jazzy stuff you get in bluegrass."

"Pretty much the same instruments, though, huh?"

I nodded. Banjo, guitar, fiddle, stand-up bass. Minimal but sufficient. Someone slid into the row ahead of us, leaving a seat between himself and Rivers.

"They're almost adequate, aren't they?" he asked, turning around to speak to us.

"We could have played circles around them in the old days," I replied.

"Except the kid on bass. He could have taken my spot away from me any day. Long time, Ted."

"So it is, Bran." Despite that, we didn't shake hands, much less embrace. Branford and I didn't do that.

The piece ended to scattered and not particularly enthusiastic applause. It was still early, after all. "This is my old friend Branford Perry," I told all. "I won't bother giving him all your names. Chances are he doesn't care."

"Except for that lovely girl at your side, Ted. That isn't the Michelle I've heard tell of, is it?"

Dorothea had to laugh. "I'm afraid not. Dot Dominguez." She did hold out a hand.

"Pleased," he said. "So, as I suspected, your fiancee is another of your fabrications."

"And what of your girlfriend?" I asked. "Pat claimed you had one but I was doubtful."

"Had to work."

"Hmm, yeah, sure." I doubt our mock sarcasm actually fooled any of those with us.

"Hi Tiff," said Bran before turning around. The band was beginning another tune.

Behind me I heard Goodpaster whisper, maybe to Tiffany, "He's cute. I hope the girlfriend *is* imaginary."

I'd best warn my best friend. And my best man? I'd best remember to ask him!

"I remember you being in a band," Dot murmured. "This was the guy you played with?"

"Yeah. It was our band, really. The others came and went." Until we went too. That was more my doing than Bran's but maybe we both were ready to move on.

It was a slower piece this time and Martin took lead vocals. The girl on guitar sang harmony. She looked even younger than him. I turned my head slightly and whispered to those behind me, "Those two could jettison the rest of the band, I think."

Tiffany giggled. "That's my best friend Amy. They've been playing together for years."

Not many years, I would assume. They didn't have a whole lot of years, even adding both of them up.

SMOKE

It was good to see Branford. It was good to see Pat. I didn't want to get either involved in what was going on right now. Best not to mention it.

Alistair and Sebastian were bent over their program, deciding where to go next. *Friend of a Friend* apparently didn't do much for them. I leaned their direction and whispered, "How 'bout going down by the river next? The gazebo."

"Sounds good," said Sebastian Furr. "I'd like to get close to the Suwanee."

I leaned forward and told Bran, "We're going to wander a little. Catch up with you later."

He nodded. "Good enough. I'll be wandering most of the day too."

Dot Dominguez rose to join the three of us. Somewhat expected, not that she had much reason to keep an eye on me now. Doctor Goodpaster also fell in with our little party.

Perhaps she could tell I was a tad surprised. I didn't think I showed it. Or maybe she was self-conscious about joining us without an invitation. "I figure you're as good a guide as any, Shaper," she explained.

"And better than most," I replied. "I'm an expert at getting lost here." I did know to go to the road running close at hand to the stage. "This is the loop that goes all the way around," I announced. "Gazebo's down that way." They believed me and followed in my wake.

Well, the guys had a map so they could check. Off on a side road, to our right, and descend slightly toward the Suwanee. It was very low in this dry season, barely looking like a river at all from the parking lot. I do think Sebastian was disappointed.

The so-called gazebo was set a short way down its bank, a structure large enough to accommodate performances and a small audience. A boardwalk zig-zagged down to it. "You can see by those markers that the Suwanee isn't always so low. Those are flood levels from the past." We all contemplated the posts for a moment, imagining the waters rising that high. The gazebo itself would be under the flood, at least in part.

"We must come back when the river is itself," Sebastian told his friend.

"Or herself?" asked Alistair. "Are rivers feminine?"

Karrie, of course, had an opinion. "I don't think so. Remember 'Old Man River.'"

A pair of performers were standing in the middle of the gazebo's plank floor, male and female, with guitars. No amplification here, just their natural sound. Sebastian came to a halt and gave them a look. Maybe a listen, too.

"I want to go down to the river edge," he declared.

There was an easy enough walkway on down to it, and a little dock as well. "I've walked enough," Alistair told him and plunked down in one of the open seats.

"I'll go with you," I said.

"Me too," added Karrie

Dot regarded the three of us for a moment. "We can keep an eye on you from up here," she decided and seated herself beside Brown.

I wasn't sure of that. The smoke was even thicker down at the level of the river, and the line of sight from Dot's position wasn't all that good. I saw no reason to worry about it, however. We wound down through the huge oak and gum trees toward the Suwanee's edge.

SMOKE

Sebastian gazed out over the river. "It's more impressive down here," he commented. "You can see how wide it is, even dried up like this."

"It is a way bigger river further south. Doesn't quite rival the Apalachicola over in the panhandle but larger than anything else in Florida."

"I've seen the Apalach," Karrie let us know. "It's pretty big. But I grew up by the Mississippi so I'm hard to impress."

I could tell she had a mid-western accent. Beyond that, I had no idea where Goodpaster originated. I didn't think further on that because someone was approaching from our right, from down river. Donny and Small Change. Rivers had said they were here and here was the proof.

Donny got right to it, barely bothering to look at my companions. "You played dumb but I knew Alyce meant this place. This festival. And I don't know whether you met her here or not but I think you know something."

"I know lots of things," I told him. "Most of them are not your business." I probably shouldn't have said that but I was a little pissed by all of this. Plus I had Sebastian to back me up.

Small Change scowled at that. "If you know anything 'bout Alice it *is* our business."

"For all we know, he's the one who killed her." Donny spoke this cooly, not actually accusing me but getting to Change. That, I am sure, was his intention.

Small Change Robinson whipped out a folding knife, flicking it open in one motion. "Put that away, idiot," hissed Donny. He eyed the thermos I still carried with a certain suspicion.

I hoped Karrie would back away from all this and get up the bank to Al and Dot. I also hoped those two could see what was going on. Probably not much hope for the first of those. Good-paster would want to gather material for her book. Maybe a poem too.

"Rex," suddenly whispered Robinson. The knife came right back out.

Sure enough, Stoddard was approaching from the other direction, up the river, alone. He wasn't a particularly big guy, was he? I hadn't realized that at a distance.

He stopped, sizing us up, and then glanced up toward the gazebo. "This ain't no place for any of us to start trouble," he said, "but I'm ready for it if you do." He patted a bulge in his pocket.

"So am I," came Donny's flat response. "So am I."

Chapter 26

So both these guys were carrying guns? What the heck have you gotten yourself into, Ted Carrol?

Small Change could barely contain himself. He wanted to plant that knife in the man who killed Alyce, that was certain. But Donny got him to reluctantly return it to his pocket. Again.

"One of you two killed Alyce," Rex stated, outright.

"No, one of you two did," came Donny's immediate retort. I assume both were including me.

I could have said the same thing but didn't.

"Ted wouldn't kill her no more'n I would," objected Small Change. "You're the one done it, Rex. I know."

"You don't know nothin' Change. I'd put my money on Donny here." There was some bitterness in Rex's sharp short laugh. "'Cept I ain't got none."

His eyes went to the thermos I clutched. "I saw you dig that up."

Donny gave it another look. "That so? What's in it, Ted?"

"Nothing for you." I held it up for them, just a moment. "This goes to the police."

Both glared at me and then at each other. Of a sudden, Stoddard came to a decision. A small revolver appeared in his hand.

Karrie Goodpaster stepped forward and her arm shot out. Rex Stoddard staggered back, his hands to his eyes. "Pepper spray," she calmly explained. "Never leave home without it."

Rex floundered into the river, dunking his head in the brown water. I don't know if that helped any and then I lost track of him. Donny had darted in and grabbed the thermos right out of my hand. He took off running up the bank and down river, not bothering with the boardwalk.

Rex's gun lay in the mud. Sebastian scooped it up. Stoddard had come ashore and was running the opposite direction. He disappeared into the brushy undergrowth almost at once.

And here came Dot and Al, clattering down the wooden walkway. Small Change Robinson just stood there, shaking his head. "I got nothin' to do with this, Ted," he said. "Don't *want* nothin' to do with it. Sorry Donny grabbed your — whatever that was."

"Evidence, Small Change. That's what it was. But it was empty so it wouldn't have done either of them any good."

The little man laughed outright at that, deeply. It took him a while to stop.

Our friends — I believed I could call them friends — were to us now. Someone else was descending to us as well, more leisurely. Dot followed my eyes.

"Here comes the cavalry," she remarked.

Gordon Rivers. "Galloping in way too late."

"What should I do with this?" asked Sebastian Furr, holding up the muddy revolver.

"I could take custody," spoke Agent Rivers, starting down the last stairs to the riverside. "Might be better if you turned it in to the local police."

"I'd recommend doing that in Cully Beach," said Dorothea. "You don't want to hang around here explaining where it came from. Let Alistair take charge of it, why don't you?"

"Gladly." Sebastian was holding the firearm gingerly, thumb and finger, and passed it to his partner. Al looked it over before slipping it into his pocket.

"I'm pretty sure Morales had a gun too," I said.

SMOKE

"Undoubtedly. As do Gordon and I." Dot turned to the agent. "Decided not to pursue Stoddard?"

"I considered chasing after him but felt it was better to watch for his next move. Good job, Miss," he added, switching his focus to Karrie.

She looked a tad embarrassed. A tad proud of herself too. "I've always wanted to do that. Carried that spray forever!"

"Where were you, anyway?" I asked Rivers.

"Up in the parking lot." He fished a small monocular out of his pocket. "Keeping an eye on things, as best I could with all this smoke."

Robinson seemed uncertain what to do but followed us back up the slope. On the boardwalk, as we neared the top, he leaned close to me and asked, "You do think Rex did it, don't you?"

Had he become uncertain? "I don't think anything. All I know is that he and Donny were both involved." And Alyce. "Is it true that Alyce was, um, in a relationship with Stoddard?"

"Uh-huh. She fell big for him. And — well, I thought he felt the same 'bout Alice." We were to the parking lot. Below us, it looked like they were switching acts in the gazebo. "I'm gonna go look for Donny," said Small Change. A narrow road — a path maybe I should say — led south, parallel to the Suwanee's flow. I think kayakers used it to launch somewhere down river. He headed that way. No one chose to comment.

We went the other direction, back toward the center of the park. There was more of a crowd now. Lots of kids too. I saw school buses parked when we got to the carillon area, which explained that. The sun had crept upward, behind its veil of haze. "I'm for something to eat," I announced.

"Aren't your pockets full of snacks?" Sebastian had seen me stuff them in.

"For emergencies," I claimed. "It's time for a real meal. Or at least ice cream." We continued in the direction of the food vendors. Agent Rivers was sticking with us, for now, and Sebastian was taking advantage of it.

"This Stoddard," he said. "I know he is a murder suspect but the robbery was a decade ago. Wouldn't the statute of limitations run out or something?"

"No, that's about being indicted. The confession by Morales was enough to formally charge Stoddard back then. He's not getting off the hook that way."

"And he can't get off on the speedy trial bit either because he was a fugitive," added Alistair Brown. It was to be expected he would know this stuff.

Dorothea Dominguez and I walked a little behind the others. "I was chatting with Mr. Brown while you went down to the river. I think he could do well in my line of business," she commented. "I might suggest it to him."

"Sebastian wants him to steer clear of a law enforcement career. He dislikes guns." That was pretty obvious.

"It's not the same. I needn't even carry a firearm, much less use one."

"But you do carry one, don't you?"

"I do today. As does Rivers, of course." She gave the man a thorough looking over. "Tucked in the back of his trousers, I see. Rivers is from the Miami office. That's why I know him. Hey, Gordon," she called, "why the hell are you here, anyway?"

He looked back at us and grinned. "Solving this case would certainly look good on some agent's record, don't you think? Not to mention recovering the stolen jewelry."

"You should know I'll be the one to do that." To me she said, though loudly enough Rivers could hear it, "The FBI's arguments for being involved seem pretty tenuous to me and everyone else, but it seems no one has told them no."

"We're just here to help," objected the agent. I am not at all certain how serious he was. "I'm going to go looking for Stoddard again. Or his chick." With that he strode off rather quickly toward the southeast.

Dot watched him go a moment. "I assume Stoddard left his cycle near the south entrance. He would pay to put it in one of the private parking spots and have someone keep an eye on it."

Karrie pulled out her notebook. "I have to jot that down," she said. "Not something I would have thought of!"

Dot gave her a bit of a smug smile. "Had I asked any one of you where Rex Stoddard would leave his bike, you might have come up with the right answer."

"But," I said, finishing her thought for her, "none of us was likely to have asked the right question."

"My only question is whether to get a root beer float or a strawberry milkshake," said Sebastian.

Chapter 27

"Isn't it inconvenient to carry that around?" asked Pat. He meant my little shovel and it was inconvenient. Too short to treat like a walking stick.

"I'm not walking all the way back to the truck just to stow it," I informed him. I'd rather chuck it in a waste can.

We had managed to converge with Branford and Pat at last, and had staked out a reasonably shady spot to eat lunch. Or whatever meal this was. One or another of us had been eating something since midmorning.

"Put it with my stuff. I'll give it to Karrie before she takes off."

"She's camping at your place?"

"Nope," Doctor Goodpaster broke in. "I'm camping here. Pat had an extra guest spot open up."

"Betty decided not to deal with the smoke and heat," he informed me. "Now Karrie is the one who has to sit up all night listening to the neighbors jam."

"The true festival experience," I told her. "But I'm surprised you're camping, Pat, what with living so close."

"Doing it for the kids. They wanted to camp." The 'kids' were not with us right then. I didn't blame them.

"I love these garbanzos and chorizos," said Pat. "Or at least I'm pretty fond of them. If I weren't getting sleepy I'd go get another plate."

That caught Karrie's attention. "Garbanzos? I always called those chick peas."

"I grew up around Cubans so they're garbanzos to me." He gave the slightest of chuckles. "Something else for you to write down."

"You're playing again today, aren't you?" I asked.

"In a couple hours. Seminole Camp." He contemplated his almost-empty paper plate again. "The band. None of us have any other commitments this weekend."

"Some people are in two or three different acts and have to run from one to another," said Bran. He'd been gnawing a deep-fried turkey drumstick, with a sip of lemonade from time to time. It gave me indigestion to watch these friends of mine.

I pretty much stuck to ice cream of one sort or another all day. Plus the snacks stowed in my pockets.

"That boy is pretty good on bass, isn't he?"

"He is," agreed Bran. "You know I mostly thumped away on a few notes. Martin plays melodically. Sort of Paul McCartney style."

"Might come from his playing classical guitar," Pat put in. "I'll be right back." He headed off toward the Cuban food vendor.

"Anyone have any thoughts for this afternoon?" asked Sebastian.

Bran shook his head. "Nothing planned. Don't have to cater to June's tastes till tomorrow."

"And Bran doesn't have any taste," I added.

"So true," he admitted. "I'm just a dumb redneck hick. Or hick redneck. Which way is proper?"

"Not so dumb," objected Goodpaster. "I know you have a degree."

"In literature, no less," I told her. I contemplated my friend — my best friend? — for a moment. "Like me, he didn't do much with it."

"And like you, I would have regretted not getting it. I know you did."

I only nodded to that. It was true. I did go back and take my degree nearly ten years late. It was unfinished business.

"Three o'clock," hissed Alistair.

Karrie looked puzzled. "It's not even One yet."

"The biker woman." He made the faintest of gestures with his head. I think the good doctor caught on then. She was walking straight toward us.

It was me she addressed, but not until her eyes had flicked back and forth taking in the others. I think she gave Karrie a rather unfriendly look. "Rex wants to talk. He, uh, didn't mean no harm before, y'know? Wants to straighten things out."

She was a decidedly normal looking sort. Aside from the clothes and maybe the dark eye makeup, she could have been any one of the normal looking middle-aged women strolling around this place with their normal looking middle-aged husbands.

I considered consulting with Dot but decided against. Rex had sent her to speak to me. You can be sure, however, that I would have Dorothea Dominguez along if I met with him. "I'm willing," I said, keeping my tone as colorless as I could.

"Where?"

That surprised me, just a bit. I figured Rex already had a spot picked. Where? "The museum," I said. "I'll head over there in, ah, about half an hour and hang a while." I turned my attention to my milkshake.

She stood there, hesitant, a few seconds before wheeling and heading off to report to her boyfriend.

"Coolly played. You should've been a cop, Ted," said Dot.

Bran snickered. "Or a criminal mastermind."

"How do you know he isn't?" asked Pat, just returned with another heaping plate of beans and sausages. He had switched out the garbanzos for black beans this time. I was glad I wouldn't be sharing a tent with him.

"I'd live in a much better house. Maybe have a better class of friends, too. So, will you come with me, Dot?"

"Of course."

"So will we," spoke up Sebastian.

Alistair grinned. "Your bodyguards."

"Not the rest of you," I said. "Too many might spook him." Damn, stop playing at being a cop, Ted. Step back. "Let's all meet when Pat plays later."

"He's right," Dot pointed out. "There's not likely to be danger but you never know. You'd best stay away." She turned her attention to Al and Sebastian. "I'm not even sure about you two."

"The criminal mastermind needs his gang," I let her know. "We might as well mosey toward the museum."

"I did want to see it," admitted Sebastian.

"And I want to see the inside of the carillon tower," countered Alistair.

"They're both air-conditioned," I told them. "That's an added attraction on a day like this." The museum was a good-sized building across an open lawn. There was some of sort of old-time craft demonstration going on there on the grass. A lot of that at the festival — it wasn't about music only.

"It's mostly a museum of Stephen Foster," I went on. "Some exhibits of pianos and period items. And —" Dramatic pause here. "Dioramas based on his songs. Admittedly a bit cheesy but fun anyway."

"He wrote good songs," in Alistair's opinion. "And not racist like some idiots claim. Sebastian can really do a great job on 'Oh, Boys, Carry Me 'Long.'"

"You guys are singers?" asked Dot.

"We met at choir practice," Sebastian told her.

Gordon Rivers was lounging near the entry. Dot went to him at once. "We have a meeting with Stoddard," she informed him. "I'd appreciate it if you kept out of the way. After that doesn't matter to me." The FBI man gave a quick nod.

It might matter to me. I didn't quite like the way Dot had asserted herself here. We went on in through the double door. No immediate sign of Rex. He could be lurking in one of the other rooms. "It might be best if you guys kept your distance," I told Furr and Brown.

"Understood," Al answered at once. "We'll stay on the other side of the room."

"Ready to leap into action," Sebastian apparently couldn't resist adding.

"There he is," whispered Dot. "Been looking at the guitars." There was an exhibition by various Florida luthiers in one of the side rooms, according to the signs. Rex's girlfriend was with him. We met in front of the 'Old Folks at Home' diorama. The old folks appeared to be fishing, way down upon the Suwanee River, but they never caught anything.

Dominguez quite surprised me with her first words. "We think you should be aware a fed is hanging around outside who may or may not have plans to take you in. A heads-up, you know?"

He nodded slowly. "Thanks." Then he took a closer look at her. "I remember you. You're a cop."

"I was. Not anymore. I'm just after the jewelry now, Rex, and I don't care what happens to you."

"Insurance," I added to this. "There's a reward."

He smiled for the first time. Not that it was easy to see with the thick beard. "I'll bet. To be honest, I don't care about them anymore. That's long past and I've —" He looked down into the face of his companion with unconcealed affection. "I've got another life now. But I care about Alyce and what happened to her. I loved that woman. You understand that, doncha Hon?"

"Sure Rex. I'm not jealous of a ghost."

"Whoever killed her is gonna pay, one way or another. I'd just as soon the cops get him so I don't have to bother." He gave me a long hard look. "I don't know about you, man. I'm not rulin' you out."

I didn't blame him. I wouldn't either. "But I think it musta been Donny. He musta thought we were crossin' him. Alyce was gonna meet me with the stuff and we would disappear if he wasn't able to show."

"Leaving Donny to sit in prison," noted Dot.

"Yeah. It seemed like the way to go when Donny became a suspect. I never heard exactly what they nailed him with. Found some sort of evidence is all I know, fingerprint or somethin'. The cops didn't know nothin' 'bout me." Rex smiled again but it was a much less pleasant smile. "Until he told them."

Dot expanded on this. "Of course, Alyce was a suspect from the start. The victim described her pretty well, even if she did use an alias."

"Donny and I wore masks and tried to make it look like she had nothin' to do with it."

"Which didn't fool anyone."

"Guess not. That's why we got her out of town right away with the jewelry." He paused a moment, maybe getting the details of a decade-old plan straight in his head. "We would catch up with her later — were all supposed to meet in Valdosta and then head up to Atlanta. That was the plan from the start. I had a buyer lined up there."

"Not Cully Beach," I said.

"I'd never even heard of Cully Beach till it was in the news and I learned about Alyce being found." He stared into the diorama window for a while before asking, "She went there to see you?"

"That would seem likely. I don't know why."

"Me neither. The last I heard was when she phoned me at the motel I was stayin' at in Georgia. The place we were gonna meet. Didn't say where she was, just that she thought someone was after her and she was gonna keep away until she was sure it was safe."

There was an obvious question here. I was surprised Dominguez did not pose it. "Do you know if that was before Donny Morales was arrested?" I asked.

Rex thought. "I'm not sure." He thought some more. "I don't think I could figure it now, either. Too long ago." The man shook his shaggy head.

I suspected we could figure it out, if we put our minds to it. There were only a few days involved and Donny's arrest date would be public record.

"If it was after the arrest, it couldn't be Donny, could it?" he continued. He gave me another unfriendly looking over.

Dot stepped in. "But we don't know, do we?"

"Maybe you and me should have a private talk," Stoddard hissed, staring into my face.

"You realize I carry a handgun, don't you?" asked Dot, quite casually.

Rex settled down at once. Settled down, not backed down — he seemed to be a man given to quick mood changes. "So did I, ma'am, till a coupla hours ago. Um, no chance of gettin' that back, I suppose?"

"Only if you want to claim it at the Cully Beach Police Station," I told him.

His eyes went from us to Sebastian and Alistair peering into one of the dioramas across the room. "I guess there's no arguin' with that," he said. "Hey, I'm not mad about the spray in the eyes. Tell your friend that, okay? I don't blame her none."

"I bet it was pretty funny to see," thought his girlfriend.

"Not for me. Let's get out of here, Hon."

The pair exited through the door opposite the one by which we had entered. Strictly speaking, that would have been the front door even if most of the traffic came and went through the other.

"I say give them a couple minutes before going outside," I said.

"Alright with me. You know," remarked Dorothea, "Alyce may have been crossing Rex too."

That didn't make much difference, did it? Unless there was someone else involved. "I'm not inclined to think he killed her, though," I said.

Dot only shrugged at that. Our companions had rejoined us. "All done?" asked Alistair.

"For now," Dot told him. "I do not think we'll see that pair again today."

"No, not today," I agreed. They were probably headed toward the south entry and Rex's cycle. Where would they go from there? Cully Beach seemed a pretty good guess. Dominguez would recognize that too.

Agent Rivers was still loitering by the doors as we exited. "You should know," he said at once, "Morales and Robinson have left the park. They might be on their way back to Cully Beach. Stoddard still inside?"

"I doubt it," Dot replied.

"So did I," came his matter-of-fact reply.

Chapter 28

"I finally shook her," I told my friends. Dot Dominguez had parted with us at the museum. She no longer had any reason to stick close.

I knew I would see her again in Cully Beach, maybe in no more than a few hours. She would want to know what was in Alyce's note. To her credit, Dot had not pressed me on this — it remained unread in my pocket.

Whether she, or Agent Rivers for that matter, had left the park, I didn't know. Either or both might still be keeping an eye on me. Or they could be sitting together enjoying a performance at the other end of the festival.

Those friends were still together, Pat, Branford, even Karrie. Apparently, she was not so easy to shake. Pat had arrived at the Seminole Camp before the rest of his group. "They're waiting on a golf cart to bring them," he said. "Martin didn't want to lug his bass all the way down here."

Mid-afternoon. Most of the stages would shut down in a couple hours, as the evening show started at the Amphitheater. I hadn't decided whether to stay for that. It might be a good idea to consult with Sebastian and Alistair.

First, Branford. The stage here was beneath a more-or-less traditional Seminole chickee, without the raised floor but roofed with a thatch of palm fronds. He was leaning against one of the thick supporting posts, watching the current act without a great deal of interest.

"Even though both our imaginary girlfriends stayed home," I said to him, "I do intend to marry mine, come fall."

There was a touch of skepticism in the look he gave me. "Never expected it from you, Ted."

"Neither did I! But since it's happening, I need a best man and I think that should be you."

"Damn right it should be me. I suppose I should congratulate you and all of that."

"Whatever." I'll admit, that cracked both of us up. It was how our friendship had always worked.

"What's so funny?" asked Karrie Goodpaster.

"We are," Branford informed her. "Or I am, anyway."

"He's the sidekick, added to the story for comic relief," I let her know.

"Whereas you're the hero, Shaper?"

"Always."

"Hmm, okay, but you should know your old friends have been telling me all sorts of things about you."

"Lies. Do not put any of them in your book."

"Here come the kids." Branford was looking toward the road. A golf cart loaded with passengers and instruments was turning onto the grass. "Will, too."

Will was the older fiddle player. He had been introduced as Grandpa Will at their appearance this morning.

"Can you believe," Bran went on, "this is Will's first time here, despite playing old-time fiddle and living an hour away most of his life? It was, ah, *good* of Pat to include him."

"Pat's a good guy. We both know that."

"Better than we are."

"That's not difficult."

"This is a new side of you, Shaper," said Karrie. "Ted's always seemed a bit buttoned down."

Bran shook his head. "More battened down, I'd say."

Probably so.

153

SMOKE

"Oh. Great line." Goodpaster jotted it down in her notebook.

The MC, a top mandolinist and a fixture of the Florida folk scene, was calling for another round of applause for the group exiting the stage. As at the gazebo, no microphones here. We sat down up closer so we could hear. A pretty good crowd had gathered.

"This next act is performing at the Florida Folk Festival for the first time this year," he announced. "Some of you may know Pat Edwards on the banjo, but the rest are all newcomers. Let's give a big welcome to *Friend of a Friend*!"

To their credit, the performance was not a clone of the morning show. They let the girl take lead vocal on a song too. The guys were pretty pitiful on trying to provide harmony. About like me.

I whispered to Branford, "You're not working at that resort anymore, right?" Pat had mentioned it sometime.

"Not for quite a while. I left *The Mooring* two years ago. Needed a change." He didn't sound like he was very serious about it all but I knew Bran. It would have been a big move for him. "Including dating again, finally. I hadn't for years."

Again, about like me. I didn't say that. "I do a little of this and that now," he went on. "Pat's even got me painting again."

Pat was making an announcement. "Hank is going to sit in with us for a tune. Come on over, Hank!"

There was scattered clapping. "Stand in with you," the mandolin player corrected him. A plain and worn F-style instrument hung from his shoulder. That didn't fool me. It was a quality mandolin, I was sure, but couldn't make out the builder's name.

Hank's lanky frame towered over the others. He stood to one side, facing them more than us. They launched into a spirited rendition of 'Oh, Susannah,' appropriate to the venue. Martin once again on vocals. They all managed to stay together as Pat and Hank traded instrumental breaks. To be honest, those breaks made little musical sense to me, more about flashy playing than the tune. But I like to complain, so never mind.

"How old is that boy?" I whispered to Branford.

"Eighteen. Graduated high school last week. His girlfriend is a year younger." I could see her in the front row, off to our left, long dark wavy hair spilling down her narrow back. "So is Amy."

"At moments like this," I said, "I am glad I did not stick with a music career."

"What, you don't want to get the band back together?"

I needn't answer as the song reached its end and applause rose.

Amy and Martin swapped instruments before launching into a slower tune. "Martin's signature," murmured Branford. "'The Rebel Soldier.'" The boy finger-picked adroitly as he sang. Miss Akin wisely stuck to thumping root-and-fifth.

"The girl is a want-to-be country singer," he continued. "The two of them have an whole other band for that. Tiffany's in it too."

"The untalented girlfriend bit?" I asked. Yeah, that's cynical but I know how bands work. Or don't work.

"She's okay. Noodles on the keyboard. I don't think her heart's in it but she wants to support her friends."

"In other words, backwards from what I was implying."

"Exactly. It's more like the sort of thing you would do."

There was fair applause as they wrapped it up and switched instruments back. Some of the listeners rose to wander off elsewhere. Maybe hoping to arrive in time for the start of some other act on some other stage at the other side of the festival. Maybe calling it a day.

I might want to do that soon. Another cart had appeared on the paved road, this one with a little wagon in tow, and a load of musicians. It turned toward the Old Marble Stage. Maybe it would come over here after unloading.

I bet we could fit in with the band if we felt too lazy to walk. "We're *Friend of a Friend*," Grandpa was saying, "and we're pleased to have been here with you today." They launched immediately into another fast instrumental, their closer.

Yes, here came the golf cart across the road and over the grass. The band finished off to applause and then more applause after Hank thanked them. Not much breaking down to do; just get their instruments into their cases and walk away.

"So what now?" Sebastian asked. "Al and I don't really care about staying for the evening show."

"I don't one way or the other myself," I admitted, and turned to the rest of our contingent. "What are you guys planning?"

"I'm for going back to the campground," announced Pat. "Relax and maybe jam some. You guys could hang there a while. Not overnight! That would get me into all sorts of trouble."

Yeah, sure. But pretty much everyone was in agreement. Even the kids, though I doubted they would stick with us very long. "It's on the way back to our vehicles anyway," Branford pointed out.

Grandpa Will was given charge of all the instruments and rode off in the cart. The rest of us took the long walk to the far end of the park. The campground was thickly packed, three, four, or more tents and campers sharing each space, all of them performers or volunteers. No room for the public on this weekend.

And no campfires. With the dryness and fire risk, they weren't being permitted. Too bad. Sitting by a fire was one of the more attractive pastimes at these affairs. Not that I have the patience to sit very long. I wandered about, said hello to a few old acquaintances, listened to folks playing here and there. Bran went with me but we didn't say much to each other.

It was darkening into dusk when we returned. Karrie sat half-inside her van, watching Pat jam with a couple guys I did not know. Sebastian and Alistair were a little aside, not talking, just absorbing the day. I asked, "Ready to head back?"

They were. "I'll walk with you," said Bran. "I might as well get home too."

"Ruby, right?" asked Sebastian. "Same as Pat?"

"Yeah. Pat kind of talked me into moving up from Genoa. Ted here introduced the two of us."

"We'll have to check out that side of the state," Alistair told his partner.

"Nothing but rednecks over there," I informed them.

"And that," said Branford Perry, "is why I fit in."

Chapter 29

Someone lurched out of the dark and into me. I stumbled and fell to the grass. A momentary thought of thankfulness that we weren't on the blacktop went through my mind.

"Check his pockets." One pair of hands grabbed at me, another groped.

"Hey!" yelled out Bran. He grabbed the one guy — two only it seemed — by his collar and yanked. By then, Sebastian and Alistair had caught up with us. They'd been trailing a little behind as my friend and I talked. My attackers might not even have known they were there.

The men who had assaulted me were large enough but Sebastian was larger. The guy Bran had engaged had risen and turned to face them. It surprised me a little when Sebastian threw a heavy punch to his sternum. He sounded like a balloon deflating as he sat down on the pavement.

Alistair took on the other one. Not that I needed help, you understand, but I'd been a bit deflated myself when I hit the ground. Brown launched himself at the guy's midsection, wrapping his arms around his torso, rolling him off me and sort of throwing him. The man got to his feet and took off, as quickly as able. The other stumbled after him.

"Nice wrestling move," observed Bran. He knew something about that, having been buddies with a few minor league pro wrestlers, ages ago. Some of them moonlighted as bouncers in clubs where our band played.

"Anyone you know?" asked Brown.

"Strangers." Who the heck would know about what I was carrying? Not those guys for sure. "Hired?" It seemed the best explanation.

"By whom?" wondered Alistair.

I shook my head. "We aren't going to find out here and now." But either Rex or Donny, right? Unless that earlier thought about someone else being involved actually had something to it.

"You okay to drive?" asked Sebastian.

"Sure. Let's go."

It was quite dark when I pulled into my drive.

It could have been darker. Guzman had carried through, in a small way, on his security light idea. Not a big one on a pole, installed by the power company, but a floodlight in his carport. Our bedrooms were on the opposite side of my place so it didn't bother me any. Now I could turn off the light by my workshop doors, which did shine into my bedroom a little.

And I'd save on electric. There was a light on in the kitchen and at the back door. It was locked. I approved of that.

Michelle had it open before I could find the proper key. The three us filed in, looking, I am sure, as tired and disheveled as I felt.

Michelle only. "We're all alone," she said. "Charlie and Shannon are sleeping at the Bells' house tonight. Patty's going to drive over in the early morning to join them." She glanced at the stove clock. "That's not so far away."

Fifty-year-old Patty with that group of young women, only one of them out of her teens. How had that arrangement happened? "I'm glad Patty has chaperons," I said. "Wouldn't want her getting into trouble." I was not going to tell about me getting into trouble, not now. Maybe tomorrow.

It was Alistair who spoke up. "We think we should stay," he said. "Just in case."

"In case of what?" demanded Michelle.

"In case someone wants to see this." I fished Alyce's note out of my pocket and unfolded it on the table top. Maybe it was time to take a look. I made a sudden decision. "This goes to the police first thing tomorrow but I'm going to write out a copy for myself right now." Note paper and pencil. Up front. I went into the shop to retrieve them.

"We could take it over now," Alistair pointed out as I sat down at the table. "Even in a little town like this the police work at night."

"I want the chief to be there." Or someone else I trusted to know what was going on. I looked at this pair of young men who had backed me up all day. I was more than just grateful for that. And I was grateful for the offer of further protection. "I do think I would like you to hang here overnight." For Michelle's sake, if nothing else.

To be honest, if these guys hadn't volunteered I might have bundled my fiancee into the truck and taken her to sit at the station with me. I did not want her alone here.

I started at once on my copy, trying not to think too much of the words as I set them down. There would be time for that later.

"We do have a folding bed out in Ted's workshop," Michelle said. "That might be better than letting you use Charlie's room."

"She'd never forgive us," I muttered and went back to my transcribing. "Why don't you take one of these guys out to get it?"

Sebastian followed her into the night. That bed used to be stored in the closet in Charlie's room, before she moved in. All the extra junk ended up in that room. I should start transferring some of it next door.

"Bastian and I will take turns on sentry duty," Alistair announced.

"Don't you think just sleeping here is enough?" I looked over the next paragraph. Atrocious spelling but I'd better set it down as written.

A thought. "Still carrying Stoddard's gun?" I asked.

He slipped it out. A small revolver. Most of the mud had dried and been rubbed off by now. Alistair's pocket must be full of dirt. "A Thirty-two," he stated, giving it a once-over. "Smith and Wesson." He broke it open. "Barrel's clear if it's necessary to use it." A grin. "But we won't let Bastian know, okay? He dislikes firearms."

I only nodded and thought of the revolver in my own bedroom. It was a bit more weapon than Rex's gun, a Thirty-eight. The door opened and Sebastian rolled the folded bed into the kitchen. Michelle closed and locked behind him. Shot the deadbolt too. I had those on both entrances. Yuccas growing under the windows as well, to discourage attempted entry.

We set up the bed in the showroom. Michelle found sheets but left it to the boys to make it up. There are limits. I finished my copying. The original I slipped back into my pocket for the moment; the copy went under a silverware tray in one of the drawers. It was handy and I could find a better place later. "I think I need a shower," I proclaimed. "We probably all do."

"It can wait," Michelle told me. "Sleep stinky."

I didn't feel like arguing. I was dead tired and fell asleep almost at once. In fact, almost before I made it to the bedroom. But, as often happens, I woke up a few hours later. The bedside clock told me it was a little before One. I decided to get up and check on things. And use the restroom, of course.

Wrapping a robe around myself first. That was one change I had to make after the Jackson girls moved in. I couldn't wander about naked in the night anymore. Well, maybe if it were only Michelle but not with Charlie around. I could see Alistair at the kitchen table as I slipped across the hall into the bathroom.

He hadn't moved when I came out a minute or so later. "Still the first watch?" I asked him, dropping into one of the chairs. He had a paperback book on his lap, one finger marking his place.

"Uh-huh. I'll wake Sebastian in, oh, an hour or so. Not much going on."

With the light on in the kitchen and Alvaro's spot burning outside, that wasn't surprising. I went to the kitchen window, above the table. Nothing to see there, nor from the one over the sink. I wouldn't go up front and disturb the sleeper there. "Later," I said, and hoped I could get back to sleep. If not, I'd just get up a little earlier than usual.

I did end up lying there. Too much on my mind. Alyce's note — I hadn't attempted to make any sense of it. That could be done later. But bits of it, lines, phrases, had stuck in my head. Alyce was stuck in my head, and the world she lived in twelve, fifteen years back. It wasn't a life I lived myself, you understand. I was an observer, watching that world swirl past me. Watching Alyce stumble through life's obstacle course like so many others.

And then I deserted her. I've said that already, yeah. I put her out of my mind, put Miami and all the rest of it out of my mind.

The docks. Did she mention the docks in her message? We spent time there when I was working on one boat or another. Dotty would show up too, on some pretext or another, and sometimes sit with us by the water. Alyce liked to stare at the oil film on those bay waters and create pictures in it. Imaginary jewels.

Dominguez became a pretty good friend of the girl, didn't she? I hadn't thought much about it at the time. She wasn't a kid, around my age, and a couple generations removed from Cuba, but her husband was born there. A barber. That's all I knew about him. I suspected she was having an affair with the Marine Patrol officer whose boat I saw from time to time. That was no business of mine but it did explain her presence.

Or maybe she was actually investigating something. No matter now, none at all.

Michelle breathed steadily beside me. I envied her ability to sleep, sleep untroubled. Voices. Subdued but I assumed Sebastian was being routed out of his own slumber. I should just get up and let both of them sleep. The clock read nearly Five when I looked at it again.

I had managed to sleep and I felt the better for it. Time to go make some coffee. Shoot, I might even walk across the street. No, get a shower. That's what I needed. Outside, so I didn't bother anyone. Sebastian was nowhere to be seen when I slipped into the kitchen but came back from the showroom as soon as I started rattling around. I got the coffee maker going, as every morning. "I'm going to go outside and shower," I informed him. "You guys are welcome to use the stall when I'm done."

"Be careful," he said, his voice kept low, little more than a whisper. "We did see someone move around out there a couple hours ago."

It was almost light now. I figured I would be safe enough. Ha, I remembered coming on Bradley Jackson camped overnight in the shower stall several months back. The late Bradley Jackson, strung out and unpredictable. I didn't expect a repeat.

Who would bother me anyway? It wouldn't do anyone any good. Only a handful knew Alyce had left something for me to find and even fewer knew it was a message. That was still tucked in the pocket of the shorts I had worn yesterday. I'd better get it out before Michelle tossed them in the laundry!

Ah! Hot water. I'd gone a decade with only cold out here. From a hose, the first couple years but I had put the shower in fairly early. I dried off, stepped out wrapped in my towel. The kitchen light shown out through the open door. Sebastian had been keeping an eye on me. Up to the north, on Eighth, I could see headlights at the Bells' place. Patty arriving? Or Jan's car leaving with all four travelers. That was a reasonably early start.

"Better keep that towel in place, mister," someone said. "No telling what effect losing it might have."

"And you're not about to find out," I told Dot. "Lurking extra-early this morning, aren't we?" I let her pass through the back door before me.

"Lurked all night. I saw Donny Morales come snooping a while back but I think all the lights discouraged him. Hi, Sebastian."

"I don't know what he might have thought to accomplish."

"I suspect he doesn't know either. Maybe just felt a need to check on you." She laughed. "Like me."

She looked bushed. Had Dot sat watching from her car all night? "Coffee?"

A bit of a face. "Maybe later. I'm filled up and spilling over with convenience store brew."

"Want a towel?" I asked Sebastian. He nodded and I went around the corner to the utility room, bringing back two. Alistair would need one also. The young man stepped out the back door.

"Smart to keep them with you last night," Dot remarked. "How soon are you going to the police?"

There was no great hurry, I realized. No need to dawdle either. Maybe I should call the station first and alert someone. I would like to have Bill Cotton there. "Don't know. A couple hours maybe." I poured myself a mug, added milk.

"And then I'll have to wait at least a couple hours more before I can learn anything." She rose, stretched. "I might as well go to my unused motel room and get cleaned up. See you later, Ted. Bye, Sebastian," she called in the direction of the shower stall, and was gone.

Chapter 30

"Chief Cotton regrets he couldn't be here," spoke Jack Saunders. Bill apparently had other pressing business — the job of police chief had its demands. But both Saunders and Blake had awaited my arrival. Furr and Brown had followed me in their Ford and now followed me into the station.

"The gun first," I stated and waved Alistair Brown to my side. He held out the revolver. "We took this off Rex Stoddard in White Springs and figured it would be best to turn it in to you." I had rehearsed that a little.

Sebastian laughed. "He dropped it in the mud and I picked it up, you mean."

Al had to chuckle too. "After Karrie pepper-sprayed him in the eyes."

I wasn't sure how these two officers took all that. Dave Blake knew Karrie, of course. Maybe Saunders did too. They took the gun, anyway. I had no doubt they would check it out in some database or another. For all I or anyone else knew, Rex might have gone on a crime spree with it.

Then I had to pretty much give them the whole story. I recognized our interrogation room as a spare office that tended to be used for whatever temporary job came up. A couple months ago, Blake was in here auditing all the department's books in an attempt to clear the chief's name. "And here," I said in conclusion, "is the note I found in the thermos." I laid it out on the table.

Blake looked at it and then at my two companions. "I don't think Mister Brown and Mister Furr need to stick around any longer, do you?" he asked his partner.

"Not at all," agreed Saunders. "We have their part of the story."

"The old brush-off, dear Alistair," remarked Sebastian.

"Now we shall never learn what was in the mysterious message," replied his friend. "So it goes! Adieu, officers."

Both those boys had seen me copy out Alyce's note so they knew they could find out what was in it, if they wished. And if I was willing. Sebastian shut the door behind him and we turned to the piece of notebook paper.

"Well preserved for its age," remarked Saunders. "Are you sure it is authentic?"

"Absolutely. It was sealed in a water-tight thermos. The metal was a bit rusty but the glass liner was intact."

"Okay. Um —" He looked to his partner. "Why don't you read it, Carrol?" Blake nodded.

I was willing and started right in.

Shaper — if your reading this something happen to me. If Im OK it can just stay beried forever. I know somones after me and dont want to get you into this Shaper. I come by your place and sit on the wall and look a wile. I see your place and the gas station. Everyone closed and dark.

"The wall?" wondered Blake.

I had already puzzled that out. "She must mean — must have meant the old motel. The seawall is still there." Nothing else remained of the place. I read on.

Didnt bother you left something and come up to park. Hope to see you Shaper but you didnt come I guess Change didnt talk to you. So I write this and hide it and fix the necklass you give me so you can find.

"She would never have meant it to sit so long, I think," I told the pair.

SMOKE

Saunders agreed at once. "If she thought she might be killed she would have expected her body to be found right away. Do you think she was on her way to your place when she was, um, caught?"

I shook my head. "I couldn't begin to guess. I *would* assume the necklace and this message were meant to be just in case something happened."

"Makes sense," said Dave.

You use to writ songs so Im writing you one. Your smart Shaper youll figgure it out.

That made both policemen smile. For a moment, me too — then I thought of Alyce and lost it a little. The first time since this had started, since I had learned what happened to her. It had finally hit me when I imagined her voice, saying these things.

"When you're ready, Ted," said Saunders. I'm not sure he'd ever called me Ted before.

"Okay." I might have been a tad shaky as I started up again.
People pull in and fill up
Wile Shaper dream the surf is up
Back and forth and up and down
Drive the streets of your beach town
Remember how we use to sit
And see how far we could spit
Long ago and far away
I remember every day
I remember the old sea cow
Everythings behind me now
Just like when it used to rain
Everythings gone down the drane

I'll admit, I've read worse. "And that is all of it," I announced. I wished she had put a 'good bye' at the end or at least signed it. It felt like an interrupted conversation.

And an interrupted life. Dave slid the paper into a plastic bag. "I'll run a few copies off later," he said. Saunders nodded before turning his attention to me.

"Officially, you're still one of our suspects, Ted. You probably know that. None of us actually believe you are the murderer. You wouldn't have brought that here if you were."

"But you shouldn't have gone off looking for it on your own," added Blake.

"Alyce gave me a job," I told them both, "and I did it. Now it's up to you. Oh," I couldn't resist adding, "Agent Rivers sends his regards to you, Jack."

He reddened only slightly and gave out a self-conscious chuckle. "We may need to bring him up to speed."

"I'll call Boris Jones, too," said Dave. "He'll want to know. And you know we're going to have to talk to you some more Ted about what all of it means. That was a personal message."

"I know. I can't figure most of it out and — well, I don't really feel like trying at the moment."

"Understood," said Jack Saunders. "Go home and get some rest."

I had to laugh. "On a Memorial Day weekend? I'll be busy all day."

I took my time driving home. Loads of traffic already along Ocean Avenue, A-1-A. But no surf. I would have a busy day in the shop and I would forget all the rest for a while. Only for a while.

Chapter 31

The 'girls' had arrived home quite late, apparently having stayed for the big Saturday evening show. Michelle and I were asleep when I heard someone come in through the back door.

I was immediately on alert. Yeah, I was pretty certain it was Charlie but I pulled out the H and R before peeking out of our bedroom. Charlie and Shannon. "Be sure to lock up," I called softly to them and went back to bed. Michelle had slumbered on.

The two girls slumbered on while I roused Michelle and headed off to church the next morning. Things felt back to normal. They weren't, of course.

"Here's Shaper," Charlie announced as we came in the back door. "You have to make us pancakes. We both want pancakes."

Shannon looked at least a little embarrassed. People didn't act like that in the Brody household.

"I can do that," I said. Michelle said nothing and headed for our bedroom. "Not in training anymore?" I asked Shannon. She was an athlete. She had also just graduated high school.

"Carbs are good," she responded. "We need fuel!"

"Absolutely agree." I began to assemble ingredients on the counter. Maybe I should change out of these church clothes first. Wouldn't do to get flour all over my slacks. I might need to get married in them! "Do we have syrup? Or honey?" I didn't use either often. If at all. I did keep molasses on hand but the girls weren't likely to go for that.

"Syrup is in the fridge," Charlie informed me.

"Okay." I lifted a large saute pan down from an upper shelf. "Let me go change my clothes."

I passed Michelle in the hall. "You can take over," I informed her.

"Unlikely, Mr. Carrol. I expect you to make me pancakes too."

"Then you'd better open up the shop," I called over my shoulder.

I was back, in surfer-approved tee and board shorts in a minute. Flour. A little oat flour. I make that myself in a coffee mill. Eggs, baking soda.

"Lemon juice?" asked Shannon.

Charlie jumped right on that. "Shaper puts lemon juice in everything. We go through gallons of it. They order it special for us at the Pig!"

I had coconut oil heating in the pan. That was something new for me but I'd decided I liked it. A little in the batter, too. "Itsy-bitsy pancakes or great big ones?" I asked.

"I want mine shaped like dinosaurs," demanded Charlie.

"Or boys," blurted Shannon. Charlie was rubbing off on her.

"Both unlikely. I specialize in blobs."

I went with medium-sized blobs. Those are easiest.

It sounded like customers had come in as soon as Michelle got the door open. "We're gonna have another busy day," I told the girls. "Are you planning to hang around?"

"John will come to pick both of us up," said Charlie. "Soon."

My first four were ready to flip. "Looks like these will come out decent. If not, I'll take 'em up to your mom."

"Don't believe it," Charlie confided. "They'd disappear before they ever reached her."

I plopped them onto their plates, two each, and started another pan-full. "You stayed for the evening show?" I asked. "All of you?"

"Yep. Karrie and Pat and their friends too. Oh, Patty liked it so much she decided to stay overnight. Even if she's not supposed to!

Goodpaster's gonna bring her back. We all sat together on blankets and picnicked."

"I liked the Seminole," Shannon Brody put in.

"What's his name? Chief something."

"Yeah," agreed Shannon.

"She liked Jeff Groves too," said Charlie.

Shannon blushed but didn't deny it.

"But Jan monopolized his time. I'll have to report that to Dave!"

"She wanted to know about his classes," Shannon added to this.

"I can understand that," I replied, and flipped the pancakes. Almost let them get too brown.

Jan and Jeff would probably share some classes come fall. Maybe a lot of classes. I hadn't even had a chance to talk to the boy, had I? He'd always been off to the side somewhere, with his camera, and I'm not one to approach anyone and bug him.

"Pat told us you had some adventures on Friday," Charlie went on. "Pretty wild stuff. I didn't know whether to believe him!"

"Oh, never believe anything Pat says." I dealt out four more flapjacks to the girls. They were probably good for a few more.

"Mom!" called Charlie. "You're missing breakfast. Shaper's gonna make you obscene pancakes!"

I hoped the customers had left.

But there would be more. The two of us were going to be kept busy today. I had no part-time kids lined up to help and Charlie wouldn't be around.

Where had I put my copy of Alyce's note? In one of these drawers — yes, there it was. I pulled it out and read through again. It still made little sense to me. It didn't actually mention the docks, did it? But the implication was clear to me. I slipped it into my wax pocket to look at again later, fastening the velcro flap securely.

Flip the next batch. *I come by your place and sit on the wall —* that was how she had started it out. Right down the road here, while I slept, unaware of her, of her danger. I wished she had come over and awakened me. Maybe it would have been different.

Things can change. I do not believe in fate. We create our own fate, with our own god-given free will.

"Don't let those burn, Shaper!"

"Right." They were a little crispy. "I'll eat these ones," I said, stacking them on a plate, and started another four. I might run out of batter before Michelle rejoined us.

"No syrup?" asked Shannon on seeing me pick one up and nibble it. She seemed a bit incredulous.

"Shaper's weird," Charlie confided. "We've got used to him." She squinted at me. "Mostly."

"Not much different from a tortilla," I offered as explanation. Too bad I didn't have some beans to wrap it around. Those I would take over syrup any day.

The girls still had pancakes on their plates so I carried the next batch up to Michelle. "I can take over up here," I offered. There were three — no, four — shoppers wandering about. All looked more like tourists than locals, not that I know everyone local.

She nodded, took the plate I handed her, and retreated to the back. She might have been looking for syrup. There was still a little batter if she or the girls wanted more. I'd leave it up to them.

I left everything back there to them for the next half-hour while I dealt with shoppers. The door remained open between kitchen and shop, for flow-through. It was going to be another hot day. I'd need to get the ceiling fans running in here.

SMOKE

That sounded like an extra voice in the back. I gave the current browsers a quick look and stepped back to see what was going on. Marty. That's what was going on. Charlie was filling her in on their day. Shannon didn't add much.

Marty wasn't her friend anyway. I'm not even sure Shannon really was Charlie's friend, though the two were closer in age. She was the sister of Charlie's boyfriend; aside from that, the two lived in different worlds.

"I wish my dad had let me go along," said Marty.

"Yes, they needed a responsible adult," I told her. It was only partly a joke.

"We had Jan," Charlie pointed out. Not Patty. I wondered when she would be back.

Not for long. There was no time for wondering about anything. The shop needed my attention and pretty much did the rest of the day. John-boy picked up sister and girlfriend after a while. Marty wandered back to her own place, before riding away with her father, mid-afternoon. Dressed nicely, I could see from the shop window. Maybe off to the Sunday evening mass, the Spanish language one. Marty did not speak more than a word or two of Spanish. Maybe three.

No police all day. No insurance investigator, no criminals. Everyone was taking a holiday.

Everyone but poor Shaper and the woman he had roped into helping him run his shop. But Michelle had been warned. Yes, she had and she signed on anyway.

Chapter 32

Karrie Goodpaster's van sat next door on Monday morning, parked behind the house as before. I could also see that Patty's sports car was no longer at the Bells'. I would expect both women to lay low this day.

I doubted today, Memorial Day itself, would be quite as busy as Saturday and Sunday. People were tired. People were winding up their weekend. Shop traffic would be sluggish by afternoon, nonexistent by the end of the day.

Then back to normal. Normal for summer. Floridians would flock to the coast on the weekends to keep Cully Beach bustling. The rest of the week, mostly families from here and there, taking in as much of the state as they could on a two-week vacation. More likely to pass through here on their way to that place with the mouse than to stick around and enjoy the ocean.

And, of course, all the local kids, the surf rats who seemed to have no better place to hang out, some days. A few of those had been in and out over the weekend.

I could get back to shaping. That would include a couple long boards for Timble, to get her started. If she liked them, if they sold, more down the line. She needed to send me some logos to glass into their finishes. In the old days, those would be decals placed beneath the final gloss coat. Now they were generally printed on rice paper, which disappeared — pretty much — under layers of cloth and resin. Those were a lot clearer than when I got started.

For that matter, maybe a stock long board or two for my own shop. A little more traditional than the one I'd shaped for myself, maybe. I wondered if Charlie was interested in doing any more custom paint jobs.

SMOKE

I'd walked across the highway this morning, back to my old routine. No waves. Lighter each day at Five AM but the neighborhood remained asleep. Only a car or two at the all-night convenience store on the corner. That place, with its gas pumps, had put the last nails in the coffin for the filling station across from my shop. It had opened and closed more than once since I'd moved here. Closed the last time, what, three years ago? Sat abandoned since.

It was to be hoped the city would buy it and add it to the projected park. I hadn't heard any more on that. Alvaro might know something, or Patty for that matter.

Alyce had mentioned the station in her message. I wondered if that meant anything. Sometime this week we'd go over that note, me and Saunders and Blake. Maybe Bill Cotton too. Who knows who else? It mentioned things Dot Dominguez knew about. Maybe she should be in on it. I had not said a word to her about being attacked while leaving the festival.

"I haven't seen much of John," I remarked over breakfast. Michelle's breakfast; I'd eaten somewhat earlier and was only drinking coffee.

"Me neither," she said. Not much help there. He'd been staying overnight fairly regularly for a while. Lately, he hadn't been staying at all.

Maybe the two were cooling. It would peeve me a tad if they were, as I had pretty much gotten them together. I didn't intend to ask Charlie. She was still asleep.

Nine AM. "I'm going to open," I said, rising. I'd finished my mug so I might as well.

"I'll come up and help later," promised my fiancee.

There were customers almost immediately. Most of these, I suspected, were the folks who parked along both sides of the highway here to use the beach, away from the downtown. The end of Eighth Street, where I checked the surf most mornings, was the only public access for a few blocks either direction. The old filling station lot would be packed with cars too.

A park over there really was a good idea. Anyway, they tended to come in to buy things like sunscreen. If I was lucky, they'd pick up something else at the same time. Rubber rafts sold well.

But in the heat of late morning the traffic began to thin. Memorial Day weekend was winding down. The only sound in the shop was the overhead fans slowly turning, the pitch changing almost imperceptibly through each revolution. They kept it nicer in here but I had to admit it was hot. We might need to use air conditioning in the back tonight.

Ha, maybe that was why John-boy hadn't been staying. Too hot!

I walked back to see what was going on. Michelle had spelled me a couple times. Hadn't seen Charlie at all. She'd obviously gotten out of bed however, and drank all the iced coffee I'd made. Oh well, better than her buying it at the convenience store.

No sign of anyone. They were somewhere, doing something. I poured a glass of iced tea and returned to the shop. A gray Miata slowed down, looking for a parking space, then backed up and pulled into the drive. I went and leaned on the door frame. Patty had the top down on her sports car and waved to me before getting out.

"No bicycle today?" I called.

"My legs are still too tired from all that walking. I should have taken my bike along," she declared. "It would have made getting around much easier."

I'd been think along those lines myself. "I'll get one too and we can race from one end of the park to the other."

Patty laughed. "I might be ready by next year!" She didn't come in but sat down on the front step. I took a seat beside her. "Not staying long. Vicky has invited me to her place this afternoon. They have a huge swimming pool."

The Ward's house was also right on the beach, several blocks south. They undoubtedly ran their air conditioning.

"I thought maybe Charlie would like to come."

"Don't know where she is. I've been deserted."

"Aw, poor Shaper. Hey, I met your friend Branford. His girlfriend too. June exists! He told me to let you know. I'm not sure he believes in Michelle."

"I sometimes find her hard to believe too."

"Keep saying things like that, Ted. Especially where she can hear you."

"Enjoy the festival?" I asked.

"It was great." She gave me a bit of a wry smile. "Except for coming home. Riding with Karrie Goodpaster scared me, as they say, shitless. She's way too easily distracted."

I could readily believe it. I waved. Marty had just come out of her house. "Hi Shaper!"

"Just the person," decided Patty. "Would you like to come to a pool party?" She didn't wait for an answer. "Run and ask your dad. Tell him it's at Vicki Ward's. He knows her."

Marty hesitated only a second or two and hurried to do Patty's bidding.

"We'll have to gab about the weekend some other time," she said, getting up. "Oh, ready already?"

Marty had reappeared rather quickly, clutching a beach bag. She must keep one ready. "Yep!"

"Then let's go." A minute later, she was backing out.

"Have fun!" I called after them. "And remind Vicki we need street lights!"

They waved and headed south. I went back inside. There was only one woman, browsing. I think she was waiting for someone and just killing time.

Noise in the back. Had my missing girls returned? Nope. It was Karrie Goodpaster, standing just inside the door. I wouldn't mention what Patty had just said about her.

"You didn't see a couple missing women out there, did you?" I asked.

She jabbed a thumb toward the north. "At Kay and Rick's place."

"Thanks. Didn't want to misplace them."

She gave me a semi-dirty look. "That's a tad sexist, Shaper-boy. They aren't objects, you know."

"We're all objects. Chunks of meat with no meaning to our lives."

Karrie burst into laughter. "You know the perfect answer! Appeal to the nihilist in me and I won't be able to argue with you." Then she sobered up, all at once. "You do have that in you too, don't you? I heard stories from your friends and, um, I think they pulled their punches a little."

"Ah. I have had some issues with depression." That was a somewhat rehearsed answer, one I kept at ready for moments like this.

"Me too. I'm bipolar."

I truly had to restrain myself from blurting, 'I wouldn't have guessed.' "Never had to deal with the manic thing myself." Not really. I did suspect that my tendency to throw myself into projects smacked of it.

"I'm bi-everything," she claimed. "Bipolar, bisexual, —" Karrie seemed baffled about coming up with another 'bi.' "Bizarre," she added, with a chortling giggle.

"But not a bicyclist."

"No, I'll leave that to my ex. Too dangerous!"

That ex, Sally Stuart, had been run off the road for digging into corruption at city hall. The incident had directly led to their breakup, Karrie proving unable to deal with it at the time. Now it seemed she could laugh — at least for the moment. That was good. I hoped Sally could too.

We both were sitting at the table by now. I'd positioned myself where I could keep an eye on the front door.

"Hey, could I borrow your extension cord sometime? I need to get my reciprocating saw over to the hedge and finish taking it down." The one I had didn't quite reach all of it.

"Sure, though I'll hate to lose some of my privacy. I leave it coiled by the back door when I have to drive off somewhere. Just come over and get it." She sighed. Yes, dramatically. "I'll need to start showing up at the college again now."

I knew that. Charlie's first class would be next Monday. Good-paster certainly had to be there sooner. There was no hurry on the hedge, of course. I'd get to it. Still a fair amount I could do with my limb-lopper too.

The lopped limbs I had dragged next door and thrown in a heap. They would bother no one there and eventually there would be a lot of stuff to haul away. Like the old shed disintegrating in the back yard, if the termites didn't finish it off first. When it finally started raining — I had faith it would someday — I might even burn a lot of it.

Probably not while Karrie was still camping there.

"How was your weekend experience?" I asked.

"Great! I think maybe I'll just drop the teaching gig and drive my van from festival to festival from now on. Or follow the Grateful Dead! Wanna come along?"

"I'll read the book you write about it."

"Hmmph. I guess that's better'n nothing."

A couple came into the shop and looked back and forth. I'd better go up and reassure them the place was actually in business. "Duty calls," I said.

She got up too. "Yep, it does, doesn't it? See y'later." We went opposite directions. It was nearly an hour before Michelle returned from her visit with Kay. I think wine had been involved. Charlie showed up later. I didn't bother to ask either of them what they'd been up to. It was good enough just to have them there.

We did use air conditioning in the back that night, for the first time. The window unit in my bedroom — our bedroom now — was the only AC I had ever installed in the place, so both bedroom doors had to be kept open, allowing Charlie to share the cool air. Perhaps it was just as well John Brody was not there.

Chapter 33

I was not at all surprised the police wanted to see me on Tuesday morning. I was also grateful they came by the shop. I didn't feel much like going anywhere and I should be working on dozens of different projects around the place. Well, four or five anyway.

"Jones says he may drive up again," Jack Saunders told me. "We faxed him a copy of the message you retrieved."

I wondered if Agent Gordon Rivers had a copy too. Or Dorothea Dominguez, for that matter. No point in asking. If they did, they did.

We went over a few of the points from my experiences at Stephen Foster Park again, clarifying this and that. They were as baffled as I by the two guys who assaulted me. "It seems like the kind of thing this Stoddard might do," Saunders thought. "And he knew you'd found something."

I wasn't so sure. "As did Morales. I think he's more the sort to hire someone to do his dirty work."

"Are your impromptu bodyguards still around?" asked Blake.

"I haven't seen them in a couple days," I had to admit. They might have recognized how busy I was and didn't bother me. "Brown said something about getting a job. Um, up in Banner Beach."

Jack jotted that down. I'm not sure why.

"We assume the jewelry was hidden somewhere right around here," said Dave Blake. "That's what the message seems to imply. Most of it doesn't make much sense. Not to us."

"There is stuff probably only I would get," I admitted. "And Dot Dominguez, maybe. But a lot of it baffles me too."

"Maybe we should include Dominguez," said Saunders. "Better you not talk to her yourself, Ted. Not direct, I mean."

I had to smile at what he was surely implying. "You're willing to share info with her but she might not reciprocate."

"Pretty much," Dave said. "Not that we can prevent either of you from doing what you want."

Jack nodded in agreement, a bit reluctantly perhaps. "We understand the, um, preamble to Norbert's message. We think. The poem, not so much."

"Some of it refers to Miami. That's why I say Dot might be able to help." Sit and spit? Old sea cow? It used to rain? Those could mean all sorts of things.

"Then we should all sit down together at the station," decided Saunders. "Lieutenant Jones, too, if he comes up."

"But if you think you have any ideas right now, let us know," Dave Blake added to this.

"She does mention the gas station across the street a couple times. There would be places to hide something over there." Our eyes all went to the abandoned building.

"We should organize a search," Saunders told his partner.

"Agreed."

I didn't really think Alyce had left anything there. It didn't fit with the rest of the note. As good a place to look as any, though. It also gave these two something to work on. They might even end up getting along.

There was time to fill after they left and before I would open for business. I decided to get into my workshop for an hour or so. I needed to get summer schedules for my employees worked out over the next few days so I could get back there on a regular basis.

SMOKE

The truth was, building boards brought in more money than the shop, so I couldn't neglect it.

Marty came over and stood watching me work for a couple minutes. She was one of those I could talk to about taking a shift. Maybe just now and then.

She spoke when I put down my router. I had been getting the board ready to install fin boxes. "I think I should have you make me a long board, Shaper. Like Kim said."

With her logo on it, no doubt. "It could be a good idea for you to simply ride mine a few times and see what you like or dislike. We could take it from there. Come borrow it anytime you want." Not that we were going to see many waves here over the next few months.

"Okay. Um, I might be taking a couple long surf trips this summer. Dad says maybe Hatteras."

Undoubtedly competing here and there, now and then, as well. "That's not exactly a long trip," I said. "Not like California. Or Hawaii for that matter."

"Oh, Hawaii. Great idea, Shaper! I'll tell Dad you suggested it." She thought a moment, perhaps imagining huge waves and palm trees. "Maybe I should have a fast board for big waves, too. A gun."

"Guns aren't fast," I told her. "The little boards you ride most of the time are way faster."

That may have gone against everything she'd been told. "They are?"

"What you're thinking of as fast surfboard shapes are actually the slowest. The purpose of a gun is to give *control* in bigger waves, so the wide point is moved forward, allowing more rail to make contact with the water."

"Oh. Makes sense." She thought a moment. "But they really are moving fast, right? Because they are on big powerful waves."

"You've got me there," I admitted.

"And my usual board wouldn't stay attached to the water. I know that from experience. I'd just be bouncing."

"I've bounced down a large wave or two myself. Bounced pretty hard!"

"I'll bet. Not Hawaii, right?"

"Never made it there." For one reason or another. And maybe some others, too. "The largest waves I've ridden were right here in Florida. Though there were some big ones in Puerto Rico. You should get your father to take you there. Tell him you want to look for your roots. Or Kim." I knew Timble traveled down there and sometimes to Central America as well.

"That's winter surf, right?"

"Yep, mostly. As good an excuse for missing school as any, don't you think?"

"I do. Dad might not." I was getting the fin boxes ready to install. This was always a fussy bit of work and the job I liked least in building a surfboard. I would get them set solidly in resin and call it a morning.

This board would move next door into the glassing room when I got back to it.

"You need to give me lessons, Shaper," said Marty.

"Surfing lessons?" I knew what she meant but decided to act dimwitted. Not so difficult for me.

"Sheesh. Shaping lessons."

"No reason I couldn't let you ruin a blank or two," I told the girl. "But you'll have to pay for them."

"You mean you wouldn't put them on sale in your shop?"

SMOKE

Marty probably wasn't serious but it was something to consider. "Honestly, if they were good, I might. But you should make sure Kim doesn't mind. She might take that as some sort of endorsement of my business." I set the last of the fin boxes into its proper position, put a strip of tape across the fin to hold everything in that proper position, and wiped away the excess resin that had oozed out around it. "I'm done here. And just in time, I see."

Lisa Deland was coming up the drive, somewhat hesitantly, pushing a bike. "I need to talk to this young lady. And maybe to you, too." I waved to Lisa. "I'll open up in a few minutes," I called, and headed for the shower stall.

Chapter 34

You could say I'd spent my whole life trying to keep my rail in the water, trying to maintain control. I wouldn't say it but you could.

And I definitely won't try to force an analogy between life and riding a big wave. I was content with the little waves of my life right now, cruising toward the sunlit sand and the girl waiting there.

That might be an even worse analogy. Never mind. I turned my attention back to Father Paul.

"So," said the priest, "we are set for the First of October."

We had decided a Monday morning was the best time for a wedding. We could take off for three or four days of honeymoon somewhere and be back in the shop by the weekend.

October First would be easy to remember too, when it came anniversary time. Not that I would forget — just thinking of Michelle. We would see the priest a few more times before then, to be sure, and at mass. I would try to drag my fiancee along from time to time.

"Do you have any ideas for a honeymoon destination?" she asked as we stepped into the morning sun. "It has to be someplace without surf. You might not be able to resist the temptation."

"For you, I would be willing to ignore the waves."

She snickered in a rather unladylike manner. "For a day or two."

Well, of course. What else could she expect? "I think Father Paul wants you to ignore me until the wedding," Michelle said.

"I'll leave celibacy to him," I replied. "And you know I consider us married. We're living together as husband and wife, and no paper nor ceremony will make us more married."

"So you've said before." She stopped walking. "Then just why are we doing it?"

"Legal advantages and protections. You know that too."

"Yeah, I guess so." We started moving again. It was already too hot to move very quickly. It would be like an oven in Michelle's van. I'd left my truck windows open. Nothing in there worth stealing. "The legal part of marriage is more like a business contract. A partnership."

"Pretty much," I agreed. "I care more about the other stuff, like one of us being able to make decisions if the other is hurt or sick." Or dead. Wasn't going to add that one.

"Okay. We'll go ahead with it! But no celibacy, now or later." We both chuckled. We had reached the vehicles, parked side by side, in the shadiest spot we could find. That was why they weren't right up by the church. Michelle rolled down her windows. "I'll let that cool a little," she said.

"But you're pretty hot," I told her, taking her into my arms. I really hated seeing her go off to work and leaving me all alone. Even for a few hours.

"Don't think I'm not aware of it, Mr. Carrol." A kiss, then another. "I'd best get to the bank," she said. "Say, you don't think Father Paul cheats, do you?"

"Cheats?"

"On the celibacy thing."

"Oh. No, I do not believe he would break his vow of celibacy. Whether he manages to stick with chastity all the time, I couldn't say. That one's harder."

We'd gone over some of these terms at the encounter in St. Augustine. Whether they'd sunk in for Michelle, I didn't know.

"He would consider it a sin if he didn't, wouldn't he?"

"I suppose."

"It's all much simpler when you're married," she decided. "Then it's a sacrament. I remember that from the class." She kissed me again — not nearly long enough — and was away.

A sacrament indeed. Marriage and the sex that went with it. The things of everyday life, of human life, made sacred. I yearned for another sacrament at the moment, a bit of baptism in the Atlantic. No sign of waves as I cruised down Ocean Avenue past the pier. I could have taken the back way, followed Michelle's route, but I decided I'd rather see the ocean.

I recognized a small dark sedan parked a block or so south of the pier, and pulled in beside it. Two men were looking down toward the beach.

"This is where they found her, isn't it?" asked Small Change Robinson as I stepped out of my truck.

I nodded. I didn't intend to point out the exact spot. Change turned back to stare at the sand.

"You're staying in town?"

Donny answered. "We're at a motel across the bridge. That's the bad side of town, right?" He sort of snickered after he said it. I don't think he saw a resort town like Cully Beach as actually having a bad side.

"Depends," I said. "There are some pretty nasty areas over there. Further south along the other side of the river." I'd lived in a trailer down there a couple months when freshly arrived in Cully, before I'd bought the house that became my surf shop. "Druggies and such. Places you'd feel at home." I gave him this with a bit of a smile, so he'd know I was joking.

And he took it without rancor. It was pretty much true. "Your friends the gay boys have a room there too."

SMOKE

"Remember they are my friends — and you're not, Donny." I didn't include Robinson in that. "Not after what happened the last time I saw you." I suspected him of sending those two guys after me too, but wasn't planning to mention it.

"I suppose not," he admitted, followed by a complete change of subject. "We saw Rex over by your place."

I felt a chill. "He was at my shop?"

"Huh-uh. He pulled in next door and talked to your neighbor for a while. His woman, too."

I couldn't imagine what sort of conversation they might have had with Alvaro. I looked at the pair. "So I assume you two have been hanging around my home too."

"We just followed Rex," objected Small Change.

"Okay. I do not want to be seeing you guys around there. You understand that, right? I will mention it to the police if I do. And I'm going to ask Guzman to do the same if you or Stoddard show up again."

Donny snickered. "Wrong neighbor, Ted," said Robinson. "We meant the girl in the van."

I didn't like that. I should warn Karrie to keep away from the man. I didn't like that her parking place was so private, so secluded, either. I should get to work on that hedge.

I remembered the last time the two had come together. "They were friendly?" I asked. "She shot him with pepper spray at the park."

Both men smiled at the memory. I might have too.

"Didn't seem to hold it 'gainst her," Small Change said. He turned to his partner. "They went on a long time."

"Maybe his chick told him he had it coming," allowed Donny Morales. "But he didn't seem to threaten her or nothin'. Your friend sat there writing stuff down the whole time."

Ah. I could picture it. I wondered a bit just where these two were watching from. I'd warn her off anyway. I definitely did not want Rex Stoddard — or his girlfriend — near my place.

"Okay. You two aren't likely to leave. I know that. I know the police probably are keeping tabs on you too, so I'll leave things to them. Bye, Change." I nodded to the little guy, got in the truck, drove home.

Chapter 35

Boris Jones. Dorothea Dominguez. They were waiting in that same temporary conference room when Blake escorted me in. "Saunders will be along shortly," he told us all.

It had taken until Thursday afternoon to get everyone together. I didn't mind that things were moving slowly but knew Morales and Stoddard might get discouraged — or run out of funds — and leave town. That wouldn't do if the murder of Alyce Noble was to be solved.

"I ran into Donny and Small Change yesterday morning," I mentioned, giving them a nod and taking a chair.

"Not surprising," said Dot. We spoke no more until Blake returned, with not only Saunders but Chief Cotton and the FBI's Gordon Rivers. The gang's all here.

And they made a bit of a crowd in the office. We arrayed ourselves around the table, a long folding metal one with a tan laminate top. I'd seen variants of that table all over the festival a few days ago. Saunders passed out copies of Alyce's last letter.

The chief, however, took the lead. "The point here," he announced, "is to get everyone on the same page." He looked down at the page he was holding and frowned. "Hmm, sorry, that sounded inappropriate, didn't it?"

"We understand what you mean, sir," said Rivers.

Heads were nodded in agreement. "So," he continued, "we're going to go through this note together, share what we know, and, well, take it from there."

"Hasn't there already been some follow-up on it?" asked Lieutenant Jones.

"Tell 'em about it, Jack," said the chief, settling in his chair.

"The note referred to a filling station, apparently the one at, um, Eight-fifteen Ocean Avenue." He looked up from the note-book he held. "That's across from Mr. Carrol's shop. We took a crew in and pretty much tore the place apart." He smiled thinly. "We had a warrant of course, but no one ever showed up to see it."

Dave Blake took up the narrative. "A drain was mentioned so we took special care to check any of those. Some were pretty nasty."

"Under the garage there was oil that had sat for years. Close to being asphalt," said Saunders. "We knocked it apart but there wasn't anything."

"Except almost two dollars in change," Dave added.

"So we can cross that station off?" asked Jones.

"Unless they missed something," said Dot. "I doubt it but it does happen, guys."

Bill had nothing to say about that. "Okay, then let's get to the note. Nothing we're missing in this, ah, opening, is there? It seems straightforward. Miss Norbert was sitting down at the *Easy Breezes* and looking up the road."

"Choosing a place to stash the jewelry," said Saunders.

"Maybe," was Rivers's opinion on that.

"So it's the poem that should tell us. And that's meant for you, Ted." Bill started reading it aloud.

"*People pull in and fill up while Shaper dream the surf is up.* That would be the gas station across the street and your own place. Simple enough there."

I agreed. "It was in operation then. Opened and closed a couple times since."

"And checked over now. Do you think we should check your place, Ted?"

193

"With all the remodeling I've done I think I would have found anything that was hidden." Not that I thought Alyce would have put it there.

"We might look through your drains anyway. Maybe that shower out back?"

"I hadn't put it in yet and, um, it didn't actually have a drain until recently." I'd just let the water run out into the yard.

"Okay." He went back to the note. *"Back and forth and up and down, drive the streets of your beach town."*

Blake said, "I guess that means just what it says. Maybe she was driving around deciding what to do."

"Or just talking about the traffic. Or about Ted," said Dot. "Like the next part."

The chief nodded. *"Remember how we use to sit and see how far we could spit."*

"That's about Miami," I said. A bit softly, I realized. Had they all caught it?

Dot took it up. "I remember you two sitting together. On the docks sometimes. On the roof of Munoz's boat house too. Remember that? It could be what she means. Meant."

"A roof? Maybe." I didn't remember spitting off it but that didn't mean much.

"So we need to switch from drains to roofs?" asked Boris Jones. No one gave him an answer.

"Long ago and far away," continued Bill, *"I remember every day. I remember the old sea cow."*

"I don't get that one at all," I admitted. "I remember manatees in the bay but I don't know what they have to do with anything."

"Maybe she just needed the rhyme," suggested Blake. That was admittedly possible.

"And the finish. *Everything's behind me now, just like when it used to rain, everything's gone down the drain.* Any thoughts?"

Saunders had some. "Back to the drain. Do we really think it could mean the jewels are in a drain pipe somewhere? Or did she mean something else entirely? Like her plans going down the drain."

"There *are* lot of drains in the neighborhood," I admitted.

"Even if we can't include your shower. You dug all that up a couple months ago, didn't you?," asked Cotton.

Blake butted in. "He did. He promised his fiancee a real indoor shower with hot water."

"Probably not your neighbors," said Saunders. "The roof thing. You have gutters, don't you? To drain the rain?" He looked at his sheet. "*Just like when it used to rain*, she said."

"You may have noticed my place is a flat-roofed Fifties Florida house. There have never been any gutters." It wasn't strictly flat-roofed, but sloped very gently, a drop of about eighteen inches, to the rear. That was echoed by the ceilings inside.

"I'd like to get up and look anyway."

"And we should check on the roof of the filling station too," said Blake. "We did neglect that."

"It's too late to check the roof of the *Easy Breezes Motel*," I told them. "Your jewels may have been hauled away when it was demolished."

They stared at one another. Hadn't they thought of that?

"That would be a great joke on all of us," said Dot. "I think Alyce would have enjoyed it." She was silent for a moment. We all were. Then she added, "I'd like to go over and poke around in what's left of that motel."

"We could get a warrant, I'm sure," felt Saunders.

She smirked. "You guys might need a warrant. I could just mosey over there like any other girl going to the beach." No comment on that.

"Anything else?" asked Chief Cotton. He looked up and down the table.

Apparently not. Not about the case. "Bill," I asked, "what will happen to Alyce's remains?"

"Nothing for a while. If the case is concluded, her family can claim them. Or if it goes cold again."

Saunders spoke up. "We haven't been able to find any next of kin, Chief."

"Neither have we," said Boris Jones. "Parents are deceased, no other relatives on record."

"Small Change Robinson might know of someone," I said. "If not, I would be willing to handle any, um, arrangements."

"I'd put something toward that," murmured Dot Dominguez.

The chief nodded. "We'll keep that in mind. Jack, Dave, you stop by my office, okay? The rest of you, thanks for being here." I shook his hand and a couple of others and got out of the place. Dot followed me into the reception area.

"You're a pretty good friend of the chief, aren't you?" she asked, fairly nonchalantly. "He seems competent."

"He is. Competent enough." Was she fishing for my opinion of the man? I was willing to give that. "Bill Cotton is a good cop but he's also a bit of a politician. You know you don't get to be chief without that."

"You've got that right, Ted. I can tell this Saunders has his eye on the job someday but I don't think he has the people skills."

"Blake does."

"Looks that way. He likes you too. A lot of these guys do." He eyes went to an officer standing by the main desk, chatting with Anna Church. "That big boy over there in the crew-cut seems to be very much on Team Ted."

Bob Redding. "We didn't get along when I first ran into him. I guess I grow on people."

"Yeah, even Saunders is okay with you now."

"Even if he does plan to come and snoop in my drains."

Chapter 36

There were ladders across the street the next morning. Policemen went up and down them for a while. Then they carried them over here. "Okay if we climb up on your roof?" asked Dave Blake. He tried to sound casual about it but I could tell there was embarrassment.

"Be my guest. It's getting hot to be walking around up there."

"A cop on a hot tin roof," said Jan. She and Charlie had been keeping an eye on the proceedings.

"A tar roof," I corrected her. "It's an old-style tar and gravel job."

"What they call a built-up roof," added Charlie.

"And how did you know that?" I was rather surprised.

"John told me about roofs. That's another business his family is in." The Brodys had a wide array and variety of business interests. That didn't surprise me but I was impressed that Charlie had retained the knowledge.

Dave poked around a bit up there. "Nothing," he told Saunders. "Just a flat desert without a drain in sight."

"How about in the sheds?" asked Jack.

"Weren't built yet," I reported.

"Shaper was putting them up when we moved here," said Jan. "In Ninety-three. My dad helped him."

"And the only other drains are inside, where Alyce definitely never ventured."

"Okay, no need to check them," decided Saunders. "You men get back to the station," he told the two officers assisting them. "Want to walk over and look at the motel site, Dave? Hmm, wouldn't mind having you along, Ted."

Dorothea Dominguez had beaten us. Her white car was pulled in at the Eighth Street beach access and she was surveying what little remained on the lot.

"Any drains here are gone," she reported. "There might be pipes underground somewhere but we'd never find them without digging the place up."

I knew where most of the outside drains had been located. Hadn't my girlfriend managed the place for months? "How about where the outside shower was located?" I asked. "It was apart from the rest of the place, near the back for beach goers to rinse off." I led the way but, no, nothing remained there either. Every sign that a motel had once existed here had been bulldozed and graded. Even the swimming pool.

All that remained was the low seawall on two sides of the site, the rear and along Eighth Street, and some plantings along the fringes.

Charlie and Jan had followed in our wake. No one told them not to, not that Dave would order his girlfriend to do anything. He'd learned his lesson there — Jan was independent.

"I hope they get that park built over there," said Jan, looking across Eighth.

"And put up street lights," I added. "Who's minding the shop, by the way?" We headed back in its direction.

"Richie," said Jan. "He's an official employee, right?"

I had entrusted the place to her little brother a few times. Briefly. "Cathy and Marty are in there too."

"Ah. Marty I trust." The police separated from us in front of the shop. Dot had lingered by the empty lot, leaning against her sedan. Maybe dreaming about that elusive reward. I wondered how much longer she would stay in Cully Beach. Her bosses wouldn't pay her expenses here forever.

It was a good time to go back and work on boards. Marty found her way out to me not much later. I wasn't doing anything creative, just tidying up, getting some newly-delivered blanks stowed away. I used to drive down to the Cocoa area and pick those up myself but couldn't find the time anymore. A truck came up now, making the round of shops and shapers, delivering what was needed where it was needed.

"Cathy kind of hates me," claimed Marty.

"I know." Richie had a not so secret crush and his girlfriend — more or less — did not appreciate it. "There's not much to be done about it." He'd been the same way when Charlie showed up.

"I suppose not. Can I try shaping now?"

Aha. "Good a time as any."

"And better than most." She'd picked up on one of my own lines.

"Okay. One thing I am *not* going to let you do is use power tools. Later on, when you are more capable, sure."

"So do I chop it out of the foam with a hatchet?"

"A block plane. I've shaped many a board with one when I didn't have a power planer available. And before I could afford one. We'll cut the outline with a handsaw, too." I looked her over. "I need to either lower my shaping stands or give you a box to stand on."

Marty Guzman was never going to be a tall woman. That didn't matter much in competitive surfing; in fact, being light could be an advantage. "Shape in high heels," called Charlie from the back door.

I had never seen either of these young ladies in high heels. It was possible to lower the stands though a bit of a bother. I soon had them at a height that should work. Charlie had sauntered out to watch us from a closer vantage. "Want me to paint it?" she asked.

"Not this one," came the immediate answer. "Maybe when I get better."

"Okay, a basic bit of wisdom from old Shaper before we start. It doesn't really matter that much if your board is lumpy and misshapen. It is still likely to work perfectly well." I knew this from experience. Clean symmetrical boards were more about aesthetics than performance. "Except maybe in really big waves."

"Why there?" she asked.

"Speed — straight-line speed — amplifies any anomalies in water-flow." I liked having the opportunity to use a big word. That was a rare event in my line of work. "Bumps or dips that keep the board from remaining in contact with the water. In theory," I had to add. "I'm not sure I believe it matters even there."

"But I want it to look good, Shaper."

"Of course you do, and it will. Just don't obsess over it."

"Marty always obsesses," remarked Charlie. "Complete perfectionist."

I figured she was probably right. "That probably hurts you sometimes in competition."

"Yeah," she admitted. Marty would be the sort to press harder than needed to win — and lose in the process. I wondered if Alvaro understood that. Or Kim Timble, for that matter. Kim, I knew, had been a fierce competitor. That's a different type.

"I prefer to be a slacker myself," Charlie told us. Not really true but I went with it.

"Good enough is good enough, most of the time," I stated.

Marty was dubious. "Most of the time?"

"Save your best for when it's needed. Trying to give a hundred percent all the time will drive you crazy." This I also knew from experience.

"Maybe so. But I'm giving my hundred percent on this board. A hundred and ten!"

Charlie gave a deep sigh. "We tried, Shaper. There's no hope for her."

We had decided to go with something similar to one of my stock thrusters. They were fairly simple. "These are my templates," I told her. I had a collection of curves, most cut out of hardboard. "Just lay the ones you want in place and trace around them to get our outline." From there we went to cutting it out and starting to roughly — and slowly — shape the rails with the plane. Charlie had disappeared but we picked up a new audience member, Dot Dominguez.

I supposed she wanted to speak with me. "I think that's enough for today," I said. "Get home and shower. You're covered with foam dust." It would have been considerably worse had Marty been wielding the power planer. "We'll finish with the plane and start with sanding blocks next time." Or the shaper's crutch, the mighty Surform. Best she not be exposed to that arcane secret yet.

I could probably use a shower myself but I only rinsed my arms off with the hose. "You haven't thought of anything else, have you?" asked Dot.

"Nope. How 'bout you?"

"Can't come up with a darn thing. We both know there's a message we should be able to figure out."

"Maybe. Or maybe Alyce overestimated my ability to get what she meant. Want to come in? You look like you could use some iced tea."

"Thanks, Ted." She took a seat at the table. I could hear the kids up front. They seemed to be taking care of thing well enough. Dot didn't start talking until I set a tall glass of tea before her and she took a long drink.

"I suppose you didn't know Alyce was an informant for me. The best I had. It was convenient to meet her at the docks." Her sudden smile subsided as quickly. Dot sounded weary. "She was fooling around with an officer from the Marine Patrol down there, too."

I sat down with my own cold glass. "That explains a few things," I said. The two women had a closer relationship than I had realized. I had thought they were both there because of me, hadn't I? That I was the connection between them. Silly Ted.

"But it does not explain where the jewelry is," said Dot.

"Nor who killed her." My priorities were not Dot's priorities.

"No, not that either."

Chapter 37

I figured I would steal Karrie Goodpaster's extension cord sometime next week. For now, I was finishing off my trimming of that overgrown hedge, lopping off all but the heaviest of branches.

It was getting late but I wanted to get as much of this done as I could. I might not have time tomorrow, Saturday. The shop would demand my time. For now, I was willing to let my young assistants keep an eye on things.

Karrie's van was over there. I could make it out through the leaves. Were there voices? Not loud. It could be the folks in one the houses behind us, maybe the Willets. I lopped some more and could see some more. I could see a motorcycle.

Call the police or rush right over there? Or go get my gun? No, that would be stupid. So was blundering in but I chose that option. There was muffled conversation coming from inside the van. Laughter? I rapped.

Silence for several seconds. Karrie, wrapped in a ratty terrycloth robe, slid the door open. I could see Rex and his girl behind her. It must be crowded in there. Smoky, too, but not much worse than outside.

They weren't fully dressed either. Stoddard slipped on a black tee and moved in beside Karrie. I guess I stared for a while. Looked pretty stupid, I'm sure. "Are you alright?" I asked at last.

"Sure, Shaper," said Goodpaster, stepping to the ground. The biker pair followed her. "Did you want my extension cord?"

"No. I wanted to know what the hell was going on over here!" I took a breath and the next line came out a little more evenly. "I was worried."

"No need," she said. "Rex and Regina stopped by a couple days ago and we all apologized to each other." A silly smile. "Now we're friends."

So I could see. "Rex and Regina? Whose idea was that?"

Karrie giggled. "Mine. I named her Regina."

"I like it better than Mona."

"Me too," said Rex.

The woman leaned over and whispered something in Goodpaster's ear, giving me an odd sort of look as she did so.

"Regina wonders if you want to join us." She shook her head. "I would greatly doubt that. Shaper is as straight as they come," she told the couple. "He doesn't even smoke pot."

I had, however, recognized its aroma. That didn't bother me any. Rex Stoddard being here did.

"I don't care what you do with your life, Karrie. Oh hell, that's not true. Of course I care. But this isn't about that. You shouldn't have let them stay over here without telling me. That's a breaking of our trust."

Rex took a step forward. "Hey, man, Karrie wasn't —"

"Keep out of this!" I turned back to Karrie without seeing how he took that. "This man is wanted. I could turn him in. I could turn you in for harboring him."

She gasped. She sobbed — one big sob, like a preparation for something more. Then she bawled. "Oh hell," I said. Again.

"I'm sorry," muttered Rex. "Didn't mean to cause trouble." Guys like him rarely did. Regina put her hands on Karrie's shaking shoulders and sort of scowled at me.

I ignored her. "I'm going to ask the Bells if you can park by their house for a few nights. I don't think it's safe for you over here. Not because of Rex." Not directly. "There's just too much going on and I seem to be somewhere near the center of it."

I turned to Stoddard. "Did you know two guys attacked me when I was leaving the park and tried to steal the message Alyce left?"

He slowly shook his head. "We were long gone," Regina put in.

"If you hired them, that would be expected," I informed her. "But I don't think you were involved."

"Donny?"

"It's the best guess. Unless —" That little idea that had nagged at me once or twice made itself known again. "Unless someone is involved we don't know about."

He considered the idea. "Wouldn't know about that."

No, he wouldn't. "You understand why I don't want you and your girlfriend over here, don't you?" I was reasonably calmed down by now and beginning to tell myself what an idiot I was for coming over alone.

"Wife," Regina corrected me.

Karrie broke in. Her tears had disappeared abruptly. "Regina is Rex's common law wife. Being on the run they couldn't legally marry."

I nodded. I completely understood the situation and was completely willing to see them as a married couple. "You can fix that, you know. All you need to do is turn yourself in. If you hang around here you're likely to be arrested anyway."

"I'm not going till I find out what happened to Alyce," he maintained, ignoring the first part of my statement.

I could only shrug. "But you're not going to stay right here. Honestly, Rex, I have nothing against you personally but if I see you around my home I *will* call the police."

I turned back to Karrie Goodpaster. "You haven't been breaking any other laws over here, have you?" It was meant jokingly, at least in part. I'd just as soon lighten things up between us.

"We didn't do any drugs except a little pot. And we compared our antidepressants. Rex has to buy his illegally."

"That must be depressing."

Karrie laughed. I don't think the biker couple got it.

"Okay," I said. "No more research for a while, right? And I expect you two to disappear by morning." It wouldn't do for Rex's cycle to come roaring out the place right now. Sometime during the night would be better. "I'll go say something to Kay about parking your van," I told Goodpaster.

She nodded. I had half-expected her to object. "Oh. I have something of yours." She climbed back into the van and rummaged about a while. "Here." It was my camp shovel, carried back with her from White Springs.

"Thanks." I'd probably never have the opportunity to borrow her electrical cord now. Oh well, I should have my own anyway. I'd visit the Brodys's hardware store sometime.

Chapter 38

it seemed unlikely to me that Alyce would hide her loot at one of the neighbors' houses but it had to be considered a possibility. There was the older house we had purchased too. Maybe that should be checked out. Someone was living there then, weren't they? There had been a succession of small businesses in recent years.

I'd mention it to someone on the force. Rex and Regina were gone. So was Karrie. I hoped she would take up the offer to park by the Bells' house, but she could be anywhere this Saturday morning.

Not a word of my encounter had I shared — not with anyone. Nor did I intend to anytime soon. I had something else to say to Michelle when she showed for breakfast. "We missed our six month anniversary."

She pondered this a moment. "You mean from the day we met, right? That would have been, what, more than a month ago?" She poured a cup of coffee and settled across the table from me.

"Something like that." I don't think either of us thought it was important to be exact about it. "Close to when you finally accepted my proposal, in fact. We'll have known each other just a tad under one year when we get married."

"We kind of rushed into this, didn't we? The relationship, I mean. I think I'm glad we had to wait on the church wedding."

"Oh, you wanted time to back out?"

"Too late for that, mister. We bought property together!"

"And who would get custody of me?" Charlie hollered from somewhere.

"We'll draw straws," I called back. "The short one is stuck with you."

"Hmmph. Maybe I'll go live with my new-found brother!" She stepped into the hall from her bedroom and disappeared as quickly into the shower room. I don't know a better name for it. It was the utility room until I built the shower stall and moved the washing machine out back.

The original shower stall in the bathroom had been dispensed with early in the remodeling of the place, years ago when I was turning it into a place of business, and converted one restroom into two smaller ones. I'd figured I didn't need it with my outdoor shower.

I should check out the plumbing next door sometime. All I knew for sure was that water did run out of the faucets and hose bibs. I'd had the city turn that on weeks ago. Plenty of time, Ted. You have all summer. And if you don't finish, you have fall.

Charlie popped back out. She wasn't one to dawdle in the shower. "Speaking of your brother," I said, "have you seen him recently?"

She walked into the kitchen, drying her hair. "Not only seen him but got him a job. He's working at the hardware store. John's sister-in-law manages the place. Ralph's wife."

"That's good of you. I should go over there and pick up a few things," I said. "Monday will do."

"He's made a good impression. Al's working in the gate house at some swanky community in Banner Beach. You need to make more coffee before I come back out." With that, she returned to her bedroom.

"You're going to need more too," I told my fiancee. "Better get busy." All I got for that was a look of disdain. And I was just trying to be helpful.

SMOKE

I rinsed out the pot, refilled the machine with water. Coffee — I almost looked for it in the refrigerator without thinking. Kept it there before the girls moved in but there wasn't enough space now. The three of us drank it up more quickly than I had on my own, so keeping it fresh wasn't as big a concern. The maker was chugging away shortly. It was a little past Eight-thirty. Early, but I could open up.

"We could do worse than rent the place next door to those boys," said Michelle. "Sebastian and Alistair, I mean. If they have good jobs now. We'd have to give Goodpaster the boot."

"Already gone." I was not going to mention her visitors. Not yet, maybe never.

"Without asking me?"

That might have been a mistake. It was hard to tell from her tone. "I was worried about her over there, with all that's been going on. I wouldn't want Charlie to move in, either."

She nodded. If Michelle had disapproved of my initiative, that was overridden by her concern for her daughter. "But the guys would be safe enough."

"I reckon so." I gave that a moment more of thought. "In fact, if they were there we might all be a bit safer." Even Karrie, if she wanted to come back.

"It would need furniture," she pointed out. There were some shabby chairs in the front rooms but little else. Those chairs should probably be added to the pile of trash I had been accumulating.

"We could lend them the folding bed." It was big enough for two. "Or better yet, take Charlie's bed over there and give her the folder."

"I'm hearing this," the girl called from her room.

STEPHEN BROOKE

"Good," called back her mother. "Then you won't be surprised when you come home and find you have to sleep on the floor!"

"Ted can sleep on the floor," Charlie informed her, coming into the kitchen. "He did over in the motel when he, um, stood guard, I guess. The night we saw Manuel."

"Couldn't figure out how to open up the sleeper sofa," I mumbled. Or was too tired to fool with it.

"Ted can sleep on the floor but I am *not* joining him," Michelle told her. "Our mattress is hard enough as it is."

"Firm. It's firm. We'll figure something out," I assured them both and went up front.

The folks in the next house south would undoubtedly be glad to see someone moving in and the place completely cleaned up. I won't say renovated. That sounds like too much work. There was a nice little cottage over there. White with green trim.

I swung the front door open. Wasn't that Dave Blake's little car up the street? Visiting Jan, maybe. A bit early unless they planned to go somewhere for the day. Two men got out. It wasn't hard to recognize the bulky Lieutenant Boris Jones.

Perhaps the black Taurus wasn't available this morning. Saunders might be off joy-riding! They came up the sidewalk toward the shop. I waved and stepped outside. I'd just as soon deal with them there.

"I'm here for the weekend and then back to Miami," Boris informed me, after the obligatory greetings and pleasantries were out of the way. "I can't justify hanging around when nothing is moving forward."

"I haven't heard from Dominguez," Dave added to this, "but I wouldn't think she'd be staying much longer either."

211

SMOKE

"Our criminal element hasn't given up yet," I informed the pair, and told them of my recent encounters with both Morales and Stoddard — leaving out Karrie, for the most part. It was then I mentioned my idea that there might be someone else.

"Maybe whoever had those thugs come after you at the park?" asked Blake.

"Maybe. It's just a thought. You guys are the detectives. You and Rivers."

"I think he already gave up," said Boris Jones. "Another man? Not a partner, I don't think. We sewed up that side of things pretty tight."

"Then someone else who knew what was going on? Any of them could have talked to a friend. Or a lover," felt Dave.

"It's possible." Jones said no more but looked thoughtful. For all I knew, that was for show and he had no ideas. "Have you given more thought to that message, Ted?" he asked. So I was Ted to him too, eh? Maybe I was on a first name basis with too many cops.

"Not as much as I should," I admitted. "It's been in the back of my head but I've been kept busy." I should read it over again. Maybe something would come to me. If not when I read it, in the middle of the night.

A city truck had pulled in across the street and a little north. Two men got out and started walking opposite directions. It took me a moment to realize they were unwinding a measuring tape between them.

"Ah," said Dave, "maybe they're finally going to put your street light in. I'd heard about it at the station. They'd asked the chief's opinion."

"I assume he told them it was essential to public safety," I replied.

"Of course. You heard the council voted on the go-ahead for your park, didn't you?"

I could only shake my head. "I've been out of that loop." I should have asked Alvaro. He would have known. Patty, too.

"Yep. The planning department has been asked to come up with ideas. Ready to go, Bo?"

"Might as well." Dave waved to the public works crew before driving off.

I would believe the street light when I saw it shining. As for the park, I knew that would take time even if it were to be built. But those guys were up to something over there, weren't they?

It wasn't the slowest of Saturdays but I can't say traffic was heavy. Michelle came up to lend assistance mid-morning. "I think I want to go to the vigil mass this evening," I told her. "Do you want to come?"

"Not all that much. Let me be lazy this weekend, okay?" Then she asked, "Isn't this one of those special Catholic days?"

I had to think. "Oh, right. Pentecost. Semi-special, I suppose. The end of the Easter season, if nothing else."

"Easter? I can barely remember when that happened!"

"Fifty days, including tomorrow. Don't ask me why I remember that, of all things. Anyway, I intend to shop a little before going to mass." That's the advantage of going to the Saturday evening service.

I'd have to arrange who would watch the shop if I took off early. Or if no one wanted to, I would just close it. Done it before, undoubtedly would again.

SMOKE

Wasn't necessary. Around Five I pulled in by the venerable *Cully Beach Hardware*, in one of the old brick buildings on the north side of Main Street — Scott City Road — between the downtown and the bridge. This place was the original base of the Brody family businesses, operating since the days of the Great Depression.

All I came for was that electric cord. But I could look at a new lawn mower maybe. I would be needing it. Hey, and they had bicycles. Later.

And sure enough, there was Sebastian Furr at the counter. No one else. They must already trust him to run the place — and to close it in an hour. "What can I help you with, Mr. Carrol?" he asked. I guess I would have to be 'mister' in here.

"Fifty foot of heavy duty extension cord," I told him.

"Fourteen gauge do?"

"Make it twelve. And, by the way, are you still staying in that motel?"

Chapter 39

"The Brodys aren't big on working on the sabbath," said Sebastian Furr.

To this Alistair Brown added, "And my shift isn't until tonight."

"So," continued Sebastian, "there's no better time than right now."

"That was quick," remarked Michelle. "It's a good thing I'm in property management and know all about this stuff." She looked the pair over. "I don't think we need a written lease unless you guys want one."

I might do well to leave all the details up to my fiancee. "And no deposits or any of that stuff," I contributed. "Really, if you two help get the place fixed up some, we can forgo a lot of the rent." Or even all of it. I had gone over some of this with Furr yesterday.

"Good enough," said Al. "We should pick a bedroom, Bastian, and start cleaning from there."

"And get a bed into it," Michelle suggested.

"I like this room with its big windows." We were in the middle bedroom. It would have been my choice too.

"The little one on the back is supposed to be mine," said Charlie. "That's what Shaper says anyway."

Moving Charlie in might be off the table for a while. I had intended to accomplish more renovation before making that move. Or any move. But *this* move seemed sensible. Not so much because they were guys but because they were capable guys. Alistair in particular. And there were two of them.

Shoot, it might even be safe to let Goodpaster return now. I had noticed her van down at Kay and Rick's place this morning.

"I'll help you get the folding bed," offered Charlie. Michelle and I went back to the shop. I recognized the older green LTD out front, with its ugly vinyl roof. Bill Cotton.

Joan sat in the passenger seat, with the engine idling to keep the air conditioning working. "Oh, there you are," said the chief, coming around from the back. "I saw the vehicles and knew you weren't off at church. That's where we're headed in a few minutes."

"Hi Bill," Michelle said, and went on inside. I chose to talk with him there in the drive. He obviously didn't intend to stay long.

"What can I do for you this morning?" I asked.

"Just checking how things were with you. Unofficial, friend to friend. Blake told me about this biker coming around."

"Dealt with, I think." I really was fairly confident about that. "And I'm moving Charlie's brother and his friend in next door. That may discourage visitors." I hoped.

"The homosexuals?" I couldn't make out just what Bill thought of them from his voice so I only nodded. "I was a little surprised Stan Brody gave that boy a job. He's pretty conservative, you know."

"Maybe he takes 'judge not' seriously," I suggested.

"Maybe so. We're both Baptists but not quite of the same sort." He shrugged and changed the subject. "I got to thinking about that place across the street."

"Another idea as to where the jewelry is hidden?"

"No, nothing like that. The building — it would make a nice substation for us. With that park a likelihood now, we may want someone down here all the time." He gazed across the highway at the abandoned gas station. "Or at least have somewhere the bike patrol can stop. I am going to recommend the place be bought."

"Wow. A street light *and* police across the street. I'll be pretty darn safe!"

He chuckled. "I would hope so. No more stumbling over bodies, okay? And do," he went on in a more serious voice, "report Stoddard if he shows up again instead of dealing with him yourself, okay?"

"I warned him I would."

"Good. By the way, there was nothing on that gun of his you turned in. Sold legitimately out in Nevada, though not to anyone named Rex Stoddard."

I could believe that. Bill and I shook and a minute later he was off to church. Yes, that old station could be put to good use by the city, I thought. No need to tear it down. I assumed the lot on which it stood extended all the way to the beach. Added to the land the city already owned between it and Eighth, it would make quite a nice park over there.

Michelle opened the door to the shop as soon as Cotton pulled away. "Not as smoky this morning, is it?" she remarked. "I haven't been keeping track of the wildfires."

Me neither. Too much else on my mind. "Maybe there's been some rain."

"I hope we get some here soon. Even your yuccas look thirsty!"

They did, a little. It was also the season for them to bloom, sending up long stalks with rows of white flowers along them. I was not going to stand there and admire those. Not for long. Time to open up.

It might have been an hour and a half later my new renters came in the front door. Alone; Charlie must have deserted them.

"Is it okay to turn on the hot water tank?" asked Sebastian.

"Sure. I tested it but there wasn't any reason to leave it running. And feel free to use the outdoor shower over here anytime."

"Thanks. We decided it's time to take a break and join all those folks swimming across the street."

"It would be wrong to live so close to the beach and not use it," I told them.

"Our feeling exactly. Oh. We've been thinking about those fellows who waylaid you at the park," Alistair said. "Whoever set them on you had to know you had taken something out of the thermos."

"Thats true," I agreed.

"So, either of your two sets of hoodlums, or Ms. Dominguez. Those are all we know for sure."

"But," Sebastian added to this, "just about anyone could have been watching. The FBI agent, included."

"Right. Lots of people knew you were involved. Mostly law enforcement."

"I find it hard to mistrust anyone from the Cully Beach force. And Boris Jones was in Miami." I gave the pair an exaggeratedly suspicious look. "You two knew about it."

Sebastian laughed at once. "Got us there!"

The reaction from Al was more subdued. "We had plenty of other opportunities. I do have to admit I've been curious about it." He held up a hand. "But none of my business. Our business."

"You can see it if you want. A copy — the original is at the police station. I doubt you could make the least sense of it."

"Probably not. Let's get to the beach, Bastian, old boy." I do think Sebastian Furr wanted to look that note over but he followed his partner.

Mid-morning, Sunday. Well, almost late morning. Peak time for the next couple hours. I hopped up on the counter and surveyed the showroom. It looked good enough but it would be better when I expanded. The spare room, no more. I wasn't likely to need more, ever.

Boards lined the room, some horizontal up by the ceiling, others upright along the walls. Not all my brand, by the way. I carried a couple 'names,' larger established surfboard manufacturers, and a few smaller regional shapers. But the bulk were my own *Secret Surfboards*. I made more profit off of those.

With the mortgage on the new house, I needed all of that I could get. A swimsuit-clad couple came in and I hopped down from my perch.

Chapter 40

Waves! Fairly good size, too, and pretty much a straight easterly swell. Storm out there in the Mid-Atlantic somewhere. Not near. It would break well enough right at Eighth. No need to drive to the pier.

I almost invited Charlie to go over with me. Nope. First day of college for her. Monday and Wednesday mornings through the summer. And shifts at *Coastal Coffee*, too. She and John and Michelle had worked out some sort of arrangement for getting her from place to place.

Old Shaper, however, did not need to be anywhere except in the surf. For three hours or so, anyway. I was the first in the water at the spot. Kids had given the break various names over the years. 'Motel' had been the most common and with a new motel expected to rise on the site of the *Easy Breezes*, maybe it would stick.

But with a park coming it was more likely that would give it a new name. Didn't matter. I paddled out on my mid-size board, the old standby I named 'Big Red.' Not so old now, since the original Big Red had been smashed not long ago. This was Big Red Mark Two. It worked as well as or better than the original; one can never manage an exact replica, try as one will. Into the first dumpy peak and short ride left. Right would undoubtedly have been as good.

Someone paddling out. "You think they'll line up better later?" called Rick Bell. Good to see him get into the water.

"Probably after you leave for work!" I yelled back.

"No shit. Isn't that how it always goes?" He reached me and sat on his board, waiting for a wave. It was the new board I had built him, a scaled-up version of my stock thruster. If Rick didn't watch his weight, I'd have to scale it up even further. "The kids will be over in a bit," he said, and whirled the board around to stroke into a wave.

Sure enough, Jan and Richie joined us a few minutes later. A couple other neighborhood kids showed up too. And then, a couple more up at the end of the Eighth Avenue access, toting long boards. Girls?

Girls indeed, I realized as they paddled out. Marty on my borrowed long board. And Patty. I'm willing to call her a girl. Anyone who will paddle out and ride a few remains a surfer girl, no matter what her age. "Hey, Ted," she called. "Marty unlocked your shed so I could get my board out."

About time she rode. Whether she rode well didn't matter much. No, that's wrong. It didn't matter at all. Patty was in board shorts and tee, which seemed sensible. I don't know why any women surf in bikinis. Completely impractical and a good way to get wax rash.

Yes, I know I made appreciative remarks about Kim Timble. Allow Shaper his little inconsistencies.

Rick left the water first. I guess he actually did have work to get to. Construction tended to be an on-again off-again source of employment. It was turning into a nice day. Hot, to be sure, but the water was still reasonably cool. Hardly any smoke at all this morning.

"I think Marty is getting the hang of your board," remarked Patty, paddling back out after a halfway decent ride. They were forgiving waves.

She was, within reason. The girl seemed to be fighting with it a bit. "It's not ideal for her," I said. "Too stiff." Like most of my personal boards. I could see where I'd need to make changes when I shaped her a long board. More rocker. Thinner, softer rails, probably. "I think this will be my last." A decent wall was rising from the depths.

Rick was right. They were lining up better. Let the hordes of surf rats enjoy them the rest of the day. I stroked in, started to fade right and then decided to just keep going that way, as it was walling up rather nicely. Even a little bit of a tube. Not a bad way to end the session. I did a lazy cutback out on the shoulder, let the white-water carry me in and managed a little wiggle or two in the shore-break before it finally closed out. As I stood in the thigh-deep water, unfastening my ankle leash, I could see Patty riding a carbon-copy of my wave. Not a carbon-copy ride, you understand, but she did okay for someone who went years without surfing. No big moves.

"I'm ready to go too," she proclaimed, hopping off her board in the shallow water. "I call first on the shower!"

"There used to be a shower right here," I said, gesturing to our right as we headed toward the street. "The motel. The kids weren't supposed to use it, of course." They still spray-painted graffiti on the seawall, I could see. The big motel moving in here was unlikely to tolerate that.

They might well put in a new wall, for that matter. It was around shoulder-height down at the beach end but increasingly low as one went west. "Hey, something's been posted," I noted. It was a small sign on a four-by-four post driven into the sand, near the entrance. What used to be the entrance. I went over to give it a look. Carefully, as I was barefoot.

"I need my reading glasses," I admitted.

Patty shook her head. "Me too."

"But I can tell it's a building permit. They're getting ready to do something here." The paper was inside a plastic bag stapled to plywood.

They were getting ready to do something on the other side of Eighth also. A trailer loaded with a curved metal pole had pulled in.

"Now I would hazard that is for a street light," I said.

"You think?" responded Patty. One would be right in guessing there was at least some sarcasm in her voice.

"That it is," said one of the city workmen. Admittedly not working at the moment. "We'll be adding more of these. All the way up to where they leave off now."

His likewise unoccupied companion added. "But not further south. This is the new end of the line."

"We're waiting for the rest of the crew and equipment."

"Gonna take a while then," I said.

"Not necessarily. It might be shining by tonight."

"Tomorrow night for sure."

"Great." I wasn't sure I believed it but it was kind of great. They were hanging the light on the existing electric pole. I'd half-expected them to put up a new one. We crossed at the corner and headed down the uneven sidewalk toward my shop. I should complain about that next.

"I'm glad my complaining finally got some action," I remarked to Patty.

"Oh, Ted, no one was paying attention to you. It's the big chain motel going in here that got it done."

"Believe that if you want," I told her. No one waiting at the front door of the shop, eager to get in and buy surfboard wax or sunglasses. We carried our boards around back.

SMOKE

For a moment I considered offering the use of the inside shower. Nope. That wasn't what Patty wanted, to be the little old lady who didn't rinse off where the rest of us did. She wanted to be one of us, a surfer again. I was pretty sure I was right about this.

While she showered I opened the shaping room. The glassing room too, on the other side of the building. Its garage doors were identical to the ones in my shaping bay but faced to the rear of my property, not forward. Patty kept her board stowed in there. I'd let her rinse it off and put it away herself.

I noticed her bicycle was in there right now. "All yours," called Patty.

She was in dripping wet clothes, the same tee and shorts she had worn in the water. "These will dry on the bike ride home," she said. "I should do this more. I sort of regret those land-locked years in Atlanta."

I had my own regrets. Doesn't everyone? "There are clouds building inland," I observed.

"Rain, maybe? It would sure be welcome."

I slipped into the shower, having popped inside to get a towel and dry clothes first. "You have to wait on Shaper," I heard Patty call out.

"I have my own shower!" came the reply. Marty, done for the morning. "Thanks for letting me use the board, Shaper."

"You'll have to give me feedback later," I called to her, and turned on the water. No sign of either when I came out. Patty's bike was gone. It was time to open up the shop, or close enough.

An old truck — even older than mine — pulled up as I swung back the front door. The lanky form of John Brody climbed out of the cab. "You aren't looking for Charlie, are you?" I called to him.

"No sir. I'll be going to pick her up shortly and take her to work. First day on the job."

I was glad all that had been worked out without involving me. He ambled on up to where I stood in the doorway. "We're going to share a shift, at least for a while. I'm not really sure it's a good idea for me to be her boss!"

"That means your free time will be at the same time," I pointed out.

"Yeah, if we want to spend time together after hours working side by side." He tried to make this sound offhand. "I'm pretty confident she'll be ready to take over a manager spot by the end of summer." When he left. Left the job, left Cully Beach, to go off to college in Jacksonville. Not that he wouldn't be back on holidays and the occasional weekend.

For that matter, it wasn't a long drive for Charlie to visit him. When she got her license and a car. She should be able to get the license reinstated soon. The car might take longer.

Would she even want to work at *Coastal Coffee* when John-boy was gone? "So what can I do for you?" I asked, stepping aside so he could enter the shop.

"For one thing, I'm finally ready to order that board I was talking about half a year ago. Charlie has to do some art work on it, of course."

"Of course."

He didn't quite sigh. Maybe you could call the expression on his face a visual sigh. "I wish she would stick with art. Does she really intend to go through with being a cop?"

Ah. So that was it. No, that's simplistic. That was *part* of it. "Beats me," I admitted. "Charlie does intend to get her degree first. A lot could change while she's at it."

SMOKE

"If she sticks with it." The boy didn't sound quite convinced she would.

"She'll stick with something," I said. "I'm sure of that. And I hope that something includes you." I suspected that would be up to John.

"So do I, Ted. Let's figure out what you're going to shape for me."

A rain shower blew in just before noon.

Chapter 41

"I could give her a lift to the college," said Karrie Goodpaster. "After all, it's my class she's attending."

"But not back, I would assume." Charlie had to be at *Coastal Coffee* sometime in the late morning. I hadn't pried and asked exactly when.

"I suppose not. I'm supposed to stay and have office hours."

"Be that as it may, I think it's safe to bring your van back over here if you want. The guys don't mind. And," I added, "you need to be near if you're going to write about me, after all."

"I have to put you on hold, Shaper. I'm gonna write Rex's story! But I do think I need to find another place to park. Maybe even a real apartment."

"Okay. As long as you want, if you want." That was settled to the satisfaction of both. I did wonder how she was going to keep Rex around to write anything about him. Might there end up being prison interviews?

"There's our girl now," said Karrie. Sure enough, John Brody's truck was letting her out in front of the shop. We were watching from my shaping bay. A part-timer held down the shop while I got some work done back here.

I looked up at the clock. I do keep one in the workroom; as much as I hate having to keep track of the time it was a necessity. "Her shift must end at Five." John's too, apparently.

Brody drove off. Charlie slowly walked back to us. She looked tired. Being on ones feet in a coffee shop for six hours or so would do that, especially if one were not used to it.

"Hi, um, Ms. Goodpaster. Hey, Shaper. Is that John's new board?"

"It is. I'll have it ready for you to paint shortly."

"Call me Karrie when we aren't at school, okay?" Karrie sort of smirked. "And it's *Doctor* Goodpaster, not Ms."

"People with degrees are picky about that," I observed. "Maybe because they go into debt to get them."

"We want our money's worth!" Karrie declared. She gave the board a looking over, not that she knew anything about surfing. "Shaper could have been an artist."

"He was for a time," Charlie informed her. "I think he really hated it. That's what Patty says."

"It frustrated me," I admitted. I figured that was enough to say.

"But he can still draw really well," Charlie went on.

Goodpaster only nodded to all this. I think she knew enough not to go poking other people's demons. "I see you got the rest of the hedge down," she said.

"Our new tenants took care of it. Al doesn't work until tonight and Sebastian has Mondays off." The two had also told me Boris Jones stopped by while I was in the water. The lieutenant was headed back to Miami.

He expressed, it seems, some disquieting thoughts on Dorothea Dominguez. Not suspicions, exactly, but questions, and the suggestion that an eye be kept on the investigator. These the boys dutifully passed on to me.

I didn't know what to do with the information. Trust Dot? I had never quite done that since she showed up. I knew her agenda was not my agenda. And I was already keeping as much of an eye on her as I was able.

Anyway, Jones was gone. He could even be back in Miami by now if he'd hurried. It was like a six hour drive. More for me; I pulled into just about every rest stop.

"Working again tomorrow?" I asked Charlie.

"Yep. I get to help John open up."

"You'll have to get up as early as Shaper," said Karrie. That was true. The coffee shop opened at Seven but there was prep work before that. I knew John-boy was entrusted with that duty at least a couple mornings in the week.

"I'm hoping John will wake me," Charlie replied. "I need a shower." In the back door she went.

"I kind of hope he does too," I said, and turned back to my board. Karrie meandered off toward her van, parked up at the Bells' house. A while later I glimpsed it pulling in next door. Easy to see now, with that darned hedge out of the way.

Also easy to see how much work awaited me over there. It was time to quit work here. Time to close the door of the surf shop too. A rinse under the outdoor shower and in the back. Michelle and Charlie were in the kitchen, gabbing about something. I hadn't noticed my fiancee arriving but I was busy.

And she hadn't come back to say, 'Honey, I'm home,' so I could blame her. I dripped my way past them and went to get some clean clothes.

"I told Lisa to go home," Michelle informed me on my return. "Didn't lock up, though." It was just about time to do that but it didn't matter much. I'd just as soon let the air flow through a while longer. I only nodded and went up into the shop, stood looking out that open door. Still quite light out at Six at this time of the year.

The new streetlight was up. Operational? I'd know soon — or when I got out early tomorrow morning. Charlie was gone when I returned to the kitchen. Moreover, Michelle had raided the workshop fridge for a bottle of merlot.

229

SMOKE

"John's coming to pick Charlie up in a bit. They're celebrating her successful first day, it seems." She poured me a glass of red. I didn't even need to ask. "Neither is being given more than twenty-four hours a week."

I understood the reasons for that. I didn't give any of my part-timers even that much work. But they were high school kids, for the most part. *Coastal Coffee* was largely staffed by college students with their shifts worked around their class schedules.

"I doubt they stay out very late," I remarked, after a sip of wine.

"Me too," she agreed.

The phone rang. Past business hours. I could ignore it. Oh, might as well. I went up and picked it up on the fifth ring. One more and the machine would have got it.

"Cully Beach Surf Shop," I answered. I didn't feel like adding 'Ted speaking.' But the caller knew who it was.

"Hi Ted, it's Dot Dominguez. I wanted to check in with you before leaving town."

"Soon?" I asked.

"Tomorrow sometime, I think. I would have got to you earlier but mobile reception in this little town is nonexistent. Had to find a pay phone!"

"Mobile?" I'd heard of it. Never seen anyone use one — maybe because, as Dot had just explained, there was no reception in Cully Beach.

"Yeah. I've gotten used to using one down in Miami. So has Boris Jones. We complained to each other about it."

"Jones has, um, expressed some doubts about you." I might as well tell her that. It wouldn't hurt me any.

"I could express my own doubts about Boris! Be that as it may, I do hope to stop by there tomorrow. Will you be around?"

"I should be. Just another slow Tuesday for me."

"Okay. Don't know when exactly, but I'll see you then. Bye."

I think she hung up before I got a 'goodbye' out. Ah, there was John Brody pulling up out front. I let him in, directed him to the back.

Before I closed and locked the door, I could see the street light come on, down on the corner.

Chapter 42

It wasn't really as bright as the security light at the old motel had been. Or maybe the street light simply didn't illuminate quite the same area. It remained rather dark down at the beach end of Eighth Avenue.

I had missed that motel light these last few months. Not that it was very dark at Five-ish, this close to the summer equinox. The skies were clear, aside from low-lying clouds, tinged orange and peach, out on the ocean horizon.

There was still a little bit of a swell. I could ride it probably but I'd told Dominguez I would be home, hadn't I? I sat down on the sea wall, all that remained of Easy Breezes, and looked south. Alyce had sat here, doing the same.

I come by your place and sit on the wall, she had written. *Everythings behind me now* — did she mean literally behind her? Behind her while she sat on the motel wall? That would mean the jewelry was hidden somewhere on the bulldozed property. Maybe it would never be found.

I'd have to let someone in on that insight, huh? I hopped down, Two figures, down toward A-1-A, silhouetted by the light. One tall, one shorter and broader. I walked toward Sebastian and Alistair.

"We saw you sitting and thinking, Ted," offered Sebastian. "Anything wrong?"

"No, no, just had some ideas about this loot that's eluding everyone."

"We wouldn't be much help there," said Al.

They crossed the highway with me, walked south along the sidewalk. "Would you like to see the note we discovered?" I asked. "If you have time."

"Plenty of time. I don't have to be at the store till Ten," said Furr.

"We both work Ten to Six today," Alistair added. "Except he's AM and I'm PM!"

"Well then, come in and have some coffee." If there was any left. John and Charlie were both up and drinking it.

Shoot, I could make more. And the kids could see what Alyce wrote too, if they wanted. Kids? All four of them were kids, really, Brown being the oldest. What, twenty-four or five maybe? I assumed six years in the marines.

I went to get the copy of the note. A copy of the note — not the one I had written out but the one that came from the copier at the Cully Beach police station. I had kept it under the counter, up front. I grabbed the extra chair while I was there.

"This is it," I announced and spread it on the table. They could look it over while I started another pot.

"I can make no sense of it," admitted Alistair. I am pretty sure the others felt the same. "But someone felt it was worth stealing."

"The someone wouldn't have known what it said," Sebastian pointed out. He looked at Al for a moment, hesitating before going on. "We both sort of suspect your, um, friend Dorothea Dominguez. She knew about it."

"And she wants to find the jewelry and claim the reward. Right. Don't think I haven't considered it, guys." I definitely had. But there were other possibilities too.

"The person who wanted to steal the message doesn't have to be anyone involved in the original crime, do they?" asked Charlie. John was pretty much baffled by all this. She hadn't told him much, it seemed.

233

"No, they don't," I agreed. Nor necessarily Alyce's murderer, even if they were involved. "Does my coffee meet your approval, Mr. Brody?"

"Not bad. We might as well get going, Charlie. There will be plenty to eat at the shop." He chuckled. "More coffee too."

The girl grimaced. "I think I am already getting sick of coffee." Both disappeared into her bedroom.

I sat down with my cup and picked up the note, looked it over once again. *Remember how we use to sit.* A place we used to sit — yes, we did go up on the roof of Johnny Munoz's boat house a couple times. But mostly we met at the edge of the boat channel, sat on the sea wall. Dot would join us sometimes. Not that often.

But spit? I didn't remember us doing that. *I remember the old sea cow.* I did remember sea cows in the water. They would slowly paddle along, right by our feet dangling over the wall. When there was rain, the fresh water would gush from a drain pipe in the wall and the manatees would come for a drink.

Alyce laughed and said it was spitting. Then she'd see if she could spit as far.

I did *remember how we use to spit*, after all.

"I think I've got it," I whispered. "I think I know where she stashed them."

"Near?" wondered Sebastian.

"Where we just came from." I rose. Breakfast? It could wait. "I think I need my trusty little shovel again." It was in the workshop. "Right back."

In the glassing side of the building. Yard tools tended to end up there, mostly because the door opened onto the yard. By the time I retrieved it, all four of them were outside. It was still a little dim out but the sun was finding its way out of the ocean.

Make that five of them. Dot Dominguez was strolling up the drive. "What's up?" She gave us all a once-over.

Furr and Brown seemed unsure whether to say anything. "We're going on a treasure hunt," I informed her.

"And we're going to work," said Charlie. "Happy hunting!" She and John headed for his truck, parked on the street.

"You've figured it out?" Dot fell in beside me, the boys right behind.

"I believe so. Alyce was referring to a storm drain, one that carried rain water to the bay. There were outlets in the sea wall." I looked across the road, toward the old motel site. "As there are in the sea wall over there, on a much smaller scale."

"Do you think maybe we should have called your policeman friends?" asked Alistair.

I stopped, shrugged. "If you want. There's no guarantee we'll find them, you know. And I don't think Dot will steal them from us if we do."

"Trusting, aren't we?" she asked.

"You had your chance at the park," I replied. "I expect you to behave now."

The slightest trace of amusement might be heard in her voice. "A guess, I assume. I admit to nothing."

"A pretty good guess," muttered Alistair.

The new light still illuminated the corner of Eighth as we crossed A-1-A. When did it turn off? I briefly wondered. Other thoughts quickly pushed that one out of my head. I led my followers across the street to the sea wall, only knee height here, and stepped up onto it.

"There are little drains set in close to the wall so water wouldn't stand behind it," I said. I led on along the top of the wall, rising higher as we approached the beach end of it. "Along the back here, the part that faces the beach. Two or three, maybe." I had never paid that much attention.

I reached the southeast corner. There was the first of them. Very small, with a rusted slotted cover, set into the narrow concrete apron. "Nothing would fit into that," said Dot.

That was certain. Nor would Alyce have easily gotten those covers off. I followed the wall north. Three more drains of the same sort before we reached the stairs. "How about the other ends?" asked Sebastian, peering over the wall. It was a bit dark yet to see much and there was vegetation growing along the wall in several spots, both above and below.

"Let's go down and look." The pipes set into the wall proved no larger than those above. It was disappointing.

"She could have meant the drain as a marker, maybe?" suggested Dot. "Buried the jewelry in the sand below?"

But which drain?

"Someone's here," hissed Alistair Brown. Two figures had appeared above us.

"Find anything?" came Donny Morales's voice.

"Not yet," Dot called. "Let's go back up," she said to the rest of us.

The pair waited at the top of the stairs. "It was just an idea I had," I told them. "Doesn't seem —" My eyes went to the short length of seawall that ran on north of the stairs. A much larger slab of concrete had been poured there, essentially a patio. Part of it had been broken off and carted away during the motel demolition.

But some remained, here on the northeast corner of the property. That I hadn't expected. A much larger drain opening was set into it. There had been a faucet and hose here, hadn't there? I stood looking at it. I assume everyone else did the same when they saw me.

"That must be the drain," stated Dot. "But are they still inside it?"

"That," said Boris Jones, "is what I would like to know."

Chapter 43

The Miami police lieutenant held up a little squarish object. I had no idea what it was. "Small Change paged me. I told him to if anything went down. I was staying just down the road in Vasco."

"Just far enough away that no local law enforcement would recognize you," said Dot.

"Exactly so, Ms. Dominguez." His eyes went from her to Small Change and back again. "Robinson has been a CI for me for years. Even when this jewel robbery went down."

Morales scowled at his companion. "Did you turn me in?"

Small Change shook his head vigorously. "I didn't even know you was involved, Donny."

"But he did give you information on Alyce," I hazarded.

A shrug of dismissal. "You think the jewelry is in that drain?"

We stood in a circle around it, staring down at a hole in the ground. It might be big enough. "They wouldn't stay put all these years," murmured Sebastian.

That did seem unlikely. I crouched and slipped the blade of my shovel under the guard. It lifted right out. There was no way to see anything, of course. I turned the shovel around and pushed the handle in. It stopped at about six inches.

"The pipe turns right away," I reported. "Let's see where it comes out."

Back down the stairs. I didn't much like being where we were. It was too hidden, what with the high seawall and overarching trees. "Here it is," reported Al. A short PVC stub about halfway down the wall. I probed it the same way I had the drain above. Again, it turned a short way in.

"Most of the pipe must slope down," I said. "I suppose some-thing could remain lodged in it." I think we all knew that was doubtful.

"Norbert wouldn't have expected her cache to remain hidden long," said Jones.

"And if it was in any sort of bag —" began Dot.

"Which seems likely enough."

"It might have rotted away by now," she finished.

As Alyce's clothes had, buried in the sand. As Alyce had herself, for the most part. Not the silly piece of jewelry I had given her. I started digging into the sand below the drainpipe.

Sebastian knelt down beside me and began using his hands, carefully checking each shovelful I removed. He held up a scrap of cloth, disintegrating into nothing but fibers and sand in his hands.

A flash of light on something. Where was that? I ran my fingers through the loose sand. There. I pulled out what had felt like a ring and brushed the clinging sand away. A diamond.

"So," said Boris Jones. "We've found them at last. I should take possession."

"No one should take possession," I replied. "We're not digging any more out until the Cully Beach police are here. One of you guys should run and phone them."

Al got up. He could call from my place. Michelle would let him in. Or there was a pay phone right at the corner, at the convenience store.

"Stop," ordered Jones. "I want to see all that's buried there before anyone else shows up."

"Evidence?" asked Al. "They wouldn't muck it up, I'd think."

SMOKE

"Yeah, evidence," I said, staring at the Miami cop. "Evidence against the lieutenant. He's afraid Alyce left something that would implicate him."

Boris swore softly. He also pulled his Glock from its shoulder holster.

Dot gave him a long look. "So you killed Alyce. How'd you figure that out Ted?"

"It had to be either you or him, didn't it? I figured you were both after her."

"Maybe we were. But I didn't know about Jones."

The man laughed. "I knew all about you, thanks to Change here."

Small Change Robinson had been staring at the policeman through all of this, maybe working out in his head all of what had been revealed. "You killed Alyce," he said, so quietly I could barely hear. "And you used me to help you." Suddenly, he lunged forward, his opened knife in his hand.

Boris Jones sidestepped him, brought a clenched fist down on the back of Robinson's head. The little man sprawled in the sand, trying to reach, retrieve his knife. Jones kicked it away and turned his automatic back on the rest of us. "Now you're going to dig up the rest of those jewels."

And after? It seemed rather impractical for him to execute all of us. Sebastian and I started digging again. "I never meant to kill Norbert," he said, his voice even, almost emotionless. "Hell, it ruined everything. I just tried to get her to give up the loot and, well, she banged her head. Uptown, that was." He made a slight nod to the north.

"You mean you banged her head into something," spoke Donny.

240

"And you were going to run with it, if she gave it up," said Dot Dominguez.

"Go back to Miami and sit on it a while. No one even knew I'd been up here. I would have let the girl go. I'm not a murderer, Dot. It just — happened." There was no mirth in his chuckle. "Now I *will* have to run with it." He looked us over. Still undecided, I felt.

"Another ring," I announced, holding it up.

"A quality diamond," murmured Dot.

"Keep digging," ordered the lieutenant.

There would be surfers showing up soon, I was pretty sure. Still enough of a swell rolling in to entice the neighborhood kids. I hoped none got involved in this.

And what was this? Something large. A chain? I pulled it from the sand. The biggest damn green jewel I had ever seen hung as pendant from a necklace encrusted with diamonds and emeralds.

Dot gasped. "The Santo Antonio Emerald."

"Bring it here," ordered Boris. "Bring everything you've found so far."

Sebastian carried the jewelry over to him. I hoped the kid wouldn't try anything. It would be pretty stupid.

The yelp of a siren. Boris glanced in its direction, only momentarily, but sure enough Sebastian took advantage of it and tried to put a shoulder into the man. Jones evaded it, for the most part, but the distraction was enough. Before he could bring his Glock around, a small automatic pistol had appeared in Dot Dominguez's hand and spoke twice.

Jones's gun went off but it was aimed at the sky.

Chapter 44

Donny had pulled a gun too but never used it. Some sort of small revolver. He slipped it back into his pocket before Officer Bob Redding reached us.

He was confused but that wasn't unusual for Bob. "Blake's girl-friend called him and said something was going down over here. Saw it from her window." Jan's bedroom was on the second floor, front, of the Bells' house. "Dispatch told me to get over here." Bob looked again at the quite dead Boris Jones. "So he killed your friend." He shook his head. Bob didn't like to think ill of fellow cops.

It didn't take long for Dave Blake himself to show up, and Jack Saunders too. The chief was only a little behind them. Brief explanations, mostly led by Dorothea Dominguez. I was willing to allow her that.

But the reward on those jewels was mine. Mine and my two able assistants. Oh, maybe Dot should get a cut. I'd think about it.

"You all might as well go home now," said Chief Cotton. "We know where to find you. There will be time enough to get together and sort this out later. Um, Dave, why don't you walk over with them?"

"Yes, Chief," he responded.

"Make sure you get all the jewelry," Dot reminded him. "You have a list, right?"

"I'm sure we do, ma'am. Saunders, you take care of it, will you?"

He also responded with, "Yes, Chief."

We slowly walked back toward my place. Not surprisingly, a crowd had gathered on the corner, including all the Bells and the Guzmans and assorted neighborhood kids. And Michelle.

"You're okay?" she asked, falling in with us. "I'd better head off to work then. Later." We parted at our driveway, but not without a fairly long kiss.

The rest of us continued to my kitchen. Too many of us! "I think I need to thank Jan," I said. "Not that we couldn't have handled Jones. I was just waiting for the right moment."

They ignored me. Skeptics. "How are you doing, Small Change?" asked Dot. "He hit you pretty hard."

He grinned at her. "You hit him harder, Miss Dot. I'm glad he got his and — and Alyce can rest now."

"Even so, it might be a good idea for you to be checked over at the hospital," said Dave Blake. "Anyone else get hurt?"

"I fell flat on my face in the sand," volunteered Sebastian Furr. "Alright otherwise."

Dave's next words came out with a touch of an apology in their tone. "I should have your weapon, Ms. Dominguez. You'll get it back in a day or two."

"Or a little longer. Okay, Dave." She handed it over.

"Thanks." He gave it a cursory look. "A Walther? The James Bond gun?"

"When he didn't use a Beretta," she replied. "Take good care of it."

Blake slipped it into his pocket.

"Jones was the last guy I would have suspected," he said. "Shows what a great detective I am."

"Ted figured it out," Alistair stated. "Bastian and I thought Dot was guilty."

"Yeah, but Jones sort of planted that in our heads," said Sebastian.

Alistair squinted at Dot for a few seconds. "But she is guilty of some other things, isn't she?"

"Hmm?" Dave had no idea what we were talking about.

"She set those two guys on me at the festival," I told him. "I have no intention of pressing charges."

He shrugged. "You'd have to take that up with the White Springs police. However, there have been some irregularities, Ms. Dominguez. We'll have to address those when we get together." He paused, thought. "Maybe this afternoon. We'll see. You at the same place?"

"I am. But I may hang here for a while."

He nodded. "How about you two? At that motel?"

Donny looked at Small Change. "Yeah, but we'll want to get out of this place now. No reason to stay any longer."

"Okay. As soon as we can sit and talk to all of you, we can probably let you go."

"Do you need me?" asked Sebastian. "I need to be off to work shortly."

"I doubt it. If we need to talk with you, you can come in later." He gave the group of us one more long thoughtful look before saying, "I guess that's all. I'll head back across the street. Jan?"

"I'm going to stay here," she told him.

"Good. See you later. And good job." I think he would have kissed her if he wasn't on duty. I also think he should have anyway.

I looked at the clock on the stove. "I guess it's too late to surf. Need to open up the shop in a bit. Coffee?"

Sebastian rose. "I need to go get ready for work."

"I'll be going too. But I need to get some sleep!" said Alistair.

"Before you go," spoke Dot, "I want to say that I wouldn't mind having you come work for me. Both of you. You would be competent investigators."

"In Miami?" asked Al.

"Not necessarily. Let's talk about it later." Both men left, leaving me with Jan and Dot.

"I really do think those boys could be useful to me," said Dot. "And why aren't you making coffee? You promised coffee."

"Yes, ma'am. The company you work for would take them on?"

"With my recommendation, I think so. But — I am considering going out on my own. An independent contractor so to speak."

Jan lifted an eyebrow. "Wouldn't that simply make you a private eye?"

A laugh. "I didn't want to use the term but yes, pretty much."

"Maybe Shaper should be a private eye."

"No thanks. I just want to go surfing and build boards."

"You did figure out Boris was the murderer," said Dot.

"And I think you might have suspected it yourself."

"It's true that both of us were in pursuit of her and both had inside information," she admitted.

"Yeah. Someone who knew what was going on were Dave's words, back at the start of this. Who knew better than Boris Jones? Who would have been more interested in pursuing the case ten years later than the murderer of Alyce Noble?"

"True enough."

The coffee was ready. I got up to serve us as Dot continued.

"I would think Jones's main concern was to avoid having the murder linked to him. That's why he came up here. But he wouldn't have minded finding the jewels too. He might even have turned them in for the reward."

SMOKE

"But we left him with no other choice than to steal them and run for it," I said, filling her cup, then Jan's.

"And who knows what other choice he might have needed to make?" said Dorothea Dominguez. "It's a good thing we did not need to find out."

That it was. I poured my own coffee, with a splash of milk, and sat down. I needed to sit. Just sit for a while.

Chapter 45

"We dug and we sifted and we found everything," reported Jack Saunders. "I was frankly surprised."

Amazed, I would have said. All those jewelry pieces managing to stay together and undiscovered in the sand for ten years.

"Norbert had wrapped them in a cloth —"

"Maybe a canvas bag," interjected Dave. "Not that it matters."

"It had all rotted away long ago," Jack continued. "We assume she slipped the whole thing into the drain and it eventually got washed through and buried in the sand."

"And Ted discovered the jewelry," said Dot. "Make a note of that so he can claim the reward."

"I want you to have a cut of that," I responded. "Brown and Furr, too." We could work out just how much later. Or I could decide. Alistair smiled a bit at my announcement.

"Here are our other, um, participants," Jack Saunders said. Robinson and Morales. We'd been waiting for them. They were accompanied by Bill Cotton and Gordon Rivers. The FBI man was only a slight surprise.

Rex Stoddard was a much bigger one. "Mr. Stoddard walked up to Agent Rivers a little while ago and turned himself in," announced Chief Cotton.

"Alyce's murderer was done for," said Rex. "I thank you for that, Carrol. You too, ma'am." He nodded toward Dot. "Time to think about my future. Mine and Mona's." A smile came and went. "Regina, I mean."

"Having turned himself in and even assisted, in his way, with this investigation, I think we can expect a fairly short incarceration," Rivers said. "Especially with all the stolen jewelry recovered."

Cotton's nod was decidedly noncommittal. None of that was his concern. "I don't know if you can add anything here, Mr. Stoddard, but have a seat." He took one himself, at the head of the table. "Now who's starting off?"

"That should probably be me," spoke Dorothea Dominguez. "As soon as I heard about the robbery and that Alyce was mixed up in it somehow, I took an interest."

"And you came up here," said Gordon Rivers. "We know that Boris Jones was also in the area. Anyone else we should be aware of?" He didn't look at anyone in particular.

"I did come up here too," admitted Donny. "Just real quick. I was following Dominguez."

Dot could not completely conceal her surprise. "Me?"

"Yeah, I heard you were looking into it." He nodded toward the small man seated at his left. "Change here told me. Knew you anyway and that you were, um, involved with Alyce somehow."

She said nothing. There was no reason to let him — or anyone — know Alyce had been her confidential informant.

Donny went on. "I could see someone else was tailin' after you. Thought maybe it was Rex but I never got a look at him."

"I was never anyways near here," said Rex. "I was stayin' put in Georgia."

"Never saw Alyce neither," said Donny. "I lost Dominguez while tryin' not to be seen myself, and ran back to Miami."

"To be arrested," put in Agent Rivers. "That put you out of the picture."

Morales nodded agreement. "For more'n five years."

"What seems likely, Dot," continued Rivers, "is that Jones knew about your connection to Norbert and followed you."

"Quite likely," she agreed. "Alyce trusted me. When things seemed to be going wrong she gave me a call and I came up." Dot turned to me. "I didn't even know you had moved up here. Not until the remains were found and your name popped up."

"But I was the reason she came to Cully Beach."

"So it seems. She was lost, panicking, but I got her to agree to a meet. I tried to get her to tell me where the jewelry was, told her it would be better if she turned it over to me. Couldn't get her to agree right then. To make up her mind."

"I would suspect she still hoped to connect with her partner," said Cotton. He didn't look at Rex but we all knew who he meant.

"I didn't intend to keep the jewelry, of course. I wanted to be the one to turn it in, to solve the case. Be a hero and get a promotion."

"And a reward," I had to say.

"Oh, sure. I was willing to look the other way and let her go."

Several law enforcement eyebrows were raised at that statement. "At the pier, it was going to be." Dot shook her head. "Alyce never made it to the meet. She spooked. We talked on a pay phone. She'd given me a number to call. Said there was someone else following her. The girl didn't know who but we know that was Jones now." She let that sink in for a moment. "Alyce ran and he got to her. That's how I figure it."

"I would guess you figured it right," said Bill Cotton. "Anyone have contradictory information?"

No offers. So it was Jones who frightened Alyce away. When the girl wrote 'someones after me' in her note, she might have meant Boris. But she could also have meant Dotty, couldn't she? Dot could even have fueled her fears. She wouldn't have known what way to turn.

She chose to turn to me. Would that I had known ten years earlier.

"Then you have been involved from the start, have you, Ms. Dominguz?" asked Blake. "Almost from the start?"

"I was. And yes, I told no one. I admit I wanted to keep my involvement ten years ago from being known. That's part of the reason I came up here now." A wry smile. "Too late for that now! But I owed Alyce, too."

And wanted to recover the jewels. No reason to point it out. Leave the bow tied on that package.

"Good enough then," said the chief. He fixed his eyes on Rex Stoddard. "You would have saved us a lot of paperwork if you'd turned yourself in down in Miami."

"At least he surrendered to Rivers instead of us," said Dave Blake. "That makes it simpler."

"True. We didn't arrest him. Or even take him into custody, did we? He's still yours, Rivers?"

"He is. I'll turn him over," said the agent of the FBI, "and head to Miami myself. I may be there before you, Stoddard. I consider you my responsibility."

Rex looked grateful but said nothing.

Cotton turned his attention to Donny and Small Change. "I doubt we need to speak with you two again," he told them. "But I would advise you to check in with the police in Miami, just in case. Okay?" In other words, get out of town.

"Sure."

"And you two —" Bill looked to the two men seated at his right hand, his lead investigators. "You need to get a full and detailed report ready. Before our visitors from Miami arrive, ideally." He looked at his watch and chucked. "But seeing as they're already on their way, tomorrow morning will do."

Dave and Jack would be busy. Possibly most of the night.

"The rest of you," said Bill Cotton. "Go home."

Chapter 46

"Pretty good job," I told Marty. "Now I need to glass it for you."

"I want to learn how to do that too!"

Of course she did. "Then first, you'll have to help me install the fin boxes." If that didn't discourage her, nothing would.

The muffled roar of a motorcycle engine. Close at hand, too. I stepped out to get a better view. It was pulling in behind the house next door, beside Karrie Goodpaster's van. And that was Karrie herself on the back, hanging onto Regina Stoddard.

Or Mona McFarland, as most official documents had it. I'd learned that from Bill. She and Rex had asked if they could be married before he was taken back to Miami but had to be turned down. We both agreed they would be likely to have a wedding before he went to prison.

I ambled on over. Marty chose to keep her distance.

"Hi Shaper," called out Karrie. "Regina is going to stay with me until her husband gets out of prison."

I had my doubts the arrangement would last anywhere near that long. Ah, one never knows.

"And I'm going to write my book from her point of view, not his," she went on.

"If Rex's name was on it someone might sue for, um, what's the word, Karrie?"

"Restitution. The insurance company that paid out the claim on the jewelry, mostly." Karrie grinned. "Dot warned us about that."

"We talked to her at the station," added Regina.

I wondered if Dorothea Dominguez would stop by here before heading south. Maybe tomorrow. She would be staying to talk to the police from Miami.

And maybe to talk to my tenants here too. If that proved to be a serious job offer, I might lose Sebastian and Alistair. Maybe these two would want to move in. Maybe I would even trust them.

It was getting late. "I wish you success then," I told them. "And don't let Karrie get distracted. Keep her working on that book!"

I went back to my place without bothering to see how the advice went over. "I'm closing the doors," I said to Marty. "It's been a long day." A damned long day!

"I should get home too." She giggled. "But I learn how to glass a surfboard first thing tomorrow!"

"Sure, kid." Why not? I got a bottle of zinfandel out of the workshop refrigerator before heading in.

"Just the thing," remarked Michelle. "So, we're going to be rich now?"

"Hmm, just not quite as poor might be more accurate."

"Maybe we should invest in Kay and Patty's gallery."

"I was thinking more along the lines of buying a couple bicycles." And putting the rest into renovations. "Anyway, we can afford to get married now."

"If I have to wed you for richer or poorer, I definitely prefer richer."

"Me too. I'll go lock up the shop." I walked into the showroom, wineglass in hand. Michelle had already sent the afternoon employee home. It was growing darker outside, the sky filled with slabs of slate-colored cloud. Lightning flashed out over the Atlantic.

A steady rain was falling. I stood and watched from the open door for a while, inhaled the cool electric air.

The brand-new streetlight came on across the road.

Afterword

SMOKE is the third novel about Ted Carrol and Cully Beach by Stephen Brooke, the followup to SHAPER and WAVES. The author is himself a surfer and has shaped a few boards in his time. He has also turned out novels of fantasy and realism, illustrated children's books, nonfiction, and volumes of poetry, all available from Arachis Press, a small publisher dedicated to presenting meaningful literature for readers of all ages.

Visit http://arachispress.com for our catalog.

Cully Beach is quite mythical. This does not mean it has no resemblance to certain towns on Florida's Atlantic coast. All we are willing to say about it is that Cully Beach would lie somewhere between Daytona Beach and Jacksonville.

The Florida Folk Festival, on the other hand, is very real. 2001 was the first year the author attended — but not the last.

the Florida Folk Festival at Stephen Foster State Park

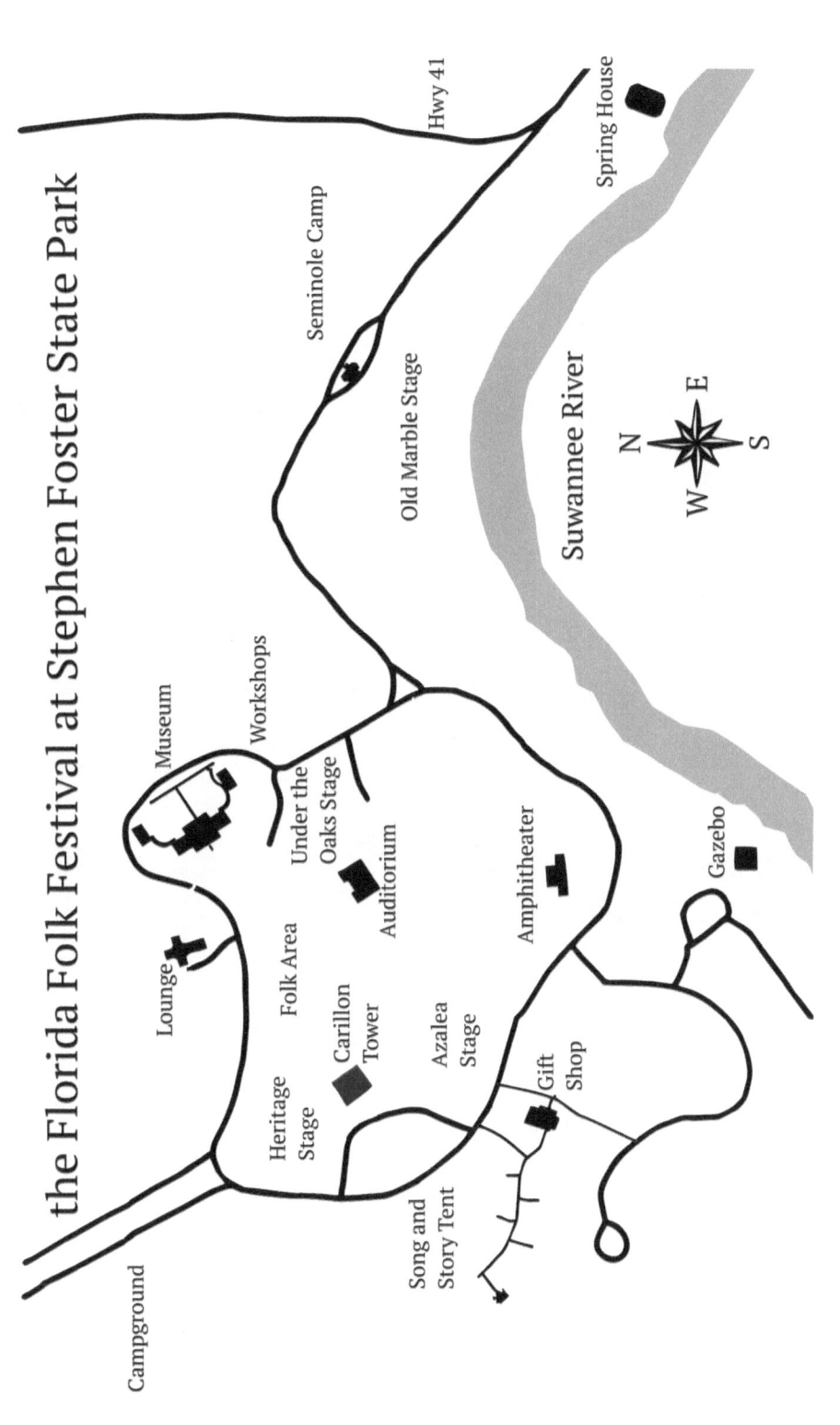